I0630840

when destinies collide

a novel by

shirl rickman

When Destinies Collide \ Shirl Rickman – 2nd ed.
Library of Congress Cataloging-in-Publication Data
ISBN-13: 978-0999368503

Selene

Huddled against the back of the couch with my knees pulled against my chest, I listen to my mother question my father about his lack of affection for me. I feel like crying, but the tears refuse to fall. They never fall, and some days I feel like my chest is a dam about to break, as if all the tears I've never cried are about to burst out of me and kill me. It scares me. I can't understand what I ever did to make him hate me so much. He's never said it, but I can feel it. I can see it from our occasional conversations when he pretends to look at me. I can see he isn't actually looking at me, but rather looking through me.

My mother's voice rises a little and pulls me from my thoughts. They don't know I'm here. They think I'm in bed. I was, but I heard them say my name.

"Mike, I don't understand why you continue to act this way. She isn't a baby anymore. Selene can sense the distance you put between yourself and her. She blames herself." A tiny sob escapes her.

I hate when Mama cries. I want to jump up and say, *Boo!* She always laughs when I sneak up on her and scare her. I love making Mama happy. I don't jump up though, because I'm supposed to be asleep.

"You don't see things clearly, Elizabeth. I'm not sure what you want from me. I was there. I congratulated her on receiving her award. Isn't that enough?" I can hear his footsteps as he walks toward her. "I love you, Lizzie. Can't you see that? You're such a good mama. Selene doesn't need me like she needs you."

I round the side of the couch and see he's put his arms around her. There's music playing in the background, just as it does every night after dinner. It's slow, and I see him trying to sway their bodies to the music. My mother appears stiff in his arms and glances up at him.

"You just don't get it. She needs you, too. She needs you like I need you. Why can't you see that?" She begins moving with him, but she doesn't relax.

"I just need you," he whispers. "I don't want to talk about this anymore. I think you're overreacting."

My mother gives him a slight nod and a tight-lipped smile before laying her head on his shoulder. He can't see her face, but I can. She isn't smiling, and I can see the tears shimmering in her eyes. "I know you love her too," she whispers back.

He doesn't though. I would know, because Mama shows me love. I don't want his love. His love hurts, and I don't like pain. I will only ever love my mama, and Great-Aunt Vi. She loves me. They love me. I won't let anyone hurt me, because when I hurt, Mama hurts too.

I watch for a while longer. My father kisses my mother softly on the lips and walks into the kitchen, leaving her alone.

Mama thinks she's the only one in the room as she covers her face with her hands.

My eyes never leave her. I don't like seeing Mama so sad.

Just as I'm about to crawl back to my bedroom, I notice reach into her sweater pocket and pull something out. It looks like a small photo.

I watch her face as she looks at it, and for the first time, I see sadness there. It's different from the look she gets when she's trying to convince Daddy to be kinder to me.

She lifts her head when she hears footsteps coming from the kitchen at the same time I do, and she quickly puts the photo back into her pocket. I want to ask her questions, but I can tell by her face I shouldn't.

I quietly crawl my way back into my room and into my bed. Closing my eyes, I pray for a strong heart, because I never want to feel the heartache I just saw on my mama's face.

L acey's tiny shadow is hanging over me when I hear her whisper my name. "Drake...Drake, are you awake?" she asks me, just as she's done nearly every night for as long as I can remember.

"I am now," I say as I yawn into my hand to muffle the sound.

Before she even asks, I slide over and push my blanket aside so she can crawl into bed next to me. My body goes rigid as I wait for her cold feet to make contact with my legs; I hate it and love it at the same time. It makes me want to smile. Lacey is the only girl I will ever love, and I wrap my arm around her as she moves closer.

I wait for it. She's sad tonight, and as hard as I've tried, I can't bring her out of it. I know she'll start asking questions, because we feel everything the other feels. Questions run through my mind too…questions I'm too afraid to ask.

She sighs. "Drake?"

I roll my eyes beneath my closed lids. Man, I'm tired. "Yes," I answer quietly.

"Do you think they ever wanted us? Do you think she has ever loved us?"

I hear sadness in her voice that echoes what I feel in my own heart. Lacey is the only person I know who would understand the pain I feel…the fear I feel of what the answers to those questions truly are. I don't want to say it out loud though. It scares me almost as badly as her asking them.

I say the only thing I can say. "I don't know, Lacey." I hug her tighter. "I love you, though, and I know you love me. You're the best sister in the whole world. You're the other half of me. It's the only thing that matters."

I feel her give a slight nod.

"Remember that girl I told you I met at Mrs. Durham's house?" she asks.

I remember, even though I was only half listening the day she told me about this funny and sweet new friend she made. It's hard—she's such a girl sometimes. Lacey just never quite understands why I don't get excited about the idea of picking flowers and playing games along the river at Mrs. Durham's house. Half the time, Tommy and I are trying to get away from her and her friends. I also don't like to hurt Lacey's feelings, so I go along with her question since she seems to want to tell me something.

"Yeah, sort of," I say reluctantly.

"Well, she has a mama, and her mama loves her," Lacey says, so plainly my chest hurts a little at the longing I hear in her voice. I feel it too. "You should see them together. I never knew a mother could love like that." The uncomfortable feeling in my chest increases a bit, and I feel a slight resentment for this girl I don't even know.

"Why are you saying this, Lacey?" I ask her, a little more

harshly than I intended to.

"I heard Mother telling Daddy we all ruined her life. Daddy was angry and said we ruined his life too." I swallow a lump in my throat as the words settle over me. "I just don't understand, Drake."

I pull her into me tighter, not sure if I'm trying to comfort her or myself more. Either way, we are all the other can really count on. I will always protect Lacey. She is the only thing that matters to me. We don't need them—Lacey is all I will ever need.

chapter 1

Selene

Ten years later

I f a heart is broken over and over, do the pieces eventually become so small there isn't hope for it ever being put back together?

At this moment, I feel like I'm never going to be whole again. In fact, I'm not even sure how my heart is still beating. I can hear it bumping against my chest, the pain increasing with each thump. Sitting in the front seat of my dad's beat-up Ford Escort, my head resting on the window, I'm mesmerized by the sound of the rain lashing the glass. I can see the gray mist hovering over the hilltops as we pass them, and it seems Mother Nature is setting the scene for how my life feels—dreary.

My dad is sitting next to me, singing along with the Beach Boys as if this day were perfectly normal...as if the world hasn't crashed down around us. I don't understand how he can do that, pretend everything is exactly as it has always been. I catch him glance at me from the corner of his eye, and his gaze lingers. For a moment, I think I see a little bit of guilt and sadness, but just as quickly, he resumes his singalong.

Since the night my mother passed away, I've never seen him miss a step in his day. I know he loved her, can remember them laughing together when they didn't think I was listening. I even walked in on them dancing in the living room a few times, my mother's head resting on his shoulder as they turned slowly in a circle. Now, to see the way he's acting…I would never know he loved her if I didn't have those memories.

I've never seen him cry or show any sign his life has been dramatically altered. The only indication that he may be grieving his wife's death at all is the gradual increase in his alcohol consumption.

The most painful part is the fact that he completely overlooks my grief. He has never once offered words of comfort or any paternal support. He has never once acted like a father.

When I think about it, it isn't like my dad and I have ever had any real lines of communication. The father-daughter relationship has always been nonexistent. He hasn't acknowledged me much over the years, hasn't put his arms around me. He's never wiped my tears, and he hasn't even squeezed my hand to show he can see it. Can he see my heartache? Does he recognize the despondency of my life now because a piece of me died with her that day?

Of course he hasn't, though. We never talked before my mother's death, so why did I expect that to change now? Maybe it's the small child who still resides in me, who wants to believe. I did expect him to be here for me. I expected comfort. I expected a father. As usual, I'm disappointed, but my mother is no longer here to make excuses for him. She isn't here to defend him and his actions.

When I was little, the explanations were easier to believe, but the older I get, the more evident the truth of our real relationship becomes. There are moments when I think I see something more in his eyes, maybe love, but it vanishes quickly into nothingness. As often as I tell myself my dad's lack of interest in me doesn't matter, I know I'm only lying to myself. I do care.

I think about the days since that fateful night. I think of what my life was before her death.

Once upon a time, I was a healthy, happy teenager, a young girl sitting on top of her world. It was my senior year, and whether or not I was going to get into the college of my choice was my only worry. I spent most of my waking hours with the same friends I've had since kindergarten. We were inseparable. I was a cheerleader, and my best friend was the captain of the baseball team. I lived a life any eighteen-year-old girl would envy. It's only now I realize it was all a disguise. I had been holding back and pretending for years. The worst part is that my mother was the glue holding my world together, and now she's gone. Now that she's gone, I'm unfixable.

I've pulled away from everyone. I try to pretend I'm fine, but it just doesn't work anymore. All the pretending is just so hard. I've always been one to hold myself at arm's length from most people, so their incessant need to comfort me only makes me push them away further. I can't help the way I feel, and for some reason, their sympathy only makes my pain worse.

I wanted more. I wanted to feel different. I've imagined my future with these same familiar faces. They are the only ones I really know. We would come home during breaks from college. My mom would dote on me just as she has my whole life. As much as I held a wall up between myself and everyone else, I wanted things to be and feel normal. I wanted them to be happy. Mama always said, "Fake it till you make it," and that's just what I've always done—until now.

I keep wondering if it's wrong that I'm not quite myself yet. Apparently my friends think I should be over losing her. It broke my heart a little more each time one of my friends stopped asking me to go to parties, movies, shopping, or even lunch. Part of me is screaming for my old life. I want to be the girl who had the strength to put on a happy face just so she could move through life. Now, I'm hardly ever happy, and I can feel how uncomfortable they all are around me. None of them knows what to say, and then they just end up saying something that makes the awkward silence worse. It's just that I don't know why I should get to be happy when my mama is gone. I stopped accepting their invitations and even began avoiding them when they came to my house.

Eventually, they all ceased trying, and then a week ago Ryan came over to confront me. Could I really blame him? He told me he couldn't wait for me to get over this, said I was selfish for ignoring him and all of our friends. He said I needed to try to get back into the real world, and then he walked away from me.

Get over this? Selfish? I wanted to scream at him, although I could see the heartbreak in his eyes. I've always known he wanted more from me than friendship, but I've never wanted more than that. I did try, and the desperate part of me wants to try now. I want to keep the boy who is so familiar in my life. Part of me feels the urge to give him what he wants, but it would be a lie. As he stood in front of me, I couldn't find the will to say anything that might change his mind. Finally, after what seemed like an eternity of silence, Ryan turned and walked away, leaving me standing in the driveway as he pulled away. I stood there, watching as his taillights faded into the dark. My mind was numb to the pain of losing someone else.

Slowly, I turned and walked back into my house. I didn't shed a single tear, and maybe that should have told me something. I felt so detached from myself as I climbed the stairs in my empty house to my room.

Later, I awoke on top of my comforter, still in my clothes, to the sound of the front door closing. I knew it was my dad, so I pulled the covers over me and went back to sleep, not even bothering to undress and put on pajamas.

The next morning I carried myself to the kitchen, only to be surprised to find my father leaning against the counter. He grinned at me—I could hardly recall a time he had ever done that before—and informed me that I was going to live with my mother's aunt, Violette. He was sending me away, and he didn't even try to explain. I couldn't believe it, although he had never shown an interest in raising me. His ability to act as if Mama had never existed was devastating—unfathomable. I felt another crack splinter its way across my heart. Once again, I was screaming on the inside, but I remained quiet. Nodding, I turned and walked back to my room without ever showing him how much this hurt me.

Now, it's like I'm waking from a dream as the car gradually begins to slow down. I notice a familiar sign welcoming us to small-town Texas. My mama and I would often visit her aunt on and off during my childhood at her home in sleepy little Montgomery, population 987. I have many fond memories of this place, but they are all with my mama, and being here without her makes the sadness I feel more acute.

Taking a deep breath, I scan my surroundings as we drive down Main Street. It's practically a ghost town, which isn't out of the ordinary. A few cars are parked in front of the local diner and the hardware store. I suppose most people stay indoors when a storm like this blows through town. It's still pouring as we turn down Aunt Violette's street and pull into the driveway.

Unfastening his seatbelt, my father sits quietly, staring straight ahead before getting out of the car. He never looks at me or speaks a single word. I watch as he saunters toward the house. The rain doesn't seem to create any sense of urgency in his movements.

I remain motionless as I take in the butter yellow Victorian house with a wraparound porch. I've always loved this old house, especially when I was younger. It reminds me of a perfect

5

dollhouse with its white trim around the windows and doorway. The white wooden rockers that line the front and the two porch swings that hang from the ceiling on the second-story balcony give it a homey feel. Everything about this place has always been comforting. Even with the dark clouds and rain, it reminds me of sunshine and happier times, but now I wonder if I will ever feel that warm, happy feeling again.

Turning, I lean over the back seat to grab my backpack then open the door and dash to the front porch. My dad is already inside and the door has been left cracked open, so I take that as my invitation to enter. Quietly, I close the door behind me and follow the sound of two voices in a strained conversation.

"Now, Mike, you know I would do anything for Elizabeth and Selene, but you can't just abandon this girl. She just lost her mother," I hear Aunt Violette say in a near whisper.

They're discussing me. Did my not father ask if I could live here before showing up? Leaning against the wall, I continue to listen. I try to slow my breathing while my heart pounds in my chest, waiting for his reply.

"Violette, she isn't a little girl anymore. Selene is strong and independent. I can't take care of her, especially not now that Elizabeth is gone. I don't know her or how to talk to her. She won't even care that I'm not around," he tells her, sounding as if he is talking about a stranger or an estranged relative, not his daughter who has lived under the same roof as him for the last seventeen years.

As if there is no need for further discussion, he changes the subject. "I need to get her things out of the car, and then I'll be on my way." He pauses a moment before adding, "Things will be exactly as they've always been between us." He leaves the kitchen and walks right past me as I lean against the wall, his indifferent gaze connecting with mine for only a moment. His eyes never betray any guilt over the words he knows I just overheard. I remain still until I hear the front door close behind him.

Pushing away from the wall, I cautiously enter the kitchen. When I'm standing in the doorway, Aunt Vi looks up and gives me a look of sad understanding. Opening her arms wide, she starts toward me. "Oh, honey," she says as she wraps her arms tightly around me. With only a moment of hesitation, I accept the warm embrace Aunt Violette is offering, and for the first time since Mama died, I lose myself in the comfort someone is trying to offer me.

Our goodbye is brief and unemotional. It's not like I expected a big, dramatic farewell, but I did expect to at least hear some regret. I mean, I'm his only child—though I'm not sure why I continue to think that even matters. I should know better.

Aunt Violette helps me carry my things up to my room, which is located in the back of the house and looks over the Pedernales River, which flows just past the large, open back yard full of mature oak trees. I've always loved this room and all its feminine touches. The walls are a sky blue, and a pure-white sheer curtain hangs over the large arched windows. The wrought-iron bed is covered with a delicate white quilt with pale blue and violet flowers giving it a more subtle beauty. I love it.

It isn't that I'm very girly, it's that this room is everything that represents my mother and my childhood spent at Aunt Vi's house. Aunt Violette insists that I make it my own, but as I slowly turn a small circle in the middle of the room, I know I won't change a thing about my new room.

Walking over to the window box seat, I sit on my knees and pull the airy curtain to the side. It finally stopped raining, and the sun is just beginning to set behind the giant oaks outside my window. The sky is dark purple and pink with hints of blue—something that only happens after a storm passes through and all

7

the clouds clear. Mama always said that when the sky looked this beautiful, God was saying sorry for all of our sorrows. For the first time, I realize I may not be able to forgive him.

An overwhelming awareness suddenly hits me that not only will I have to move on without my mama, but now I will have to do it in a new place without everything and everyone I've always known. How am I going to get through the night, let alone the next year, without my mama or friends, or even Ryan?

My heart tightens in my chest. A single tear slips down my cheek, and I quickly wipe it away. *No. No crying*, I tell myself. If I allow myself to cry and feel the devastation of my situation, I know I will never be able to stop, and if I don't stop, I won't just break...I'll shatter.

Once again, I wake up fully dressed, but this time I'm curled up on the cushion of the window seat, in a new place. I feel every stiff movement as I sit up. Rubbing my eyes as they're hit by the light coming in through the window, I observe my surroundings. A crocheted afghan is now on the floor beside me, and I realize Aunt Violette must have come in at some point and laid a blanket on me. The corner of my mouth slightly tips up at the thought of the sweet, elderly woman who has always been so nurturing and gentle. I know I have a few hours of unpacking to do, but first I need a quick shower, and maybe I'll even try to eat a little.

Walking through the doorway, I turn back and look at what will now be my room. Maybe, just maybe, I can keep myself together here. I just have to keep from feeling or caring about anything, and I will be just fine.

chapter 2

Drake

I don't care about anything, or so everyone thinks. It's something I'm not interested in changing their opinion about, either. The one thing I did care about, I destroyed.

Pulling the weeds that have grown up around the stone since my visit the week before, I talk to her as if she were right next to me. Today, I brought lilies to replace the already wilting daisies in the permanent granite vase. There is a slight breeze, and I can't help thinking Lacey would have loved a day like today: the sun shining, the smell of spring blowing through the trees, and the quiet whispers of nature surrounding me.

As I lean back against the headstone, I open her favorite book and begin to read. She loved to read. It was one of the many differences between us, although most never noticed it. It didn't matter how long people knew us; they only ever saw our similarities. Before everything happened, I was more of a CliffsNotes type of guy, but things are different now. I read to her when I visit, getting through at least one book every few weeks. I only have time to read one chapter today. With some reluctance, I close the book.

I make a joke about the hero of the book and how weak he is for chasing the girl. Lacey would love it and every sappy word. I do all of this because she always loved when I teased her, even though she pretended she didn't. Knowing this doesn't make up for anything that has happened, and I still come here every week. It's where I can be alone. It's the only place I can be who I am and feel what I do without holding back.

Everyone has always known me to be in the center of the action. I was always the life of the party—I *was* a party. I had it all, but that was before, before everything changed—well, before everything changed for me. It seems life continues on around me as if that night never happened four months ago. My parents constantly talk about it and expect me to carry on in the same way. My friends were sympathetic at first, but now they just carry on as usual. I mean, she was their friend too. They loved her too, but it's easier for them to move on.

For me, moving on feels impossible. I'm not sure if it's because my parents covered everything about that night up. They made sure our family name was protected by keeping everything out of the papers. Keeping secrets in a small town is hard for the average person, but my father isn't an average person. He's the mayor.

It's because of this that I'm different. No one has even noticed how I've changed. They don't see me, and frankly, I don't care. I let them see what they want to see. My parents have always seen what they wanted to see. The fact that they ignored my recklessness gave me permission to act and do whatever I wanted without consequence...or so I thought. In reality, consequence came in the hardest form imaginable, and now I've slowly distanced myself from everything I was before, because I owe it to her to be better.

I stand up to leave. "See you soon," I whisper. The now familiar squeeze around my heart tightens in my chest. I've never been able to say goodbye.

———————— • ————————

As I pull my car up in front of my father's office, I sit and stare at the sign hanging over the door: *Mayor Gregory Thomas welcomes you to Montgomery, Texas—Hill Country Heaven.* My dad has been mayor for the last ten years, the people of Montgomery voting him in year after year based on his family values and honesty. I feel nothing but disgust at the idea of my parents' supposed morality and family values.

Before the accident, I never gave a second thought to people's blatantly misguided beliefs about our family. I only saw the benefits of riding the power of it, using it to my advantage every chance I got. After all, that was what I was taught my whole life.

Suddenly, I'm pulled from my thoughts by a loud knock on the window of my truck. I look up to find my mother smiling at me as if she has never been happier to see anyone in her life. I know it isn't true, thought; it's always an act with her.

Reluctantly, I play my part too and place a broad smile on my face. I wonder if my mother can see the truth behind the smile. I wonder if she can see what I actually feel when I see her. Even more than that, I wonder if she even cares.

Opening the door, I get out of my truck. "Hello, Mother," I say as I step down out of my black Ford F450. Placing a kiss on her cheek, I pull back and place a happy expression on my face once again, doing as I'm expected to, as I always do.

"Hello, Drake, dear. Where did you run off to so early this morning?" my mother asks as she turns away and heads for my dad's office.

She sounds as if she doesn't care one way or the other what

I've been doing this morning, her tone giving the impression that she's just asking because she feels it's what she is supposed to want to know as my mother.

Shaking my head, I speak the lie to her back with ease. "I went up to the track at school to run." I stand still and wait for her reaction. I'm always waiting for her reaction.

She keeps walking and doesn't even acknowledge that I've spoken as she enters the building. I followed behind her, giving Marilyn, my dad's secretary, a sincere look of friendliness as we pass her and walk into my father's office. Marilyn has known me most of my life and has always been kind. I often wonder how much she actually sees and hears but keeps to herself.

My dad looks up from his desk as we enter. "Claire, Drake, glad you could join me." He always sounds so serious and businesslike, I constantly feel as if I'm about to be let go from a job. I always sense his detachment from our family more than I can see it. I've always wondered why but have never had the courage to ask.

I watch my mother as she walks around his desk and leans forward to place a stiff kiss on his cheek. "Hello, darling," she states without feeling.

"Dad," I say with a nod in his direction before sitting in the chair across from his desk.

Without any other pleasantries, my father gets right to the point. "Drake, your mother and I want to be sure your head is on straight for the start of football season and school this year. We know the school year ended badly last year, but it has been four months."

I feel gutted as the shaking in my hands begins to move up my arms. For a moment, I think I see regret in his eyes, but he drops his gaze from mine.

My mother continues for him. "You still seem to be a little...should I say, withdrawn? We discussed the necessity of continuing life as we always have and representing a united front with the election coming up."

I stare in complete disbelief at the man and woman across from me. Hatred builds in me for these two people who are supposed to love their children unconditionally, the people I'm supposed to love with the same intensity. They show no compassion at all. All I can do is stare and blink, searching their faces for something—anything. I linger on my father's because sometimes I feel he holds his real feelings back. I need to believe he cares. The longer I remain silent and watch him, the more I recognize a flicker of my pain reflected in his eyes. I shift my gaze to my mother's, and there is nothing, so I move back to my dad's, willing him to confirm what I think I see. Then he blinks, and it's gone.

Since I don't respond, my father clears his throat and continues. "It's not that we expect you to carry on as if nothing happened, but we need to present ourselves as if, despite this loss, we're strong enough to get through anything. It's also imperative that you remain in good standing in school and sports, because of your scholarships. Your success means everything to our family." Again, my dad pauses like he is expecting a reaction from me.

When my mother realizes I'm not going to say anything, she looks from my father to me. "Is your father making himself clear?"

The beating of my heart picks up the pace, causing me to feel a little dizzy. Clenching my fists at my sides, I try to maintain my composure, because losing it will only mean more pain—except I can't hold back any longer.

Abruptly, I stand up without taking my eyes from my father's, which are the same emerald green as mine. I feel bile in the back of my throat, and my control is slipping further and further away. Dammit, I want him to say something, anything to let me know he is a man. He won't, though. He never does.

Suddenly, I slam my fist down on the desk, startling both of my parents. I no longer think about the consequences of my actions. I gaze red-faced at them both, deep breaths rapidly coming in and out as I try to hold myself together.

Through clenched teeth, I utter, "Sure, you're both clear. I'll start school, I'll be happy, but with an underlying sadness for effect. I'll focus on school, on sports, on the election, because we wouldn't want anyone to think we're not strong enough to get over the death of a daughter...of a sister." With that, I turn and slam the office door.

As I walk past Marilyn once again, there is an apology in her eyes, and for a second I wince at the thought of what my actions just now will mean for me later.

chapter 3

Selene

It's been two days, and I finally finish unpacking then decide to take a walk along the river to a hidden spot Mama always took me to on our visits to Aunt Violette's house. Aunt Vi sweetly packs me a little picnic, and I dash back upstairs to grab my guitar before heading out the door.

Aunt Vi has been so wonderful over the past couple of days. From the moment my father dropped me off and I began crying on her shoulder, I haven't been able to stop. It's like coming here has made me more vulnerable. The numbness is beginning to subside, and it scares me a little to allow myself to feel. I just need to get out and take a step back.

It's a typical hot, humid August day in Texas. I'm wearing my favorite pair of old cutoff shorts—which my mother hated because she thought they were too short—and a seafoam-colored tank top she bought for me last summer. She always said it made my catlike eyes even brighter.

I make my way down the river and take in the familiar surroundings. It's been a while since Mama and I have been to visit Aunt Violette, but it's easy for me to remember the way to our favorite spot. Finally, I reach the secluded area where the cypress trees grow tall and the branches hang low over the river's edge.

Looking around, I try to remember the last time Mama and I were here. It was a day similar to this one. We picked some of the yellow flowers that always bloom along the river; I think she called them sour grass. On that day, we chewed on their stems before picking some to braid together into a crown. After years of trying to convince me, I finally believed her when she told me I would actually enjoy chewing on the green stems. The funny thing is it's good and disgusting at the same time. I remember it being a good day. It was the last day of our visit before we had to go home because the school year was starting in a little over a week.

I can remember how excited I was because I was going to be a freshman that year, and I could feel that my life was going to change. I remember telling Mama I was nervous things would change too much, yet I was also impatient for something new to begin. She pulled me into her arms and told me things would change, but were going to be good. She said high school was going to be the time of my life. I can recall smelling her hair and thinking the lavender scent was so comforting. I felt so safe. My lone dimple deepens at the memory. This is what I needed.

Opening my eyes, I lean against one of the enormous cypress trees. The sense of hope I felt stirring in me when I was getting dressed that morning seems to linger. I unpack my picnic lunch, taking a small bite of the PB&J Aunt Violette made for me. The peanut butter combined with her homemade plum jam is the best thing I've tasted in weeks. I haven't had much of an appetite, and this hits the spot. I take a long drink from my water bottle to quench my thirst from the heat.

I'm thankful I piled my wild auburn hair in a messy bun on top of my head. This humidity has always been the bane of my existence, but today I'm sort of enjoying the heat. The warmth on my skin feels pleasant. It reminds me of good times and makes me feel alive.

It's quiet except for the running water pushing over the rocks in the most shallow areas of the river. I picture my mother leaning against this exact tree, looking on in amusement as the nine-year-old version of myself tries to skip every last flat rock I could find across the water. The image makes my heart tighten in my chest, but it also brings me a sense of happiness at such a fond memory.

Although I feel hopeful, I can't help but wonder how I'll be able to start over. I'm not even sure how my father thought moving me here to a new town—away from everything familiar, away from all my friends—was supposed to make things easier for me. I've been trying to justify it, but who am I kidding? I know the truth. My move to Aunt Violette's isn't to make things easier for me; it's to make things easier for him.

I begin to wonder if Ryan has tried calling me. I know we left things in an awkward spot, but we've been best friends since we were five years old. I would think at some point he would notice I'm not around. I would think he would forgive me for shutting him out. Ryan has a good heart, and I feel confident he'll eventually see that I have every reason to grieve the unexpected loss of my mother for as long as I need to.

I do wonder if I actually pushed him away, but then I think, if he loved me, wouldn't he have been more supportive? And if I loved him, even if only platonically, wouldn't this all feel even more unbearable? Losing him doesn't feel unacceptable; at least I don't think it does. I don't know how I actually feel because frankly, I don't feel a whole lot of anything anymore. I can't. If I do, there won't be anything left of me. When I feel even a stirring of grief within me, I close it off—at least I did until Aunt Violette allowed me to briefly lose myself in her comfort, but it can't happen again. I need to build that wall higher before it all comes flooding back into my thoughts.

Pulling out my guitar, I gently strum my fingers across the strings. I'll lose myself in this and not think too much, because every thought is like an ice pick chipping away at my heart. I'm still hurting, but this day seems a little less tragic…a little different.

I'm standing frozen in place, hidden behind a giant cypress, listening to a beautiful and surprisingly gentle voice floating through the air. I can't see who is making the music that has me so riveted, but I need to. My heart begins to beat a little harder, and my palms are getting clammy. It feels like fear, but I'm not afraid.

It's something completely different, something foreign. Something changes as the guitar plays. The soft voice surrounds me, and that is all I know. It's strange, but I can sense that my life is about to shift in an unexpected direction I'm not sure I'm ready for, especially now. I'm not sure I'll ever be ready for it.

The music suddenly ends, and it pulls me from my thoughts. I remain still because I'm not sure if I should reveal myself. I feel a little embarrassed to be eavesdropping on this private moment.

I lean against a tree as quietly as I can so I don't give myself away then peek around to see what has captured my attention. Instantly, my breath catches in my throat, and a warmth I've never experienced begins to spread through me. It's a girl I've never seen before. I watch her move around as she packs up her guitar. A light breeze blows through her hair, the highlights from the sunlight looking like spun gold. It's the most beautiful color

I've ever seen. Her skin appears soft and delicate as I move my eyes up her body, from her legs to her shoulders. My hands ache to touch it. I want to see her eyes so terribly, want to see their color. Mesmerized, I shift a little. My body involuntarily leans toward her, and a twig snaps beneath my feet.

I freeze as her head whips around toward the sound. I hold my breath and wait, not moving again until I hear her resume packing up her things. Once again, I shift back to a position I can watch her from. She stands up and looks briefly out over the river then reluctantly turns as if she is about to leave someone behind on the opposite shore. Before I know it, she's walking away from me. I want to call out to her, but what would I say? Stepping out from my hideout, I watch her silently until she disappears entirely.

Sighing, I shake my head and try to grasp the sudden loss I feel at this mystery girl's departure. I'm not sure what has come over me, but I know one thing for sure: I need to find out who she is. It may sound crazy, but I know I'm supposed to know her. I have a feeling I didn't walk up on her by accident, and that only makes this encounter more extraordinary.

Selene

By the time I get back to the house, I'm sweating and bleeding. I decided to take the longer route home to see if the fort we built when I was ten was still standing, and I ended up tripping over a rock and cutting my knee open. I've always been a little clumsy—it wasn't unheard of for my mama to teasingly call me Grace. The endearing term was a sort of a joke between us. She loved teasing me, and I loved it right back.

I limp my way up the back porch steps and through the screen door, into the kitchen. I look down, trying to make sure

I'm not dripping blood all over the place, when I run into some-thing—or should I say *someone*—coming around the corner from the hall with a big box. It knocks us both back and I land hard on my bottom. Hardwood floors are not forgiving, and I scream out as the box and all of its contents hit the floor beside me.

"Aunt Violette, I'm so sorry," I instantly exclaim as I look up to find a set of eyes, the most unusual shade of green, staring at me with intense familiarity. "Oh…uh…I…" I can't seem to form a coherent word.

It isn't Aunt Violette, but the most stunning person I've ev-er seen. His eyes are so indescribable, I feel my cheeks heat as they freely roam over my body. It's like they're marking their territory, and I can feel it move through every part of me.

As if he suddenly remembers his manners, the stranger steps forward and reaches his hand out to me. My gaze moves from his eyes to his hand and back. My mind seems to be moving in slow motion, and a beat later I finally snap out of my thoughts and accept his help. He grips my hand and pulls me up with such force that I'm now almost pressed entirely against him. Our hands drop to our sides, and we're standing so close I can smell a mixture of soap and sweat. I never knew the scent of sweat could be so appealing. I look up to find him gazing down at me, send-ing chills up my spine.

Looking me straight in the eye, the stranger steps back a lit-tle and takes my hand again—this time without permission. "I'm Drake…Drake Thomas." He keeps my hand in his, making it hard for me to think. I feel like I'm on fire.

"I…" Before I can finish, Aunt Violette walks into the room and interrupts.

"Oh, Selene, dear, I see you've met Drake." She begins pulling vegetables out of her basket and setting them on the counter before washing them off.

We don't take our eyes off of one another. *What is wrong*

with me? I suddenly feel an awareness that my life is about to get a little more complicated. A fluttery sensation moves from my chest to my stomach then I abruptly pull my hand away and take a step back, immediately feeling uncomfortable. He's staring at me so intensely, I'm not sure if I want to run or lean into him. I'm beginning to feel something…something I know is dangerous. My only thought is that I can't allow myself to feel this much or I will break. I need to get away.

"Uh, yes…I did, Aunt Violette. I made him drop the box he was carrying by accident. You know how clumsy I can be." I keep taking small steps backward, as if I'm afraid to turn my back on him.

All of a sudden, I notice his eyes dart to my knee then back up to my face. He steps toward me before I can stop him and drops to his knees, lightly touching the skin around the cut.

"You're bleeding, and you have a knot on your knee." His hands begin to roam over other parts of me. "Are you hurt anywhere else?"

His touch feels like it's setting small fires all over my body. I can see the worry etched on his face, and I can't help thinking how bizarre his concern for me is, yet I stand there frozen while he continues to touch me. I feel an internal struggle about asking him to stop and move away.

Before I know it, Aunt Vi is at my side, saying my name and touching the back of her hand to my forehead.

I turn my head to look at her worried face. "Selene, are you all right? You seem a bit flushed." I push her hand away gently. Once again, I find myself taking a step back from this handsome stranger.

"No, I'm fine. I just tripped over a rock when I was walking back and scraped my knee. In fact, I was on my way upstairs when I bumped into…Drake." I look over to Aunt Violette and take the wet cloth she is now handing me. "I'm fine. It's no big deal."

Aunt Violette shakes her head and cackles. "As you said, you've always been a bit clumsy. Well, go get a bandage on that before it gets infected." She turns to Drake, who is still on his knees with his gaze trained on me. I'm trying hard to not look at him. "Drake, do you think you can get that stuff back in the box and out in the shed for me? I believe we can finish the rest next Saturday."

"Uh, yes ma'am," he says, and I can't keep myself from glancing his way. He's still watching me, and the shock I feel as our eyes meet has me instantly averting my attention to the floor. "You best take care of that knee. It's a pleasure to have met you...Selene."

It's as if his voice is caressing me when my name leaves his lips. I glance up, a shock coursing through me. What is he doing to me? I need to get away, but I don't want to make it seem like he is having such a strange and uncomfortable effect on me. "It was ni...nice to meet you too, Drake," I stammer out before I turn toward the stairs.

As I climb the steps, I can feel his eyes on me. What is it about this guy? I don't know, and I can't find out, because if this one brief encounter causes me to lose this much control over my emotions, then Drake Thomas will be nothing but trouble for me.

I make it to the top of the landing, rush into my room, and shut the door. As I lean my back against the door, my breathing is labored, as if I just ran a marathon. I'm feeling something I've never felt before, and it seems out of my control. *What the hell?* I just ran away from a boy.

I walk over to the dresser and pick up the picture of Mama and me. I'm looking at the camera, and she is looking at me. We're both wearing our golden hair down around our shoulders, and our green eyes are shining. We look more like sisters than mother and daughter. I wish she were here so I could talk to her; my emotions are all over the place, and I don't know how to handle what I'm feeling.

Carrying the picture over to the window seat, I peek out and see Drake entering the garage out back. The sight of him sends chills across my flesh. Yep, Drake Thomas is definitely going to be trouble.

chapter 4

Drake

The tips of my fingers are still tingling from touching her skin as I carry the box across the back lawn to the shed. I can't believe the mystery girl is Mrs. Durham's niece—such an unbelievable but welcome surprise. I unlock the door while propping the box against the wall with my knee.

Walking to the back of the room, I place the box in an area I cleared last weekend for the things Mrs. D wants to keep out here.

I've been helping her with handiwork and other things she needs done around the house. It was always Lacey's thing to come here. She spent at least two hours with Mrs. D every weekend, sometimes more before the crash. Lacey said it was her civic duty as the mayor's daughter, but deep down we both knew she loved it. About a month after the accident, I showed up on Mrs. Durham's doorstep, asking if I could pick up where Lacey had left off. She didn't even say a word, just opened her screen door and stepped aside for me to enter. I was stunned at first, unsure of what to do, until she said, "Well, don't just stand there like a bump on a log. Get in here. I need help boxing up things in the attic."

I had no idea her attic was full of at least forty years' worth of stuff, but I've been here every week since that day. We both just fell into a comfortable pattern. Although our relationship might seem odd to an outsider looking in, I don't care; helping Mrs. Durham is just one more way for me to keep Lacey close.

I shut the door behind me and turn to lock it up, hesitating as I feel a prickling on the back of my neck. I glance over my shoulder, but I don't see anyone. I raise my eyes to the second story of the house and see the curtain stir against the window. They're sheer, so I can see the outline of her figure behind them. She's watching me, and I can't help the sudden happiness I feel at the thought.

I'm not sure what it is about this girl, but the moment I heard her voice, I knew there was something...something I wasn't going to be able to ignore. The feeling only intensified when I looked at those stunning catlike eyes up close. The way I felt being that close to her didn't make sense, but I realize not everything makes sense all the time; sometimes things have no explanation, they just are.

I look back toward the window, and this time she doesn't pull back quickly enough. I caught her. Giggling to myself, I decide to see how far I can take this little game I feel we're playing. I pull my shirt off and wipe the sweat from my brow, and then I slowly raise my hand in a sort of a wave to let her know I see her. I can barely see her face, but I can imagine she's turned the most incredible shade of red. I grin then turn back, locking the door before walking across the lawn. I take slow strides back toward the house. Although I can feel her still watching me, I never look back up. *Oh yeah. This is going to be fun.*

Selene

*S**hit, shit, shit*, I chant over and over to myself as I continue to stare at Drake walking across the lawn. He saw me, so I'm not even going to try to hide now. I can't believe it—he actually took off his shirt. He did that on purpose; I could see it on his face. Then he had the nerve to wave with an amused look on his face. I may be fifty yards away, but I can tell his grin says he thinks I'm watching because I want him. Well, I am watching him, but not…not because—crap, I don't know why. *What a cocky ass.* Look at him, sauntering across the lawn without a shirt. He thinks I want to see his tan and obviously—even from this distance—hard abs. He does look good…*oh my God! What is wrong with me?* I'm still bleeding, for crying out loud.

I quickly pull the gauzy fabric closed again and back away from the window then slowly limp my way over to the side of the bed so I can sit.

This is just great. I've just been caught staring at Aunt Vi's helper boy…or whatever he is. The scary thing is if I really feel so…*whatever* about him, why does every place he touched my skin still feel like it's in flames?

Putting my face into my hands, I shake my head. This isn't what I need. For the first time ever, I feel an immediate attraction and connection to someone. I can't even think clearly, but one thing *is* clear: this boy is doing something to me. I've felt more in the last twenty minutes than I've felt in the last four months.

chapter 5

Drake

It's been three days, and Selene is still on my mind. I've gone back to what Lacey and I called "our spot" along the river every day, hoping to run into her. I want to find an excuse to stop by Mrs. D's house, but I can't seem to come up with even one good non-stalker-like motive. So, instead, I'm stalking her in my dreams.

Yeah, pathetic, I know, but I haven't wanted something— someone—so badly, ever. I'm just a little afraid to give in to that need. Maybe I recognize the same grief in her voice, or it could be this unexplainable familiarity when I look into her eyes. I've been trying to rationalize the way I feel, but I can't exactly pinpoint it.

Lacey would giggle at me and tell me to get over myself. It wasn't often I left myself vulnerable, even to her. She waited for situations like this so she could tease me, and I didn't typically give them to her. Usually, she would give me shit for being a jerk. The truth is, I'm an asshole. I never had to be anything else. Everyone in my life has allowed me to act this way and loved me for it. I often find myself wondering why, but I usually shrug it off because I don't want to think too much about it.

My family let me because, well, they're assholes too, every last one of us, except for Lacey. She wasn't anything but good. We were the epitome of good twin and evil twin. Being connected to her was my only redeeming quality. Now the only part of me that's left is hanging on for dear life to any goodness that might be lingering in me.

My whole life, my friends let me act like a dick because someone decided I was cool, and it allowed them to be assholes, too. For some reason, teenagers—especially guys—love to be little bastards. I was so cool I could act any way I wanted to, and I would never fall from grace. What kind of stupid shit is that? Girls let me be a dick because I was wealthy, popular, and good-looking. I don't even have an explanation, but if it weren't for Lacey, I would think all teenage girls were clones of stupidity.

Regardless of how my attitude has changed, I'll always be the person who made those fatal mistakes. Everyone will continue to see me the same way they've always seen me. I'll always see myself in that same light too, except now I don't see it as an opportunity or a fortunate circumstance. No, it's just a reminder of everything that led to Lacey being taken away.

Pulling up in front of the school, I switch off the ignition, pressing my forehead against the steering wheel. I'm exhausted by the thought of all these expectations my parents and everyone place on me. Sighing, I recognize there isn't a choice. It's time for me to get my classes squared away. Plus, I have a meeting with the team because two-a-days will be starting in a week. I used to look forward to the practices and workouts, but now they're just another aspect to the old Drake, the one who thrived on being the star quarterback, the one who doesn't exist any longer. Jumping out of my truck, I head for the front doors that lead to the school office.

As I pull the door, something pushes it from the other end. Having expected a little more resistance, I pull too hard and lose my balance, falling backward and landing on my back. To my surprise, something lands right on top of my stomach, knocking the breath out of me.

In an instant, I realize it isn't something, but someone—the very someone I've been unable to get off my mind. My arms instinctively wrap around her, trapping her arms and body against my chest. I stare up into her shocked green eyes, and *fuck*, those eyes are even more dangerous up close than I realized. It's like my hands move of their own accord as they reach for her face, pushing the golden strands of hair behind her ear. At this point, I'm not sure if the lack of air in my lungs is due to the impact of the fall or being in such close proximity to her.

She is staring at me silently, but I can feel her breath moving rapidly in and out of her partially opened lips. It's tickling my skin, and the scent of sweet mint swirls around me.

"Selene," I whisper.

It's like her name pulls her back from wherever she went just now, because she begins to push against me. The only problem is my arms are reluctant to let her go, and she is struggling. I realize I need to get a hold of myself. I can see the panic in her eyes, and I don't want to scare her. Finally, I loosen my embrace and release her. Our gazes remain locked as she gets to her feet.

Slowly, she begins to back away, speaking rapidly under her breath. *Is she just saying "shit"?* I think she is, and I can't help the small chuckle that escapes. I pick myself up from the cement sidewalk and watch her.

As I dust off my beige cargo shorts, I say, "We really need to stop running into each other this way. One of us is bound to get hurt."

As I say the word hurt, something pricks my heart, and my smile fades. Why do I suddenly feel like this girl standing in front of me, looking so vulnerable, has the power to hurt me so severely that I would never recover?

Finally, she speaks, breaking through my thoughts. "Look, I'm sorry." She sounds annoyed, and I'm not sure why. "I will admit I wasn't paying attention. It's just that I came all the way here to register for school, and I forgot the one paper that would finalize everything. So now, I'm still not registered, and I have to come back."

I hold my hands up and take a step back as if fending her off. "Sorry to make things worse," I say. I can't help the smile that begins to widen on my face again. Damn, she is cute when she's flustered.

"It's not you, I was just hoping this was going to be easy. I gotta go. See you around," she stammers out as she turns on her heels and heads toward the parking lot.

I watch her ass do this cute little back-and-forth sway. "Looking forward to it," I say as I tilt my head to the side to see how nice it is from another angle. Yep, just as I suspected—it looks just as good from that perspective too. I imagine myself looking like a dog angling my head to the side when its owner is talking about it, and I don't give a damn. The thought makes me laugh out loud.

She stops and looks over her shoulder, giving me a confused look, then turns back and leaves. As I continue to watch her walk away, I know I need to learn more about Selene the mystery girl.

Selene

As I turn the car at the corner, I allow myself to relax. My body is a traitor. I'm pretty sure I could light the whole town with the amount of electricity I can feel shooting through it. What the shit? It's his fault—why does he have to be so cute? No, wait, not cute; Drake is much more than that. A puppy is cute. He is like Channing Tatum, Ryan Reynolds, and Ryan Gosling all rolled into one—beautiful, mouthwatering, hard to resist, and he knows it.

He was actually checking me out. Well, I'm not interested. He is all charm and arrogance like he is used to having his way. It's like he's always on, except for that one moment he dropped the smarmy smile and looked like he wasn't quite in control of everything around him. Before I even had a chance to blink, his usual façade was back.

I pull into Aunt Vi's driveway and notice she is watering her plants along the front porch. I hop out of her '58 cherry red Chevy Impala convertible. I can't believe she let me drive it. Riding in the Impala was one of my favorite things to do on our visits when I was little. We would go to the local drive-in, which was still open, and all sit in the back seat together, stuffing ourselves with popcorn and candy.

I rub my hand along the side as I make my way to the porch. "Hey, Aunt Vi," I say as I take a seat on the steps that lead up to the porch. She stands at the top in her soft, A-line floral-print skirt and white cotton button-down blouse neatly tucked in. She looks like she belongs in a home and gardening magazine.

"Hello dear, did you get all registered?" She continues to move around to the different potted plants that line the railing of the porch.

I shrug. "No ma'am. I was missing one paper I needed with Dad's signature on it. I know I had it this morning, but I guess I left it on my bed by accident. The counselor told me to just come back and they would have everything ready for me." I stare out over the front lawn, wondering how she keeps it so green in this sweltering heat.

I notice a pitcher of lemonade sitting near the steps and

reach over to pour myself a glass. I take a drink, and it's the most refreshing feeling as the liquid slides down my throat. It's just like Aunt Vi to have this made and ready for anyone who might stop by. There isn't anything more refreshing than her fresh-squeezed lemonade.

Interrupting my thoughts, she stares down at me and says, "Well, don't wait too long, Selene. It will be better if you just get that taken care of. Then you can enjoy the last few weeks of summer." I nod as I stand up and make my way up the steps to the front door.

As I reach for the handle of the screen door, I stop and turn toward my aunt. "Aunt Violette, what's the story with that boy who was here a few days ago?"

I don't want to let her know I remember his name. I don't even know why, it just seems like it would make my question more important if I did.

"Are you talking about Drake? Drake Thomas?" She is now looking at me with tenderness.

"Uh, I—yeah, I think that's his name." I try to sound casual as I speak.

She watches me with a knowing look. I need to set her straight. It's not what she thinks—I'm not interested, I'm just curious. Is that the same thing?

I speak again before she can say anything. "It's just that I ran into him at the school just now." *Literally*, I mutter under my breath.

She sits her body carefully into one of the wooden rockers and uses one foot to gently rock herself as she replies, "Well, Drake is the mayor's son. He is quite the athlete, and I hear very popular among his peers, especially the girls."

I notice a gleam in her eyes as she mentions the girls. Of course he's popular with the girls—who wouldn't want hotty toddy, ChanRyRy? *Well, I don't*, I tell myself quickly. Of course I don't.

"Anyway, you may remember his sister, Lacey. She always came around and helped me here at the house. She was here a few times when you were visiting with your mama." At the mention of my mother, a knot suddenly forms in the middle of my chest, and I subconsciously begin to try to rub it out. Aunt Vi continues, "She was a sweet little blonde thing with the prettiest hazel green eyes."

I think back over the years, and I do remember a girl my age. She was sweet. In fact, she was the one who told Mama and me about the hidden spot on the river we loved so much. How did I forget that? It might be nice to see her again. I could always use a friend, and since I sort of know her already, it would make things less awkward once school starts. So, she's Drake's sister…but that doesn't matter.

"I do remember—"

I'm cut off by the phone ringing.

Aunt Violette pushes herself up out of the rocker. "I better get that. I'm expecting the roofers to call about that leak in the shed."

She disappears inside, leaving me thinking of a new school, old acquaintances, and seemingly dangerous boys.

chapter 6

Drake

I tell Lacey about Selene today. As I read the next chapter of the newest romantic adventure to her, I can't help imagining myself and Selene. Inevitably, fate puts us together, we fall in love, I rescue her, and then we live happily ever after.

I'm pathetic. I mean, where are these pansy-ass ideas coming from? Like any good brother, I blame my sister. *This is your fault*, I tell her quietly, and I release a small snort.

Seriously, if she didn't love these ridiculous love stories so much, I wouldn't be spending every weekend brainwashing myself into becoming some mushy, lovesick, feeling shithead. I tell her as much, which leads me to the story of seeing Selene in our secret spot then running into her at Mrs. D's. I talk and talk until I realize I've told her every detail of each meeting and how it made me feel. I tell her about Selene's sun-kissed skin, long golden hair, and fierce green eyes. I give her every detail, knowing I will never hear her teasing laughter, but I feel it down to my core anyway.

Closing the book, I stand and stretch. "Gotta go before Mrs. Durham begins to wonder if I've left her hanging today. See ya, sis."

───────●───────

As I pull into Mrs. Durham's driveway, I can't help hoping for another run-in with Selene.

I back my truck in so I can load up the scraps of metal and junk I promised to take to the dumpsite outside of town this afternoon. As I hop out of my truck, I notice Mrs. D stepping out of the kitchen door onto the covered porch. She cheerfully lifts her hand in a good-morning salute.

"Good morning, Drake dear, how are you?"

"Good morning. Sorry I'm a little late. I lost track of time with Lacey."

Mrs. D is the only person who knows how I spend my Saturday mornings. I confided in her when she told me just a couple of weeks after I started coming around that she went to visit Lacey every Sunday after church. She didn't actually ask me if I went, and honestly, I didn't come out and tell her. She only said that the flowers I left were exactly what Lacey would have loved, and she never said another word after that.

She has never asked me what happened the night of the accident. There was one day I know she wanted to ask, but when she opened her mouth, nothing came out, and she immediately closed it before walking away. I could see it was too painful for her, and I'm glad she didn't ask. I need her, and I'm afraid if she knew the truth, she wouldn't forgive me.

"Drake, you don't have a set time, and I will never reproach you for spending time with Lacey. In fact, I look forward to visiting her tomorrow. I miss having her around here." She sighs, and I notice a bit of sadness in her eyes.

Love isn't something we were shown very often at home, and it's such a wonderful feeling to know that Lacey was so loved by this woman, although I do hate seeing Mrs. Durham hurt.

I suddenly remember Selene and wonder where she is right now. Does she like to sleep late? Is she an early riser? Does she drink coffee? There are so many things I wonder about her. It's strange; I've never wanted to know so much about any one person before, especially a girl.

"Well—uh, you have Selene now. Uh…where is she, anyway? Did she get registered for school?" I sound like a complete fucking moron. I can't even look up at Mrs. D for fear she will see the pathetic cream puff I'm becoming.

I think she knows anyway. I'm pretty sure she just giggled, but she quickly presses her lips together before saying, "My niece is all registered, and as to her whereabouts, she went for a walk about an hour ago." Handing me a piece of paper, she changes the subject to our tasks for the day. "This is a list of what I would like to get done today. I have a few more boxes upstairs in the attic, and then I would like to move the garage sale items into the shed, but put them closer to the front so we can get to them." She sits in one of the rockers she has on every side of the house.

"Yes ma'am." I turn to enter the house through the kitchen.

As I pull the screen door open, Mrs. D stops me. "And, Drake, be careful with my Selene. She isn't one to open up and trust quickly. She has suffered many heartaches and has been let down by one person or another for her whole life."

I stand still with my back to her, unable to move. What does she mean, "be careful with her"? I don't even know what I want from her. I'm not even…*fuck*.

"Yes ma'am." I walk through the door and get to work.

Selene

I notice the familiar black truck parked in the driveway as I walk back up to the house. Stopping dead in my tracks, I dart behind one of the huge oak trees. *Damn.* What the shit am I supposed to do now? I'm not ready for this—whatever 'this' is. I just know being around him makes me feel too much.

I forgot he was coming here today. I can feel the pull already, even though I can't see him as I peer around the tree trunk. My body is so close to the tree that I appear to be hugging it. I don't have my game face on; I'm not ready to see him. When I say game face, I mean my asshole-repellant war face. *Grrr. Grrr*, I keep saying to myself, trying to work up my angry-girl attitude. *Grrr. Grrrrr.* I peek around the side of the tree again—still no sign of ChanRyRylicious. I turn back around.

"Grrrrrrrrrrrrrrrrrrrrrrrrrrrr." A loud growl erupts in my face, so close I can feel the warm breath against my cheek.

I scream and stumble backward over an enormous root protruding out of the ground. As I'm falling back with my arms flailing to help keep my balance, I feel two large hands encircle my wrist and pull me forward with so much momentum I fly forward into a rock-hard chest. It all happens so fast, I barely stop screaming before I hear a roar of laughter.

The body holding me is shaking so violently with amusement that when his grip relaxes on my forearm, I jerk away from his hold.

"What the hell, Drake? You scared the shit out of me." I want to be pissed. *It's not funny, asshole*, I think as mirth tickles my throat. I fight to keep my face straight. He has no right to sneak up on me. The worst part is he heard me growling, and now I'm mortified. I can't let him know I'm embarrassed, but I'm pretty sure my cheeks are the color of a ripe strawberry.

At this point, Drake is bending over, clutching his stomach

as if in pain—I hope he is. He looks up and starts to say some-thing, but before he can get a word out, another full-blown fit of laughter overwhelms him.

"Nice. Real nice." I abruptly turn and begin to walk toward the house, trying my best to appear offended to hide my embar-rassment. Why am I an idiot around him?

I'm walking as fast as I can without running. I hear him calling my name between rounds of laughter. As I hear him get-ting closer to me, I turn my head over my shoulder and yell, "I don't know you very well, Drake Thomas, but you're a shit-head." This only causes him to laugh more. I can't take it any-more, so I whip around to face him. He is only two or three feet behind me.

"It's not funny! Are you always this way? Do you think people should just fall at your feet?" I try to sound angry and severe—try being the key word. "I have news for you: I will never fall at your feet. I don't think you're funny or charming, not one bit." Of course, the fluttery feeling in my stomach and my irregular heartbeat are contradicting every word I'm spout-ing, but I continue anyway. "So, if you will excuse me, I have things to do, and I know you have things to do too." *There! I told him. Yes, I sure did.*

As I begin to turn around again, his arm flies out and he grabs my wrist, whipping me around to face him. "Look, Selene, don't be mad—please. I'm sorry." He puts on a pouty face with his lips sticking out slightly. I wonder how soft they are, and my hands itch to reach out and touch them.

"Do you forgive me? Can we start over?" Drake bats his eyelashes at me as he puts his hand out so I can shake it, his lips tipping up at the corners. "Hello, I'm Drake Thomas. Welcome to Montgomery," he says, his hand remaining suspended in the air between us.

His eyes never leave mine, and I decide to just give in to his little game, though God knows I'm going to regret it. My hand slowly moves to his, and now we're palm to palm. My god, I'm in trouble, but he doesn't need to know that. "Hi, I'm Selene Chandler." I hesitate before adding, "This is much better, but I'm still not falling for your shit."

"You say shit a lot," he states in a matter-of-fact tone without letting go of my hand. His smile is wider now.

"And?" I retort as I yank my hand out of his grasp. It was beginning to feel too comfortable.

"Just noticed, that's all." He still wears a smirk, like he's won something. It irritates the shit out of me, but it's irresistible at the same time. *Ugh*, I want to smile. I hate being a girl.

Taking a few steps back, he continues to beam at me. "Well, Selene Chandler, I better get back to work before Mrs. D has my hide." I can't help but stare at his mouth as he speaks. "Oh, by the way, we're going to be excellent friends—magnificent."

This sends my walls back up. I've never been trusting of people, especially a handsome guy with a cocky grin and oozing charm, but damn if I don't want to give in to him.

"We'll just have to see about that," I yell over my shoulder as I hurry up the back porch steps, into the house. I don't even sound convincing to myself, and I can't help the pleased look that spreads across my face.

I'm finally done putting every last scrap of metal and junk into the back of my truck, so I hop out of the back and lift the tailgate closed. Taking off my gloves, I put them in my back pocket before wiping a trickle of perspiration from my brow. The temperature has reached a record high, and I'm dripping with sweat.

I've been working hard for several hours without stopping, and there hasn't been any sign of Mrs. Durham or Selene. As I was working, I thought about the confidence Selene tries to display when I'm around her. She is so different from any girl I've ever met. It's refreshing that she doesn't fall at my feet—well, at least not in the same sense as most girls. She is a bit accident prone, but it only makes her more adorable and interesting.

Lacey would have really liked her, and I can't help but laugh to myself imagining how they would have ganged up on me. It was always Lacey who kept me grounded, and since she's been gone, I haven't been able to keep myself there. Since meeting Selene, I feel that same sense of calm.

I was serious when I said we were going to be friends. I know without a doubt after today, when I caught her talking to herself and growling, I have to know her. I chuckle a little, thinking about her growling. I'm not even sure what she was doing, but damn if it didn't make her more appealing. There is no choice for me; I need her to be in my life.

I walk up the porch steps and pour myself a glass of lemonade from the pitcher Mrs. D always leaves out while I work.

"Are you hungry?"

I whip my head to the left with a start. She's sitting in one of the rockers that line the porch, her legs pulled up, her knees to her chest. She looks so peaceful sitting there, and I have a hard time forming a coherent thought. I'm not even sure how much time passes by before I notice her waving her hand in my face. "Hello, Drake? Are you in there?"

"Oh, uh, I'm sorry. I didn't see you there. What did you say?" Great, I sound like a fucking idiot.

Her lips spread into the first genuine smile I've seen directed my way. Once again, my brain begins to lose all ability to function. "I asked if you were hungry." She continues watching me. "Soooo, are you?"

I can't take my eyes off her lips. "Am I what?" I lick my

own, because suddenly my mouth feels dry.

"For shit's sake, Drake. What's wrong with you? Were you out in the heat for too long?" There's a mischievous gleam in her eyes. "ARE. YOU. HUNGRY?" she adds sarcastically.

I want to laugh out loud at the way she is speaking to me. No one has ever spoken to me this way—no one except Selene Chandler, apparently.

"Starving," I state plainly, and again my gaze remains on her lips before I quickly dart my eyes up to hers.

She begins to fidget with her hair, twisting it around her finger as if she is suddenly nervous. "Okay, well, Aunt Violette made some sandwiches and fruit salad. I'll go get them. You sit down, and I'll be right back."

She steps around me, and I can tell she is very careful not to touch me. I turn and watch her enter the house before I carry my lemonade over to the nearest rocker and sit down.

Letting out an exaggerated breath, I lean my head back and close my eyes. I begin to drift to sleep then the slam of the screen door wakes me. I look up and watch her walk toward me. As she nears me, Selene holds the plate of food out, and I gladly take it.

"Thank you," I say before laying the plate in my lap. I reach for the sandwich and take a big bite. It's so good. I love the way fresh vegetables taste on a sandwich, and I grin with my mouth full, making it hard to chew. I feel so relaxed, something I haven't felt in a very long time. I hear a quiet giggle escape Selene's lips.

"What's so funny?" I say with a mouth full of food.

She giggles again, and the sound is so sweet that I can't help the toothy expression that makes an attempt to spread across my face despite the large amount of food in my mouth.

"Seriously, how do you fit so much food in your mouth?" She takes a dainty bite of watermelon, and I can see the juice glistening in the sunlight on her lips. I nearly choke on my food,

41

finally managing to swallow hard.

"I have a big mouth." As if to prove my point, I stick what remains of my sandwich in my mouth and smile with full cheeks.

Selene just shakes her head, and a soft look appears on her face. She seems more relaxed around me. I wonder what happened in the last few hours. Maybe it's the fact that we didn't knock each other over in that span of time. She was sitting so quietly up here on the porch that I didn't even notice her—was she watching me the whole time? I almost crack up at myself for having such a self-centered thought.

We finish the rest of our lunch in silence. It's not awkward, and I don't feel the need to fill the lull in our conversation. She seems to feel the same.

Finally, I stand up and reach out for her plate. "I'll put these in the kitchen." She hands it to me without a word, and I turn to enter the kitchen. The pleased feeling I get when I'm around her returns.

As I walk back out onto the porch, I decide to ask Selene if she wants to ride with me to dump the junk piled in my truck. "Hey, would you want..." I stop midsentence as I realize she's gone.

I suddenly hear the sound of the front screen door slamming close and feet running up the stairs inside. I feel my happiness disappear, and it almost hurts.

I want to follow after her and demand to know why she snuck away from me, but before I make a move, Mrs. D's words from this morning drift through my mind: *And, Drake, be careful with my Selene. She isn't one to open up and trust quickly. She has suffered many heartaches and has been let down by one person or another for her whole life.* I'm not sure what scared her off exactly, but I'm determined to prove she can trust me.

I don't know why, but I need her to trust me, to open up to me, because something is telling me I'm going to have to trust her too.

Selene

I lean back against the door of my bedroom. I ran from him again. *Oh God.* I'm such a coward, but I was losing all sense being around him. I listen carefully at the door, waiting for the sound of his footsteps following behind me. He wouldn't do that, and although I'm the one who chose to run, I can't help the hint of disappointment I'm feeling.

Walking over to the window, I peer out, trying to see if I can catch a glimpse of Drake leaving. I notice him securing everything he loaded in the truck one last time. It's as if he didn't even realize I disappeared, and that thought bothers me. I was watching him all day, telling myself I was indifferent to his charm and good looks. He is full of himself for sure. The way he acted this morning, sneaking up behind me and then having the nerve to laugh at me, *to my face*—he has to be the most frustrating human being I've ever met. And yet, thinking of his laughter fills me with the urge to giggle. I stop myself. I don't know him, and from what I know of most guys, I'm not willing to allow myself to be vulnerable.

He is a jerk. He has to be because—well, he is a guy. Yes. A jerk…a jerk who spends his Saturdays helping an elderly woman, whom he isn't related to in any way, clean out her attic and shed? Yes, an arrogant, inconsiderate, charming, polite, beautiful jerk. *Shit.*

This is precisely why I had to get away from him. He is unintentionally funny and adorable. I actually felt joy and forgot everything for one tiny moment. I forgot I don't trust people, and worst of all, I forgot Mama. Sitting in that rocker on the porch next to Drake felt good. He's weaseling his way into my mind; nearly every thought is of him. I'm not ready for that, and even if I were, it wouldn't mean he is interested in more than harmless flirting. He was flirting…I think, but maybe he wasn't and I'm reading this all wrong. *Ugh.*

The rumbling of his truck starting breaks into my thoughts. I pull the gauzy fabric back again and watch as he looks out his driver's side window in my direction. He isn't smiling, just stares, and I swear, even from this distance, I can see the disappointment in his eyes.

———————————•———————————

A few hours later, as I sit on the porch, reading and drinking some sun tea I made that afternoon, Aunt Vi pulls into the driveway. I watch her climb out of the car, smiling as she sees me.

I close my book as she steps up onto the porch. "Hi, how was your day?" I ask as I lean back and begin rocking the chair.

"It was nice, and I got a lot of errands done. The only thing is I didn't make it to the grocery store like I wanted, so I thought we might go out to eat tonight. What do you say?" She takes a seat in the rocker next to me and reaches her hand over to cover mine.

I stiffen a little before I relax into the comforting touch. I don't know why I react that way to any sort of contact or affection, especially when it's from her, but I just can't help it. Smiling over at her, I nod my head. "Yes, that sounds good. I'm starved." I allow a smile to spread across my face.

"Great, let me go in and freshen up. Then we can be on our way." She stands and heads for the house.

I follow behind her, carrying my tea to the kitchen, and then run upstairs to put on some shoes and change my top. I pull the brush through my hair and swipe some pink gloss across my lips before heading back downstairs.

Aunt Violette emerges from her bedroom as I hop off the bottom step. "Ready?" she asks in her tender voice.

"Yes ma'am."

I really am looking forward to dinner out with Aunt Vio-lette. It's the second time today that I feel like things have a chance to be normal.

chapter 7

Drake

I spent the rest of the day at the dump, unloading my truck, and now I'm making my way to dinner with my parents. I don't want to go, but I wasn't exactly given a choice. Of course I wasn't—I've never been given one about anything, so why would they start now?

I'm a little late, and I know it isn't going to go over well with Mother and Mayor Thomas at all. I usually refer to my parents in a more formal way when I'm not around them. I'm sure if I were analyzed by a doctor, they would say it's a form of disrespect and that I have anger issues when it comes to my parents, and they would be right. Then again, my mother has anger issues too.

I pull into the parking lot behind the local Italian restaurant, Romeo's. Lacey always loved this place, and we came here often, although my parents weren't doing it for that reason. They only cared that it was the nicest restaurant in town.

As I pull the keys from the ignition, I glance down at the time on my phone: I'm ten minutes late. I lean my head against the steering wheel and take a deep breath. This can go one of two ways: terribly, or really terribly. I can only hope she waits until we're home.

I get out and lock the doors. Walking with my head down, I don't even see her standing at the end of the building near the alleyway that leads to the front of the restaurant. It's dark, and the alleyway is only dimly lit, so I'm startled when she suddenly speaks.

"You're late," I hear her say coldly.

I flinch, but so slightly no one would notice. I continue walking toward her without saying a word. I learned long ago that saying anything at all only makes things worse.

"How many times do I have to remind you that when I give you a certain time to be somewhere, you're not to arrive even a second after? You've embarrassed us once again."

I'm standing directly in front of her and decide now is when I will make my first apology. "I'm sorry, Mother. I didn't manage my time well while working today, and I still had to shower and change."

I hold my breath, waiting for her next action. She is always so unpredictable. Her hand flies out and connects with my cheek before I can even register what's happening. The sting sends a shiver up my spine, but I hold steady.

"Don't let it happen again. Remember, Drake, this is election season."

I keep my head down because I don't want to give her the satisfaction of seeing the dejection I feel in my eyes.

"Yes, Mother."

I watch her as she turns and walks back down the alley to the restaurant. I feel a little sick, and my cheek is still burning. God, I hate her. I hate how she makes me feel helpless and weak. What's more, I hate that I still let all of this get to me.

47

Clenching my hand into a fist, I begin to swing it into the brick wall but stop just before I connect with the hard surface. Instead, I slap both hands against it and lean forward. I let my head hang down in between my outstretched arms as I take several breaths—several long, deep breaths, because I can feel that the dam is about to break if I don't get a hold of myself. Sometimes, it's just too hard. I can't always hide the pain.

Suddenly, I feel a hand on my shoulder, and I freeze.

"Drake?" I hear a sweet, familiar voice whisper.

I can't move. *What is she doing here? How long has she been here?*

"Drake…are you all right?" I can hear the uncertainty in her voice.

She's quiet, but I hear the tremor in her words. She's rubbing her hand over my shoulder, and her fingers brush my neck. I shiver involuntarily. I can't look at her; I'm afraid of what she'll see, and I'm sure my cheek is red from my mother's hand.

"How long have you been here?" I ask, already knowing the answer. I know because I can hear it in her voice.

If she heard everything, I can only be thankful that this was one of the less severe displays of punishment. It's hard enough thinking she witnessed any of it. She doesn't say anything.

"Selene, how long have you been standing out here?" I ask her again, with a little more bite than I intend.

She drops her hand and takes a step back. "The whole time. I didn't mean to eavesdrop, I just…"

I turn and face her. She has her head down and is wringing her hands together. I reach out and stop her, taking her hands in mine. I stare at our entwined fingers before looking up and meeting her gaze. Selene watches me, her eyes wide, and I can see something in them I never expected—understanding.

"Selene, I'm sorry I just snapped at you. It's not you, but—"

"Drake, don't explain. I understand more than most that sometimes parents are not what a person expects them to be. I'm just sorry you know it too."

My only focus is the words coming out of her mouth. She slowly, almost timidly reaches her hand up and gently lays it upon my still tingling cheek.

"Does it hurt?" she asks in a hushed tone. She takes my breath away.

"No," I lie, but only a little. "Don't worry about me, Selene," I tell her as I cover her hand with mine. "I just need you to promise you won't tell anyone what you heard or saw—not even Mrs. Durham." I notice her eyes widen at the mention of her aunt. "Please. Please promise me."

I can see the reluctance in her eyes before she drops her hand and turns. I wait for her to speak.

When she remains quiet, I beg again. "Please."

"I promise," she finally whispers.

It's as if I hear the click of a lock to my heart being opened with those two words. At that moment, I know without a doubt, Selene holds the key. I may have thought I'd lost my other half when Lacey died, but in reality, I've been waiting to find it.

I step behind her, our bodies almost touching. I wonder if being this close is having the same effect on her that it is on me. I timidly place my hand on her shoulder.

"Thank you," I say, choking on my words a little.

The emotions I feel are building, and once again, I'm afraid I might break.

"Drake, why does she do this to you?" The concern is evident in her voice.

I want to answer her, but I've waited long enough, and prolonging joining my parents any longer will only make things worse.

"Selene, I—I want to tell you, but I really need to go in."

She turns and faces me again. Our eyes meet, and I can see the worry has come back. She seems to realize we've been standing out here for a while, and I know she knows it's the whole reason for my trouble to begin with.

I speak before she can say anything. "It will be fine, don't worry. She didn't expect me to follow right away." Changing the subject, I ask, "What were you doing out here alone, anyway?"

"Aunt Violette and I are having dinner here. It's a little chilly in there, so I ran out to the car to get my cardigan."

She is playing with her hair, twisting it around her finger over and over again. It's something I've noticed she does when she is nervous. I can feel my lips tug at the corners just watching her.

"Well, then, shall we go in?" I ask as I reach out and take her hand in mine.

I start to lead her to the front of the restaurant without waiting for a response. She doesn't seem to mind, but as I look out of the corner of my eye, I can see something in her eyes that looks almost like fear. She is even walking a little stiffly.

As we come to the front entrance, Selene stops walking. It pulls my arm back a little, so I turn toward her.

"Drake, I won't forget that we didn't finish our discussion back there."

She pulls her hand from mine and quickly enters Romeo's, leaving me standing on the sidewalk, staring at her.

Selene

I haven't heard a word Aunt Vi has said since I came back from getting my cardigan. My mind is consumed by what I witnessed between Drake and his mother. She hurts him. It makes me want to weep, and I barely know him.

I can see how much sadness and despair he holds inside. I recognize it. I feel it. And, because I know his pain matches my own, I feel an unexplainable need to take it away.

"Selene...earth to Selene."

I snap out of my daydream and turn my attention to Aunt Vi, who is staring at me with questions in her eyes, questions I know she wants to ask but never will.

"I'm sorry, Aunt Vi. What were you saying?" I move some food around on my plate.

"I said you've barely touched your food. Do you not like it?"

I look down at my spaghetti as if only just now realizing it's in front of me.

"Oh, uh...no, it's good. I'm just not as hungry as I thought," I lie, although a voice inside me is screaming for me to tell her about Drake.

"Are you sure you're okay? Did something happen when you went to the car? I saw Drake came in after you—did he bother you?"

She saw us. I wonder if his mom saw us, too. I hope I didn't get him in any more trouble than he was already in.

Shaking my head, I place a tight smile on my face. "No ma'am. We only said hello. I think we may be friends after all. It's just..." I almost begin to tell her but realize I made a promise, and I never break promises.

"Yes...it's just what?"

I look up to find her watching me with a slight crease between her brows, as if she is trying to figure me out. I work harder to appear like everything is fine.

"It's nothing. Everything is great. I'm just not hungry."

I see the disappointment cross her features, but I keep my smile in place.

"Okay, if you say so...but, Selene, you know you can always tell me anything."

I reach across the table and place my hand on hers, feeling the fragile bones beneath her delicate skin.

"Yes, I know," I say with gratefulness. *But this isn't my secret to tell.*

Drake

I don't even know why I'm here. I just felt like I needed to finish the conversation we were having outside the restaurant, and...okay, if I'm honest, I wanted to see her again.

It's late, but I knock anyway. When I drove up, I could see that there were still lights on throughout the house. After a few minutes, the door creaks open slowly until Selene appears through the screen door. She looks shocked to see me, and I can't tell if she's glad or not.

"Uh...hi," I say, almost shyly, as I peer down at her.

She smirks. "Hi." She pauses and pushes the door open. "Do you want to come in?"

"No. I...do you think we can talk out here for a minute?"

I see her hesitate at my question, and she glances back behind her like she might get in trouble. I know that isn't the case, but she seems hesitant about something.

I quickly add, "It will only take a minute."

She looks back once more before turning to me and nodding her head slightly as she joins me on the porch.

Without a word, Selene slowly walks to one of the wooden rockers and takes a seat. I follow her and sit in the chair next to hers. We both remain silent for a few minutes. She doesn't push me to say anything. It's a comfortable silence, and as much as I know wanted to talk, it feels nice just sitting here with her.

The night air is warm, and I notice lightning bugs dancing across the darkened lawn in front of us.

I have no idea how long we've been sitting here, but I'm

glad Selene doesn't rush me. We both release a deep sigh at the same time, and she looks over at me before laughter fills the air. It's the sweetest sound I've ever heard. I'm stunned by her beauty, and by the warm feeling I get just being around her. I watch her as she giggles, studying the lines of her face and the way her delicate shoulders shake. Dear God, this girl is everything I want but don't deserve.

So lost in my thoughts, I don't realize she has stopped laughing and is now watching me.

"I'm enjoying the quiet, but are you ever going to tell me what you came to say?" she asks matter-of-factly, amusement still playing at the corners of her lips.

A smile forms on mine in response.

"I just wanted to say thanks for tonight. Thanks for listening, and for keeping my secret."

I watch her face as I thank her and see the emotions play across her features. It doesn't make her happy to keep my secret, but she'll do it. Looking back out into the night, I wait for her to say something.

"Drake, you don't have to thank me. It's what a friend does."

I look over at her again. "Oh, so we're friends now?" I tease, because I don't want to admit what her saying we're friends does to me.

She grins. "Yeah, I think we are."

A funny feeling fills my chest. The sensation isn't one I recognize, but I know I like it. I'm just not sure how to feel about it, though. I quickly stand and walk across the porch and down the steps. I can feel her staring holes into my back before I turn to face her.

"There's something about you, Selene Chandler. I wasn't ready for you," I tell her as I run my hand through my hair. She starts to say something, but I put my hand up to stop her. "Let me finish. I've never met someone who sees the real me. I'm going to screw this up because that's what I do, but I need us to be friends."

I feel some relief, but there is still a part of me screaming to ask for more. I think I might want more, but I'm not sure. I'm unsure of how it will work, and right now, I'm not willing to take the chance it might not.

Slowly, Selene pushes herself out of her seat and walks toward me silently. The glow of the porch light surrounds her, making it hard to see her face, so I can't even get a feel for what she's thinking.

She keeps walking until we're toe to toe, carefully taking my hand in hers. Her gaze drifts up to mine. I think I see fear when I look at her, but her touch tells a different story.

"Drake, I have to admit you scare me. When I'm around you, I feel so out of control, and that is something I've spent my whole life avoiding. That being said, I believe to my core that you and I were meant to be friends. Be exactly who you are and you can't screw this up."

I squeeze her hand and pull her into a quick embrace. I feel her stiffen a little, but I ignore it and wait for her to relax. Once I feel her give in to my touch, I lean my forehead against hers, our faces mere inches apart. I feel her release a massive breath and suck it back in as if she were going to say something, but decided against it. I don't want to push us further than we're ready to go.

Feeling content, I take a step backward. "You know, I think we're going to be great friends." I hop off the porch and walk toward my truck. When I reach the door, I look back over at Selene. She's standing on the porch on the edge of the top step, watching me.

"Goodnight, Selene," I say.

"Goodnight, Drake," she says back, and then she lifts her hand in a slight wave.

As I drive away, I glance in the rearview mirror. I can just barely make out Selene's silhouette still standing at the top of the steps, watching me leave.

chapter 8

Selene

It's early, and he's standing on the other side of the screen door, smiling. If I didn't know any better, I would say no one else has ever seen that look. The thought makes my chest ache a little, but in a good way. The sensation is so new, and I think I may be in a little over my head.

Thinking back to last night, I almost wish I had said no to friendship and yes to everything else I felt when our faces were mere inches apart, almost being the key word. When it comes down to it, I'm too scared, too afraid of what Drake might say or do if he knew just exactly how he makes me feel, too afraid of the reaction he might have if he knew just how broken I really am. He said friends and seemed all right with it, and I know deep down I can't do more. I wouldn't be good at more.

I also recognize I want him in my life in any way I can get him right now. There is something about the way he makes me feel, something that tells me I can trust him, and I feel this overwhelming need to protect him. So, friends it is.

"Good morning," he says through the door as I push it open.

Taking a step back, he puts his hands in his pockets. I notice he does this every time he feels a little unsure, and I allow myself to feel happy. I'm not sure I could stop it even if I wanted to.

"Good morning. I didn't realize you were helping Aunt Violette today." I allow the door to slam behind me.

"Oh, well, I'm not. I actually came to see you." He doesn't look me in the eyes.

"Really?" I say before I can stop myself.

He looks up, and I can see the crinkles around his eyes. "Yes, really, Selene. I wanted to see if you want to go fishing." I can't control the smile that threatens to take up permanent residence on my face any longer.

"Drake, I think you may need to come around here more often if you continue to put that expression on my niece's face."

We both jump and turn to find Aunt Vi watching us through the screen door with a pleased look. I feel guilty. Why do I feel guilty? Probably because I was starting to have very naughty thoughts about my "friend", and my aunt was standing behind me while it happened.

Drake's chuckle brings me back to reality.

"Mrs. D, I don't always make her smile. In fact, it took me a while to figure out how to get just one out of her."

He slings his arm around my shoulder and I instantly stiffen. Drake doesn't seem to notice because he leaves his arm draped around me and continues talking to Aunt Vi. I can't move, but part of me wants to punch him right in the face, and the other part wants to bury myself a little farther into his side. I've often wondered what makes me so anxious when it comes to physical contact. My mama and I discussed my inability to trust people. She always said one day someone would break those defenses, and before I could even comprehend it, I would long for their presence. Is that what's happening with Drake? I'm so lost in my thoughts, I don't even notice Aunt Vi has asked me a question.

"Earth to Selene…Selene, would you like me to pack a lunch for this little fishing trip?"

I just blink at her. "Fishing trip?" I ask as if it's the first time I'm hearing of it. I can feel Drake's stare burning into my cheek.

"Selene, dear, are you all right?"

Shit, Selene! Get a hold of yourself. He just put his arm around you, and this is just Aunt Violette.

"Oh, yeah…yeah!" My voice comes out overly cheerful. I'm sure they can see it's forced, but neither says anything. "Of course I'm fine, and I think lunch would be great. I can help you."

She pushes the door open for us to come in. "No, of course not. Go get changed and put on some shoes, and I'll get it all together. Drake, wanna grab the basket off the top shelf of the pantry for me?"

"Yes ma'am. I'll give you a hand, and I definitely think Selene needs to change her outfit."

He gives me a onceover and looks pleased before he walks through the door. I look down at myself and realize I have on my pajama shorts, a tank top, and bare feet. My cheeks flush red, which is silly since it's far too late to worry about the way I look now.

Drake looks back over his shoulder with a huge grin on his face. "I think you look just fine the way you are, by the way, but you can't go fishing in that," he says, like he can read my mind. Just as quickly, he turns and walks in the direction of the kitchen, leaving me staring at his back, entirely unsettled.

Drake

This girl has me coming unglued. I said friends, and I can tell that is all she's comfortable with, although occasionally I can see something in her eyes that says she may feel more. Hell, it's all I'm comfortable with, and I know without question I feel more.

That is precisely why she has me in knots, yet I can't stay away from her. It's the reason I was at her door at nine in the morning. It's why I've wanted to be near her every second since I drove away from her last night. There is something about Selene that just won't go away, and the overwhelming need to protect her from everyone—from the world—just gets stronger and stronger as the days go by. Suddenly, I'm pulled from my thoughts when I feel a thump against the back of my head.

"What's wrong with you and Selene today?" Mrs. Durham asks as she lowers her hand back to her side. "I've been saying your name over and over."

I rub my head. "So you felt the need to slap me upside the head to get my attention?"

"Well, you weren't listening, and frankly, I've always wanted to do that to you," she states stoically, but I hear the humor in her voice.

Just as I'm about to respond, Selene walks into the room. Her hair is back in a high ponytail, and she exchanged her pajamas for a pair of short khaki shorts and a purple tank top. Every time I see her, I'm surprised by her subtle and unique beauty.

"Let me just say now, I don't skin fish. I catch them, and I eat them, but I absolutely don't skin them. Comprende?"

I'm a little taken aback by the return of her confident attitude. I like it, but it's a complete one-eighty from ten minutes ago.

"It's nice to see you haven't completely lost the *I'm in charge* attitude. I've grown so fond of it," I say as I pick up the basket of food Mrs. D put together for us.

Looking up, I find Selene staring at me. "What? Oh, come on, Selene. You won't have to skin any fish we catch—if you even catch any…" I trail off when I realize maybe I've said too much.

The look on her face is priceless, and I think I just unintentionally threw down the gauntlet.

"I'm going to fish circles around you, Drake Thomas!" she states confidently as she strides to the back door, yelling over her shoulder, "See you later, Aunt Vi! Thanks for lunch!"

She's leaving me, but at the moment I don't care, because the view she leaves in her wake looks perfect in those little shorts she's wearing. Once again, I feel a sudden slap on the back of my head.

"Drake Thomas, you better quit staring at my baby girl like that and get your butt out there before she leaves it here!"

Rubbing my head again, I just laugh and follow Selene out the door. She isn't waiting for me.

"Come on, Selene! Wait up!" I yell as I watch her striding across the back lawn with increased speed. "I need to grab our poles out of the truck!"

She stops but doesn't turn around. Is she mad at me? The thought only makes me chuckle. I run over to the truck and grab the poles and tackle box out of the back. She's still standing in the middle of the lawn with her cute little backside to me.

"Would it kill you to give me a hand?" I ask with a little sarcasm in my voice.

I'm hoping it will get her a little fired up again. She is so damn beautiful when she gets irritated at me. Selene whips around and glares before walking up to me and taking the lunch basket out of my hands.

"For your information, I don't have to be in charge!" she

shouts, and then she turns on her heels and heads toward the river.

I just smile and shake my head before silently following behind her. I definitely hit a chord with my little comment back in the kitchen. The funny thing is, I would willingly let her be in charge of me any time she wanted.

Once she reaches the river, she stops and asks, "So, where exactly are we going?"

I keep walking past her toward the spot beside the river where I saw her for the first time three weeks ago. Of course, I don't say this. She still doesn't know I was there that day behind the trees, mesmerized by her.

"Follow me. It's just a little down river."

We don't say much after that. It actually feels nice to be with her and not have to talk. She seems to be comfortable with our silence too. I noticed it when we sat on the porch yesterday, both before and after she discovered my secret; our silences are never awkward.

As we reach the small clearing beneath the cypress trees, I set our poles and tackle box down before turning toward her. She's standing at the edge of the clearing, and I can see she is upset.

"Selene?" I take a step toward her.

She looks up at me and shakes her head before taking a step in my direction. I watch her wipe the uneasy look from her face and replace it with a calm one. It tugs at my heart because I can see she is used to hiding her real emotions.

"Where should I put this?" she asks me as she moves toward one of the larger trees lining the river's edge.

I answer quickly her to put her at ease. "I think under that tree so it's out of the sun."

I walk back over to the poles and pick them back up. Selene comes to stand next to me and is watching as I bait our poles with the live worms I picked up at the bait shop on my way to her house this morning.

"I could've done that myself, Drake. I've been fishing before," she says as she takes the pole from me. She sounds a little annoyed, and it rubs me the wrong way.

"Look, Selene, if you don't want to be here with me then just say so, but I thought we would have fun."

I'm beginning to feel a little frustrated with her. I love her spunkiness, but she seems pissed at me. I don't know how to read her. I mean, *fuck!* I'm having a hard time keeping my emotions in check, and I'm going to screw this all up. I turn my back to her because I can feel all the blood has rushed to my face. I just wanted today to be perfect. I wanted to make her happy, and it seems I may have just made her feel worse. Can I even be friends with a girl I'm attracted to? I close my eyes just before I feel her hand on my shoulder. I tense up.

"Drake, are you all right? I'm sorry. I do want to be here, but like I told you last night, I'm just not very good at things like this."

I nod and turn to the water. As I cast out my line, I let the doubts that had begun to rise up in me drain away. "Then let's catch us some dinner!" I can feel her watching my face before turning and casting her own line into the water.

I peer over at her, and there is a tenderness in her eyes. I want to know her. Maybe we can do this after all; it will just take some time.

"What's that look about?" I ask her, grinning.

Her smile widens. "I just…"

Before she can finish, Selene begins screaming and slicing her hand through the air. "Shit! A bee! Shitty shit shit!" I'm howling as I watch her karate chopping the air and running in a small circle. "This isn't funny! I hate bees! Shit, is it in my hair? Drake! It's in my hair! Get it out!"

I regain control of myself. "Selene, the bee is gone."

I'm trying to reassure her, but then I start laughing again.

She stops running around and glares back at me. She calmly picks up her pole before reeling it in and recasting it again as if nothing happened. I snort one more time and then look at the water.

"It's not funny," she says, but then I see her lips are tugged up in both corners.

I look back over the river and feel peace take over for the first time in a long while. Another fifteen minutes go by before I feel a tug on my pole, and I begin reeling it in slowly.

I whisper, "Selene, stay quiet."

She quickly whispers back, "I haven't said anything for nearly twenty minutes. Why…"

I huff out a breath of air. "Because I have one tugging on my line, and it's not quite hooked yet."

I begin walking backward and continue reeling. Just when I feel another tug, I yank back and reel quickly. What I didn't anticipate is the large root protruding out of the ground behind me, and I feel my line snap when I trip over it.

"Fuuuuuuuuucccck!" I roar out in frustration.

I lie there looking up at the sky, wanting to scream some more because a fucking fish just got the best of me. "Fucking fish!" I say just as I hear a burst of laughter echo through the air.

Any frustration I was feeling instantly dies, and I push myself up on my elbows to find Selene doubled over, holding her middle and laughing hysterically. So she thinks this is funny, huh? I watch her. I feel paralyzed as I follow the curve of her face, so I remain there on the ground, taking in how beautiful she looks when she is unguarded and carefree. Suddenly, she catches my eye and abruptly stops, as if just remembering I'm there.

"Uh, sorry. It's just that…that…well, you know you shouldn't say fuck. It's not very nice."

She looks so serious I almost burst into laughter myself.

"Oh, really?" I say as I stand up and walk toward her until we're toe to toe.

We both put our hands on our hips, staring one another down.

"And what is wrong with the word *fuck*?" I ask with emphasis.

She twists her hair around her finger nervously. "Uh, it's a bad word."

I nearly crack at the ridiculousness of this conversation and her reason. What are we, five?

"Well, so is shit! And you say that all the time," I respond.

I got her there. She looks appalled. "No, it's not! And...and I don't say it that much!" She is so cute right now, I don't care how absurd this argument is.

"Oh no? Then what would you call it?"

She pauses for a minute, and I can see the wheels turning in her head, searching for a comeback.

"It's...a natural bodily function!" I can tell she feels like she just came up with the greatest comeback known to man. It's so damn adorable. I let her bask in her glory for a moment before leaning in as close as I can get without our lips actually touching. I can feel her breathing speed up as it hits my face.

"So is fucking," I state candidly as I stare back into her eyes and feel a tremor roll over my body.

chapter 9

Selene

I can't breathe. I really think my lungs have forgotten how to function. Drake's breath is a sweet mix of mint and a cherry cough drop, and as the scent continues to swirl around me, I'm not even sure what we're talking about anymore.

Wait, did he just say fucking is a natural bodily function? The content of our entire conversation hits me, and I can't hold back the bubble of happiness that pushes its way free. I bend over at the waist, holding my stomach in a hysterical fit of laughter. I'm pretty sure I just spit on Drake's gorgeous face, because he is taking a step away from me.

He is standing in front of me, blinking as if I've lost my mind. Then, suddenly, he doubles over in amusement, which only makes me laugh harder. I need to sit down, so I lower myself to the ground as Drake says, "So much for catching any fish today."

This only makes us laugh harder. I don't think I've felt this carefree in…well, ever.

"I'm sorry," I manage to say when I finally stop.

It seems he is regaining his composure again as he takes a seat next to me. He shrugs his shoulders. "It doesn't really matter to me, but I guess we will need to make it up to Mrs. D."

He watches me carefully, almost as if I might break, then suddenly he turns back toward the water again. I look over at him then, and I can see his eyes are shimmering with unshed tears.

"My sister and I used to come here all the time. This was our escape," he tells me.

"She's the one who brought us here the first time. She brought me and my mama here. She told us it was special, and she felt she needed to share it with us."

I wipe a tear that slips past my lids. He stares at me again, but this time with a little confusion.

"Why didn't I ever meet you before, Drake? I never even knew Lacey had a sibling. Of course, I didn't know her too well, but we did play together off and on over the years."

Drake lets out a sincere but clipped laugh. "You're that girl." He smiles, and it fills me with a warmth I never want to leave. "She talked about you all the time. Of course, I'm a boy and never really paid any attention. I guess we never met because I never came around back then."

"I've been so caught up in me, I haven't had time to think about anything else. I haven't even asked Aunt Vi about Lacey. Why hasn't she been coming over?" Immediately, I regret asking, because Drake's face suddenly turns completely white. I know I've said something wrong. "Dra—"

"Selene, didn't you know? Lacey died four months ago."

I'm seized by an incredible sense of anguish. I can't believe Aunt Vi didn't tell me. I've been so caught up in my own grief, I never saw it in Drake, but now...now I see every bit of despair in his eyes. This explains every lost look I wondered about last night over dinner. Lacey was Drake's twin, and a piece of him is missing.

Without me realizing it, tears begin streaming down my face until I feel his hand cupping both cheeks and wiping the tears with his thumbs.

"Selene, I didn't mean to make you cry. I didn't realize you were close to Lacey."

I look into his eyes and shake my head. "No, it's not that. I mean, I'm sorry for your loss, and it does make me sad to hear about Lacey, but I'm just realizing how lost in my own grief I've been. I didn't even notice yours."

He drops his hands and chokes out the words. "What do you mean you've been caught up in your grief?" His eyes are glistening again with tears that just won't seem to fall.

"My mother died. It's why I'm here…why I'm living with Aunt Violette now."

A shocked look crosses his features. "Don't worry about me. I'm sorry, I didn't know about your mama." He swallows hard before continuing, "What about your dad?"

"He didn't want me. Honestly, I don't think he ever wanted me."

Another tear slips down my cheek, and I wish like hell I could take it back so he wouldn't see that my father's lack of parental love has such an effect on me. Again, Drake reaches up and cups the side of my face. I lean into his hand a little and close my eyes, shocking myself as I begin to relax into such intimacies.

"I can't imagine anyone not wanting you." His voice sounds low and raspy, and I look up at him again.

We both stare at one another for a moment before he pulls his hand back and stands up. I sit there watching him, still a little stunned by our close and honest conversation.

"Okay, up, Chandler! We're getting up and we're fishing, if it's the last thing we do. We promised Mrs. D a fish dinner, and that's what we're going to give her."

He is talking loudly, and the sound of happiness in his voice would never give away the seriousness of the conversation we were having only moments ago. I stand slowly, wiping the dirt away from my shorts and hands. "Well, if you don't quit talking so loud, you'll scare the fish off again!"

As I pick up my fishing pole, I look back up and notice Drake shaking his head, grinning. "You really are a smartass, aren't you?" Then he casts his line back out into the river and turns away from me.

Maybe Mama was right—letting someone in isn't as scary as I imagined.

T he sizzling and popping of fish frying is almost as appealing as the smell of dinner wafting through the windows from the kitchen. I take another long drink of my tangy lemonade as I watch the sun set behind the hills just on the other side of the river. I stretch my legs out in front of me and rock myself as the music drifts out from inside.

I haven't actually enjoyed myself in a while, and it feels good. Smiling, I think about our day, remembering the way Selene looked when she reeled in her first fish, the way she giggled when I couldn't get mine off the hook.

"You know, if you keep smiling like that, I just might wonder what secrets you're keeping."

I turn my head at the sound of her voice. "No secrets here. Just thinking about our day."

A blush creeps across her cheeks, and she quickly says, "Yes, well, speaking of our day, Aunt Violette says it's time to eat. I set the table in the dining room, so come on."

I sit for a moment longer then push myself out of the chair and head for the house. Selene and Mrs. Durham are carrying dishes into the dining room as I enter.

"Drake, be a dear and grab the pitcher of lemonade for me," Mrs. D says as she balances two plates in one hand while holding the door for Selene with the other.

"Yes ma'am," I reply as I grab the pitcher and follow them into the dining room.

Everything is set neatly on the table, and the white and red gingham tablecloth gives the place a picnic feel. This is something I feel is uniquely Mrs. D—she is the only person I've ever known who can make any setting feel like home.

I'm about to tell them how great everything looks when I notice them both sitting and holding hands. Each of them reaches out their empty hand for me to take. As they look at me, they both grin, so I sit down and take their hands in mine. I watch them close their eyes, and Mrs. Durham says a blessing over the food, the town, Selene, and even me.

When she's done, Selene gives my hand a light squeeze before saying, "Dig in."

Throughout our dinner we talk and stuff ourselves full of delicious food. I can't remember the last time I sat around a dinner table and actually had a discussion, especially one that wasn't centered on politics or my plan for my future. When I can't take another bite, I stand up and begin clearing the table.

"Drake, you stop what you are doing this very instant!" Mrs. D demands as she places a hand on my arm. "You caught this meal, so I expect you to take Selene out to relax on the porch. I'll clean this up."

I look over at Selene, and she just shrugs her shoulders before leaning down and kissing her aunt on the cheek.

"You heard her, Mr. Thomas. It's time to relax!" Selene teases as she sticks her arm through mine and pulls me with her toward the door.

Pushing the door open, we step out into the night air. The sun is still hovering over the horizon, so we're still able to see our surroundings.

"Let's go for a little walk," she says, turning her face to look up at me.

She is so beautiful I can only nod my consent. It feels good being with her. I think this just might work out after all.

Walking around to the front of the house, I come to a dead stop when I spot a car sitting up the street that looks familiar. I abruptly pull away from Selene, causing her to stumble a little, but she catches herself.

"Drake! What the shit! You almost knocked me down!"

I can hear the smile in her voice, but I feel nothing except dread in the pit of my stomach. She looks up at me, and her contentment begins to fade.

"Dra—" she starts, but I quickly cut her off.

"You know, I just looked at the time, and I really should be going. I…I'm sorry."

I can't even look her directly in the eye, so I keep my eyes down. She looks up at me, and just when I think she is about to say something and call me out for my abrupt change in mood, she looks over her shoulder and turns back to me.

"Okay," she says, nodding her head slightly. "Whatever you need to do."

I know she can feel my panic, but I'm glad Selene is going to let it pass. I just can't talk about this now. I need to leave as quickly and quietly as possible, because I'm 100% positive my mother's car is parked up the street.

Selene

When Drake said goodbye, he hurried off toward his truck, and I rushed inside. I'm trying not to feel hurt, but I know something is wrong. I don't know what it is, and I hate that he felt like he couldn't tell me. I hold the soft linen curtain in my hand as I peer out the window at Drake's retreating figure. The uneasiness in my stomach intensifies with each step he takes away from the house. I'm not sure what changed, but something did.

A hand gently squeezes my shoulder. "Did something happen between you two?"

Aunt Violette always gets right to the point. I let the curtain fall and shake my head.

"No, he just suddenly said he had to go. I don't know, Aunt Vi. I thought my life was complicated, but Drake Thomas is definitely giving me a run for my money."

Aunt Vi lets out a long, sympathetic sigh. "Selene, I hate that you see life as complicated. I'm sorry for all you have been going through, but you're right—Drake Thomas is most likely only going to cause you more complications."

I begin to defend him, but she keeps going before I can say a word.

"Now, don't get me wrong. He is a sweet, loyal, and hard-working young man...now. Maybe he has always been just like Lacey, but that family...it's tainted by all the wrong things, if you know what I'm getting at."

I lean in and hug her. "I think I do, Aunt Vi, and that's exactly what worries me. The only problem is I think Drake Thomas is one complication it's too late for me to avoid. I like him, and he's my friend. Plus, I'm excellent at handling anything that's thrown my way."

"I'm glad to hear you say that," she says as she pulls back, brushing the hair out of my eyes. "You're a good girl, Selene, always have been. Drake is a good kid, too. He carries a lot on his shoulders for a young man of his age…a lot of guilt and heartache."

When I look into Aunt Vi's eyes, it seems she is trying to tell me something about Drake. I know about Drake and what he is going through…does she?

It kills me to not be able to talk to her about what I saw. I'm scared to say anything and scared to keep it to myself, but I'm more afraid of Drake never forgiving me for breaking his trust. It's a chance I'm just not willing to take, because regardless of whether or not I'm ready to admit it out loud, Drake is important. I'm just not sure what he is beyond that, and the more I think about it, the more I worry about just how important he is becoming to me.

chapter 10

Selene

Two weeks and a day—that's the length of time that has gone by since I've seen or spoken to Drake. It isn't like he didn't call. He did, but it wasn't to talk to me. He only called to make his excuses to Aunt Vi for not being able to make his usual weekly visit with her.

I don't know what happened. I've gone over and over in my head what I could've done. I know he's avoiding me, I just can't figure out why. I've gone through many emotions about Drake's sudden disappearance, and anger has definitely made its presence known. I've been so angry with Drake for pulling me into his life and then leaving without a word. It's exactly why I tried holding back at first. Most of all, I'm mad at myself for allowing my guard to drop and opening up to the possibility of…friendship.

Who am I kidding? I opened myself up to the possibility of more.

So here I am, standing in the middle of the crowded hallway

of my new school, alone. One would think I'm a huge beacon of light shining brightly with the way everyone is staring at me. As everyone passes, I see them look briefly in my direction then quickly look away. As much as I hate to admit it, I search through every face that passes me, looking for his, but he doesn't appear. It's probably best this way.

Putting my head down, I walk in the direction of the school office. I can only hope I'll be able to avoid Drake entirely, because I'm not sure how I'll feel about seeing him, especially if he continues to avoid me.

Drake

I'm not surprised I can spot her out of all the heads bobbing up and down, making their way to their first-period classes. I haven't seen her in two weeks, and now I'm standing only fifteen feet away from her. I'm having trouble remembering why I'm staying away from her in the first place.

I watch her glance around as everyone is passing her, and I can see the fear she is so desperately trying to hide. Is she searching for someone? Is she searching for me? My heart speeds up a little at the thought. Then the shadows return to her eyes, and she puts her head down before walking through the crowd.

I feel a little disappointment, but what do I expect when I haven't spoken to her in weeks? I have my reasons; I knew that night when I left that if I didn't hide the way I felt about Selene, she would end up getting hurt, and hurting her is the last thing I want to do.

Selene

I made it through my first three classes without seeing Drake, though I've walked through the halls and into each room filled with anticipation of coming face to face with him.

As I head to my last class before lunch, someone bumps into me, knocking my books from my arms. "Sorry," echoes through the hallway as the guy continues running. I watch him in shock until he disappears around the corner. Turning back to pick up my things, which are now scattered across the floor, I nearly bump into a petite blonde girl smiling brightly while holding my books out to me.

"Hi. You're the new girl, right? I mean, I know you are because...well, I know everyone since I've lived here my whole life. Anyway, I wanted to introduce myself and see if you have anyone to sit with at lunch. I'm Emme."

I'm not sure I've ever met someone who talks this fast, but I still caught every word. She continues smiling as I take my books.

"Uh...umm...hi, I'm Selene...and...uh...no." Her happiness fades, and I suddenly realize she thinks I'm declining her invitation. "No, what I mean is...no, I don't have anyone to sit with at lunch."

Her face lights up again. "Oh, good!" she says as she slips her arm through mine. "I took a look at your schedule when I picked it up, and we have next period together. It's fate!"

I can't even form words or thoughts to respond, so I just allow Emme to drag me to class. I'm pretty sure my mouth is still hanging open. *What is even happening?*

Emme continues to lead me down the hall, chatting away, but I'm not sure what she's saying because I'm still looking for Drake in the sea of teenagers we pass. Not one face is his. Maybe he didn't come to school today. Perhaps I could ask Emme, but I don't know her well enough, and she would probably get the wrong idea, would probably think I like him. When we enter the classroom, I look around. From the back of the room, a tall, muscular guy with dark hair looks up, and a smile spreads across his face.

"Hey there, Emme girl! Who's your new friend?"

Ugh. Who is this guy? Why is there one in every school? The teenage boy who thinks he is God's gift to the opposite sex. I want to laugh.

"Hi, Tommy! This is Selene Chandler. She just moved here from…where did you move here from?" she says as she turns and looks at me.

Before I can answer, Tommy is right next to me. He is so close I can feel his breath against my ear.

"It doesn't matter where sweet Selene is from, Emme. It only matters that she's here now."

I can't move. Why do people around here think it's okay to just invade a person's personal space? Even though he appears to be harmless, all I can think about is the fact that I don't want this guy anywhere near me.

I'm standing just a few feet from the doorway as Emme Fleming leads Selene into biology. *Fuck!* We have a class together—I should've known my luck wouldn't last.

Taking a deep breath, I follow behind them. She has no idea I'm here, and I kind of like it that way. I really like the fact that I can watch the sway of the cute little butt I've often admired over the last month. She's going to hate me.

Suddenly, I'm pulled from my thoughts when I hear Tommy Phillips say Selene's name. He's standing way too close, and I can tell from here Selene is uncomfortable with his intrusion into her personal space.

As I begin to make my way toward them, all thoughts of Selene's reaction to me disappear. I can only think about the fact that Tommy is now reaching up and rubbing his knuckles against her shoulder. He may be my best friend, but that doesn't mean I won't put him in his place. I don't even say a word before grabbing his hand in a hard grip and twisting it behind his back.

"Tommy, I suggest you keep your hands to yourself." I let go of him, pushing him forward into the desk across from us.

"What the fuck, Drake?"

I don't even answer him because I can't look away from Selene, who is staring directly into my eyes. She is so beautiful, and for a moment I want to say to hell with my mother. As our gazes remain locked, I try to figure out if she hates me or not. She should, because I asked her to be my friend and then vanished without explanation. It was a dick move.

Our trance is broken when I feel a hard punch on my arm. "Drake, if sweet Selene is your girl, then dude, you could have just said so."

I can see Emme's eyes flashing at me and Selene trying to figure out how we know one another. Before I can say a word, Selene speaks up first.

"I'm not his girl. We aren't even friends."

I hear the words and feel the knot that has been tightening in my chest for the last two weeks get a little tighter. Her eyes never leave mine. I just nod, and she seems to take that as a sign to leave.

She turns and walks away, taking a seat on the other side of the room. Emme takes one last look at me and then follows Selene. When I finally look over at Tommy, he has a smirk on his face.

"Dude, that was a dick move. What did you do to the new

girl, anyway? It's only fourth period."

The thing is, I haven't done anything to Selene. She has done something to me, and I'm not sure I can let go as easily as I thought I could.

chapter 11

Selene

I keep my attention to the front of the class as Emme pulls her desk closer to mine.

"Oh my gosh, Selene! Drake Thomas just defended you like you were his property, and you walk away!"

Does she always talk this fast? She says Drake's name like he is a god or something. Well, I can admit he looks like one— I'm pretty sure his godlike features were one of the things I noticed about him the first time I saw him. I sigh and close my eyes, taking in a deep breath.

"Seriously, Selene, do you know Drake?"

I want her to leave me alone. I mean, we have known one another all of fifteen minutes. The only problem is I kind of like her and the way she is completely herself and friendly. I'm trying to be better. I need to be better.

"Hello! Earth to Selene!"

I finally look over at her. "Sorry. Yeah, I kind of know Drake."

I immediately see her eyes light up. She's getting the wrong idea. *Shit!*

"Oh reeeeally," she says as her eyes drift in Drake's direction.

"Emme, don't look over at him. I'll explain later, but…well, let's just say I don't think we will be friends or anything else."

"Well, I believe you're wrong, especially with the way he hasn't taken his eyes off of you."

I want to look over at him, but I stop myself. Why is he doing this? Did he think he could blow me off then just show up today and act like we just spoke yesterday? Mrs. Peterson, our biology teacher, walks into the room, asking us all to pull our books out. She greets the class as she sits on the edge of her desk. I can barely focus on what she's saying because I'm entirely consumed by thoughts of Drake.

Surely he has a good reason for completely ignoring me for two weeks, but this isn't how I wanted to start a new school year at a new school. I don't want to feel totally wrecked over a boy. *Shit.* I've never allowed myself to care this much, and I refuse to do it now. Glancing in Drake's direction, my eyes connect with his, and I feel my face betray me. I straighten up in my seat and turn my attention back to Mrs. Peterson.

Drake Thomas may have chipped away at my walls, but I can't let him knock them down. After the look he just gave me, I'm confident I wouldn't survive the devastation.

Drake

*F*uck, I really hurt her. She's trying to pretend otherwise, but I can see it in her eyes. Can I do this to her? Wouldn't it be worse if my mother came between us?

She would make Selene's life hell, and I would never forgive myself for that.

I just need her to understand. I need her to know the time I spent with her meant something, especially every honest confession we made to one another.

The bell rings, and I'm pulled back into reality. I notice Emme already has Selene by the arm and is dragging her out of the class, so I grab my bag and dash after them.

"Selene!" I shout. "Selene, please wait! I really need to talk to you...to explain."

She stops abruptly, which jerks Emme back, nearly causing them to fall. She remains standing with her back to me.

"Explain? You want to explain now." Her breathing comes out in a huff, and I can tell she's frustrated with me. "Why should I listen to anything you say?"

I take a step forward, and my hand twitches to touch her. "I know I've handled this all wrong, but I had my reasons. You of all people *know* my reasons," I say with emphasis so she understands what no one else will. I notice we're beginning to draw attention, and Emme is standing next to Selene, her eyes darting between us.

Selene slowly turns around. "What happened? Did... Okay, I'll listen," she says, finally looking up at me. "But just for the record, this isn't how friends treat one another, Drake."

"God, Selene. I know, and..." I trail off, once again realizing we're not alone. "Uh, can we go somewhere else to talk about this?" She looks around and nods before turning to Emme.

"Hey, I... Thanks for the lunch invitation. See you later?"

A knowing look lights up Emme's face. "Yep, see you next period." She turns and practically skips away before stopping and calling over her shoulder, "Oh, and Selene?"

Selene looks over her shoulder. "Yeah?"

The smirk on Emme's lips grows even wider. "I think definitely friends...or something." Then she turns and heads toward the cafeteria. Selene's cheeks flush pink as her eyes follow Emme then look my way.

I can't help but smile. "Something? Sounds interesting...very interesting."

Selene

I kind of want to smack that grin right off his face...then curl up and hide. Why is it every time I'm around Drake, my sense takes a vacation? I look up at just the moment he smiles again and takes my hand in his. My heart flutters in my chest, and I'm pretty sure that's my answer. My heart is a traitor.

"Come on, I know a place where we can talk," he tells me as he leads me down the hall behind him, leaving all the gawking teenagers standing in our wake. Once we're out of the building, his hand loosens and drops mine. I feel the absence more than I'm willing to acknowledge.

"This way," he says as he leads me through a gate and up the bleachers of the football field.

We walk all the way to the top before he turns and faces me. I can't read the look on his face. He seems to be conflicted, and I'm kind of over it.

"Okay, start talking. I'm giving you five minutes to convince me of why I shouldn't think you are one of the biggest assholes I've ever met."

"I never said I wasn't an asshole, Selene," he says, and the corner of his mouth tips up on one side.

"Hysterical, Drake. What do you want from me?"

Drake sits down and puts his face in his hands. "Aaaahhhh-hhh!" he yells, and it echoes around us.

I reflexively flinch away from him. "I shouldn't..."

He reaches toward me and grips the back of my shirt.

"Please, wait. There are things that…well, there are things I need to explain."

I stop, keeping my gaze focused on the bright green field, releasing a long sigh. "I'm listening," I tell him, holding my body stiff and facing away from him.

I feel so vulnerable with Drake, something I'm not used to allowing myself to feel. I slowly walk up a step and lower myself to the bleachers behind him.

"God, Selene. I'm so sorry. I…I know I pushed my way into your life, asking for this friendship and your trust, and then I threw it back in your face like it meant nothing."

I can feel his eyes on my back. Slowly, I turn to face him. "Why, Drake? Why did you just leave that night and then not even acknowledge me for two weeks? You even disappointed Aunt Violette."

Drake stares at me. I want to ask him so much more. I want so much more, but I can't do this back and forth. I wait, and he says nothing.

"You know what? This doesn't even matter. We only just met…there were no promises. Shit, we were only friends for like a second."

My words hit me square in the chest. Why does this hurt so bad when I only just met him? He just watches me, and once again I have a hard time reading him. I can't muster the energy to stand here and wait for him to explain.

I'm having trouble keeping my thoughts clear. Selene is so vulnerable. I see she's hurt, but trying hard to not let it show. I hear everything Selene is saying, but she's wrong. I made promises, and it definitely matters, every minute…every second she listened and trusted me.

She looks like she is about to run, and it takes everything in me not to grab a hold of her and never let go. How am I supposed to explain my reasons for pushing her away?

"I'm leaving. I can't do this," she says. I knew it; she's about to bolt. I can't let her leave, because I still haven't explained. She stands abruptly.

"Wait!" I stand up, and now we're face to face. I hear a gasp slip between her lips. "You're wrong, Selene. We may have only just met, but it did matter…it does matter." I take in the way her eyes are darting around, trying to avoid direct contact with mine. "I need you to understand…I thought it would be better if I didn't get any closer. You see, my mother was watching me that night, and she doesn't want me around you. She's afraid it'll affect my focus on football and the things my parents feel are important. Don't you see?"

Selene eyes connect with mine. "Did she hurt you again?"

I snicker before answering. "No, that isn't my point. I'm not staying away from you to keep the inevitable from happening. That will happen no matter what."

She reaches her hand forward and brushes her fingertips against mine. "Then what are you saying?"

"Selene, I'm afraid she'll cause trouble for you. I don't think you understand. It's beyond what she might do to me physically. This is a small town, and she can make things miserable for you." I slowly extend my hands toward her face and cup her cheeks, forcing her to look into my eyes. "I couldn't—I can't let her taint this thing between us like she ruins everything else in my life. I can't let her hurt you."

I want her to understand—no, I need her to understand. She begins to shake her head slowly from side to side.

"No. You don't get to do this. You made me trust you, and I trust no one—no one, Drake. Do you understand that? I was beginning to let you in, and you just walked away like it meant nothing. I think I should get to decide if I want to be friends with you."

There she goes again, being all adorable and hard to resist. I let go of her face and walk up to the top of the bleachers again, my back to her. "I ca—"

"Please, don't. We will be friends. That's what we agreed, and nothing more, so I can't get hurt. I won't let myself get hurt."

I turn to find her standing right behind me. "Selene, I want—"

Suddenly, the bell rings in the distance and interrupts me.

"I gotta go," she says. I watch as she rushes down the bleachers until she reaches the bottom and stops. She looks back up at me, reluctance clear on her face, and asks, "Friends?"

This girl is everything I can't resist. "Okay, friends."

"Promise me," she says. "I need you to promise me you won't ever do this again."

She looks so hopeful. I want to know what that feels like, so I give in to what my heart is telling me and block out all of my doubts.

"I promise," I say.

A relieved look lights up her face, and then I watch her disappear around the side of the bleachers.

Selene

I can still hear his cackling as I walk back through the gate to the school. I swallow the knot that formed in my chest. My emotions are all over the place, and all because of this guy. *A guy? Shit!* He wanted to protect me. I can only think of two people who have ever protected me: Mama, and now Aunt Violette.

I tread around people so carefully when it comes to my emotions that I keep up a wall in every relationship I've had. He sees that, and I'm not sure how he knows. I'm scared because I'm letting him in, and everything I've built up is falling away from me. He wanted to walk away, but I can't let him. This is the first time I haven't stopped someone from trying to get close. Actually, I tried with Drake, it just didn't work. There is something between us even my stubborn fear of allowing people in can't stop.

As I make my way down the hall, I hear my name being called. Turning, I notice Emme coming toward me with a huge grin on her face.

"Tell me everything!" she exclaims when she finally reaches me.

Taken aback, I take a step away from her. "There's nothing to tell you." I try to sound nonchalant.

A frown forms on her pixie-like face. "Seriously, I know Drake, and that look doesn't say *nothing*. In fact, that is a look I've never seen him direct at any girl. So, it isn't nothing...it's something." She pauses for a split second, which I'm almost certain she never does in a conversation. "It's something, even if you don't want to admit it. I haven't seen this much life in Drake since Lace..." She trails off, and her face turns slightly pink.

I instantly feel his presence. It's like my whole body is magnetically charged by him.

"Emme, I think Lacey would be happy to see you've made a friend like Selene," I hear him say behind me. "You know, Lacey and Selene knew one another. You have that in common for sure."

Emme's face brightens once more. "Really? Lacey and I...well, she's been my best friend since kindergarten. She is...was..." Her light dims a little.

"It's been a few years since I spoke to Lacey, and we didn't know one another all that well, but she was always fun and sweet."

Her features brighten again. "Let's get to class. See ya, Drake!"

I finally turn to face him. "Bye."

He shakes his head as he says, "Nope, I believe we have this period together. Lucky me."

A slow smile creeps across my face before I follow behind him with Emme beaming at my side as we all head to class. "Told ya," she whispers.

I can't help the warm feeling that begins to burn in my chest. Yes, Drake Thomas is definitely melting my defenses.

chapter 12

Drake

The rest of the day goes by quickly. I hadn't realized just how miserable I've been the last two weeks—maybe because I'm used to being miserable, something I only realized today when I saw Selene again. I'm pretty sure I was only living half a life before I met her.

Looking up and seeing my mother and father watching practice from the stands reminds me of what I was worried about. She is always watching my every move. She has expectations, and she likes control. The only problem is, I can't let Selene go again. I hurt her when I was trying to protect her. We agreed on friendship, and as much as my heart begs for more with every beat, the only way I can have her and protect her is by putting my wants aside.

I walk off the field, and my father nods at me as they stand and leave. My mother doesn't even acknowledge me. I push aside the uneasy feeling she leaves me with. I realize I need to change into my clothes, quickly. I owe one more person an apology before I head home for the night.

This apology may be harder than the one I gave Selene. In fact, I know I'm not going to get off as easy. The only thing that makes it okay is the fact that I know I will see Selene, too.

Selene

I hear a car pull up to the house, and instantly I know it's him. The sun is just going down, and I hear Aunt Violette walking to the door from the den, so I creep slowly out of my room and sit at the top of the stairs. The knock on the door is light, and I listen as she greets Drake.

When I hear his voice, my heart stutters. I realize every time he's near, the door to my heart opens a little more. I'm becoming less of a ghost of the girl I became when Mama died.

I listen to Drake and Aunt Violette as he apologizes to her. In her usual Aunt Violette fashion, she isn't cutting him any slack. Although she isn't making it easy for him, I can hear the fondness she feels for him in her voice. I find myself feeling happy, something I haven't felt for a long time.

My feelings are so conflicted, especially when I think of Mama. I know she would want me to carry on with my life, but I can't help the guilt about doing it so soon.

 Drake

I'm not surprised by Mrs. Durham's gentle but blunt reprimand of my behavior. She lets me know breaking promises isn't any way to show maturity or the kind of thing you do to a friend. She sounds like Selene when she says it.

"Okay, young man, now that you have apologized for your rudeness, did you want to speak to my niece?" She opens the door wider, finally inviting me in, then says, "Selene, you can stop eavesdropping from the top of the stairs now. Mr. Thomas and I have made our peace."

Mrs. D looks over at me and winks when we hear a tiny gasp from the top of the stairs. I'm not sure how this woman does it, but she is amazing. I look up at the stairs just as Selene moves off the last step.

Her cheeks are bright red, and she lifts her hand in a slight wave that leaves me captivated.

"Hey," she says when she's standing in front of me.

"Hey, do you think we can really do that talking thing now?" I ask her as I see Mrs. D turn and leave the room.

"I think I would like that," she says with a slight smirk.

We both make our way back out onto the front porch and sit in the same wooden rockers we sat in just a couple weeks ago.

"Look, I'm willing to do this friendship thing, Selene. I just need to warn you that if my mother sees you as a problem, she won't hesitate to make your life miserable. It's not beyond her."

Selene takes a deep breath and begins rocking the chair with her foot while the other is curled beneath her. "Drake, I don't understand why she is the way she is, but why would I be a problem? Don't you have friends? Haven't you had girlfriends? It's not like we have even been seen with one another. I only just moved here."

I want to tell her my mother knows more than I've even allowed myself to acknowledge. I could tell her she is a master at seeing through the smoke, but it wouldn't make any sense to her, and not only that, it might scare Selene off—it might even scare me off.

Instead, I'm vague in my explanation. "Just believe me when I say she notices everything. Especially now that Lacey is gone, all of her focus is on me. Plus, I'm different, and she sees that. She sees I'm not the same son she had before Lacey." I stand up, walk to the railing, and grip it tightly. "I'm not good, Selene. I wasn't a good guy. I wasn't a good brother, and I definitely wasn't a good friend."

I can tell she has stopped rocking her chair because I no longer hear the creaking of the wood against the porch. We're both silent, letting what I just said sink in.

Selene swallows hard. "Why are you telling me this?"

I feel a sudden frustration, not at Selene, but at myself. I wish I could change who I was then. If I had been different, things would not have happened the way they did. Lacey would still be here. I wouldn't have to feel like shaking some reality into Selene—the reality that I'm not good enough for her.

I spin around to face her, and the words stick in my throat. She is sitting with her knees pulled up, hugging them to her chest. She looks so fragile. This girl definitely has a hold on me. Could this be happening? I don't deserve to have her, but I'm not sure I can find it in me to give her up. So, all I can do is warn her. I sit back down and rest my elbows on my knees.

"I'm telling you so you know what you're getting into. I don't want to keep anything from you, and I need to know I did everything I could to warn you."

Her feet drop to the porch, and I feel her hands wrap around my wrist as she leans into me.

"I want you to listen to me, Drake Thomas. Before we met, I was walking around an empty shell of a human being. You have no idea the person I am…the person I was, either. Sure, I was what most would call a good girl. My mama would have called me a good daughter, and hell, my friends would have said I was a good friend at one point. It was all a lie. I've been cold, closed off, and unfeeling to just about everyone I was supposed to be close to except my mama—you should know!" Selene's voice begins to rise a little, and she pushes back from me without loosening her grip on my arm. "I was the biggest bitch to you, and it was only because you made me feel. You make me feel so much, and it scares the shit out of me."

I look up at her, and I can see her eyes are glistening. "You think I'm immune to it. From the first moment I saw you, I had to know you. I've never wanted to know everything about a person before, mainly because I don't allow anyone to know me. The only person who truly knew me is gone."

Selene

I know how you feel, a voice whispers in my head, but I don't say it out loud. I'm too afraid. He can tell me he is no good over and over, but it's too late to listen.

"It's too late," I say in a near whisper.

"Too late for what?" he asks, turning his body to face me.

"I want to know you. I don't know what it is, but I finally feel like things will be okay, and it's because of you. I need you, Drake, and I think you need me, too."

He pulls my chair closer, never taking his eyes from mine. He's leaning toward me slowly, and just when I think things are moving in a direction I'm not ready for, he leans my head onto his shoulder. He pulls me into him tighter and releases a long, low sigh.

I've never felt more comfortable or safe in my life. I can

hear his heart beating against his chest, and it's the first time I've allowed myself to be close enough to a person to actually listen. I'm not sure how much time has gone by when I hear Drake whisper, "Thank you." The strange thing is, I'm not sure if he's talking to me or not. Something tells me he isn't, so I keep quiet.

We sit like this for a long time, neither of us saying a word. Subtly, the porch light flickers, bringing us both back to the present.

"I think that's my cue to get going." I can hear the humor in his words.

"Yeah, Aunt Violette has a way of getting her point across."

We separate ourselves and stand up. Looking down at me, Drake smiles before pulling me into a hug once more. "You're never getting rid of me now...friend."

I laugh out loud. "I thought I made it clear I don't want to get rid of you, friend."

As he pulls back again and makes his way to the steps, I'm relieved by our comfortable banter. You would never know the last two weeks happened.

When he reaches the bottom of the steps, Drake turns back to me. "Goodnight, Selene. See you tomorrow."

"Goodnight, Drake."

He heads to his truck. I lean against the post of the porch, watching him until he pulls out of the driveway. He waves one last time, and I turn to go inside. I stop midstride when I notice Aunt Vi watching me from the doorway.

"Honey, I'm glad to see you two came to your senses. Now I won't have to spend another Saturday cleaning out the attic all alone."

I wrap my arm around her shoulder, and we both go inside for the night.

chapter 13

Drake

As I lean against the lockers and watch Selene pushing her way through the crowded hallway this morning, I'm amazed at the difference one day can make in a person's life. So many things can change, including ones' whole outlook on what life may hold has hope.

When she finally sees me, a smile spreads across her face. I don't think she even realizes how much power that look can hold over a person. I'm sure it isn't just me who has been changed by that radiant glow, but that doesn't matter because here, in this moment, it's just for me.

"Hey," I say as she reaches me.

Smiling, I lean forward to take her backpack. She smells like flowers and sunshine, and I inhale slowly through my nose.

"Hey yourself. Do you always sniff people when you greet them?" she asks, pushing me away from her.

"I would if they all smelled as good as you do." Selene

pushes me again and rolls her eyes as she starts to walk away.

"Seriously? A little lesson in friendship, Mr. Thomas: friends don't say things like that to one another."

I laugh out loud before jogging after her.

She stops in front of her classroom door and holds her hand out for her backpack. Placing the strap in her hand, I lean in close, giving her a kiss on the cheek. I instantly feel her stiffen, so I pull back relatively quickly.

"They do in our friendship," I say as I turn and make my way toward my own first-period class.

Once I round the corner of the hall, I peek back around to see her staring at me. She is red and stiff. Yep, she is pissed at me already, and it's not even eight fifteen in the morning. *This is going to be an excellent day*, I think as I feel a blissful look spread across my face.

Selene

I squeeze my eyes shut. I think my heart just forgot to beat when Drake's lips met my cheek. They were as warm as I imagined…and as soft. *He is my friend*, I repeat to myself several times before opening my eyes and heading to class.

I take the same empty desk in the back of the class I sat in yesterday. As soon as I sit down, I look around the room and notice many of the other students are watching my every move. I'm not sure what makes me feel more uncomfortable, their prying eyes or Drake's tempting lips.

Okay it's the lips, definitely the lips.

The bell rings and pulls me from my thoughts. I look up and notice a pair of eyes staring at me from across the room. They are some of the most beautiful blues I've seen. I focus on the face they belong to and take in all of the features. It's a hand-

some face, but there's something about it...it's almost too perfect. A smile curves his lips, and I instantly look away. I begin
cursing my inability to keep from blushing, so I put my head
down on the desk. He may be gorgeous, but he knows it, and my
blushing cheeks will give a guy like him the wrong idea.

"Hey, no need to hide from me, new girl," I hear from right
next to me. I'm almost afraid to look up, but I know if I don't, it
will only make things worse.

"Uh, hey," I say. *Ugh*, he isn't going away.

He extends his hand toward me. "Hi, I'm Jared. So, you're
new, right?"

I'm struck by how his eyes look even more blue close up.
"Uh, yeah." *Shit*, why can't I speak like a normal human being?
He's definitely going to get the wrong idea.

Snapping out of it, I reach my hand to his. "Right, I'm Selene." A smile spreads across his face. He turns in his seat and faces the front of the class as the teacher begins writing the date on
the chalkboard.

I watch his profile, and immediately my mind begins com-
paring him to Drake. Jared is everything a girl would dream
about in the all-American guy, while Drake is more rugged and
handsome in a natural way.

I feel a tingling sensation again where Drake kissed me. I
put my hand on the spot, willing it to stop. I don't want to feel
this way. *He is just your friend.* I keep repeating that to myself
for the rest of the class.

I walk around the corner, smiling at the thought of see Selene, even though I'm sure she is still mad at me for this morning. When I look ahead toward her classroom door, I see Jared Mitchell standing entirely too close for my comfort. I lengthen my stride toward her. I can't see her face, but I can't imagine her feeling comfortable with him being so close.

Once I reach Selene, I toss my arm around her shoulders, startling them both.

"Jared, I see you met my Selene," I say with a little too much emphasis. I instantly know Selene is going to be irritated, but at this moment, I just don't have it in me to care.

Jared doesn't move or take his eyes from Selene. "Yeah, Drake. I met Selene."

I notice her gaze bouncing between Jared and me. She is just about to say something when I chime in with, "We need to get to class."

I grab her hand, pulling her down the hall. I hear Jared laugh out loud, and it takes everything in me not to turn around and punch him in his smug face.

As we reach her next class, Selene pulls from my grip. "What the hell, Drake?"

I turn, looking at her in complete innocence, although I know she is about to give me an earful. I just stare at her, my mouth shut, waiting. I mean, what would I say? He dated my sister. He hurt her and used her. Or, maybe I could do with *I know we're just friends, but I didn't like seeing you talk to Jared the asshole.* I think this might be one of those things she will not feel falls under the friendship-relationship category.

"Don't give me that look! I don't even know what to say about the way you just acted, because I know you're going to

97

charm me into forgiving you." I blink at her but still remain silent. "Ugh! You are so frustrating!" She brushes past me, leaving me standing outside her classroom, staring after her.

I smile while shaking my head. I'm really bad at this *just friends* thing. For the second time today, I've gotten under Selene's skin, and all before ten o'clock in the morning.

Selene

I've been watching the clock since I left Drake standing in the hallway. I swear the more I stare at it, the slower it moves. My nerves are on high alert. I can't focus. All I can think about is Drake's reaction to me talking to Jared. We're supposed to be just friends, but his actions and my feelings keep blurring the lines.

We have next period together, and I haven't figured out how I can make it clear I can't go there. The thing is, I'm not sure if all of this means he wants to go beyond friendship. If I say something and he doesn't want more than friendship, I'll look like an idiot. I don't know how to handle these emotions because I've never opened myself up enough to feel them.

I wish my mama were here. I can't help but think how she might react. She always told me one day I would meet someone that made me feel alive. In my mind, I can see her smiling and comforting me in the way only she knew how, soothing the pain of the internal conflict about these feelings Drake has awakened in me.

I made it perfectly clear I didn't like the way he acted in the hallway. I was annoyed with him, yet I almost like the idea of him being jealous, which only makes me more uncomfortable. I'm so messed up, which is exactly why we can only be friends. Isn't that what he said he wanted, only friendship? My heart aches a little every time that thought crosses my mind. *God, I'm so confused.*

The bell rings, and I quickly stand up and make my way toward the door. I really need to get a grip on my feelings.

eciding it's best to skip meeting Selene in the hall, I opt to head to our next class instead. She was obviously irritated at how I interrupted her and Jared, but I couldn't help myself; something burned in my chest when I saw the way he was looking at her. He used to look at Lacey that way, and look where it got her. I just don't like it.

I look up and see her walking through the door with Emme, and I realize my reason for not liking it is something I'm not ready to evaluate yet.

She's laughing at something Emme said, and I feel a flutter in the pit of my stomach. In the moments she lets all the worry and walls down, the most attractive glow shines in Selene's eyes. She is always beautiful, but there is something different when she's unguarded.

When she's near my desk, her gaze connects with mine, her laughter instantly stops, and her happiness fades. It kills me that I'm the one who makes that light disappear. I start to say something, but she beats me to it.

She looks nervous when she says, "Why didn't you meet me between classes?"

She covers her mouth with her hand as if those were not the words she intended to say. I'm a little surprised by her question since I could have sworn she was angry with me when I last saw her.

"I didn't realize you would want me to after…"

She puts her hand up, stopping me. "I didn't…I mean, I…uh…I just thought you might."

Emme coughs, and we both look at her. "What? My throat was itching," she says as she takes a seat diagonal from mine.

I look back up at Selene; she is still looking at Emme. I reach my hand up and take hers, instantly shocked by the electricity that passes through our simple touch. I wonder if she feels it too, but her expression doesn't give anything away.

"Selene, I wan—" As soon as I begin to tell her I want to meet her, Tommy walks in and slides his desk against mine, almost knocking me into Selene. "Fuck, Tommy! Watch what you're doing!"

"Dude, chill," he says with his typical egocentric attitude.

As I turn back to Selene, the bell rings, and the teacher walks in and closes the door. "Ms. Chandler, please take a seat." She looks down at me, her cheeks flushing red, before sitting at the desk across from me.

As Mrs. Peterson begins the lesson for today, I write Selene a note and pass it to her. She looks at me like I scare her but then quickly hides her uneasiness. I hate when she gets that look on her face. I want to make her happy. I watch her as she begins to unfold the note. Briefly, she glances my way and gives me a small smile. Again, I realize I've never met anyone like her. *Friends…just friends.*

Selene

I can feel his eyes on my face while I slowly unfold the piece of paper he passed me, so I give him a slight grin before turning my attention back to the note. Once I open the letter, I suddenly burst out laughing, causing the entire classroom to turn and look at me.

Mrs. Peterson stops midsentence and quickly addresses me. "Selene, is something funny?"

I can't help the last giggle that slips past my lips before replying. "No ma'am. I apologize."

I hide the paper under my book so she doesn't see it. I look over at Drake again and notice both he and Tommy are staring at me. Tommy has a smirk on his face and winks, while Drake's smile is spread wide across his face.

I roll my eyes at both of them and slip the note from under my book. I roll my eyes as I read the words written in the most perfect print: *Will you be my friend? Check yes or no.* I was right earlier—I knew he'd charm his way back into my good graces. I slowly take my pen and circle yes then pass the note back to Drake.

He beams at me again, and there is no doubt this boy has changed me forever. The question now is just how I'm going to handle this change, because so far I'm failing miserably.

chapter 14

Drake

I got to her. The day progressed with my push-and-pull relationship with Selene. When I wasn't annoying her—which
wasn't very often—I would amuse her. It really was all I've
wanted to do since the first day I met her. I just want Selene to
be happy.

She made me forget—forget Lacey was no longer here, forget my parents weren't Mr. and Mrs. Brady, forget all about the
pain of the last five months and the fact that life can be really
fucked up sometimes.

I wander toward Lacey's grave. I don't typically visit her
during the week, but I felt compelled to come today. It's almost
as if my car steered itself here. My parents once again sat up in
the stands, watching every play we ran, and I could feel their
eyes boring into my every move. Their focus is solely on me. Of
course, growing up, that was always my goal. I did whatever I
could to take their focus off Lacey...to protect her. In the end, it

appears they weren't the ones she needed protection from.

I sit down in my usual position and lean back against the stone. "I miss you," I whisper as I close my eyes and take a deep breath. "This isn't my usual day to visit, but I needed to come. God, Lacey…it was a good day. I'm sorrier than you can even know for that be—" I choke on my words midsentence, unable to speak for a moment. "Because you deserved to have a lifetime of good days. You should have had so much more than you did."

I let the silence comfort me before I continue. "I'm beginning to feel a little hopeful that there is more to this life than the hand we were dealt. She's the reason. I know I don't need to tell you who. I'm sure you sent her to me. You just couldn't leave me in my misery…always so unselfish. The only thing you forgot about in this scenario is that she deserves someone better than me."

I feel the threat of tears. Even saying it out loud to Lacey doesn't change the fact that no matter how wrong I think I might be for Selene, friend or something more, she has invaded every part of me, straight to my core.

I pull out a flashlight and pick up from where we left off in our romance novel. After a few sentences, I say, "You know, no matter how I'm feeling right now, this shit's still ridiculous."

Then I resume the story, reading well past my usual one-chapter-per-visit rule.

Selene

I tried calling my dad again. He didn't answer. I guess I'm not really surprised, but I wonder if he intends to ever see or talk to me again. Losing every tie to that part of my life only makes the pain of losing Mama worse. It has been a month now since I came to live with Aunt Violette, another month of feeling like I lost a piece of myself I'm not sure I can ever get back.

As soon as the thought crosses my mind, I think of him. *Drake*. He has changed so much for me. Gradually, he has torn away the wall I've spent years building around my heart, the wall only my mother could scale.

"No answer again, huh?" Aunt Violette's voice startles me from my thoughts. I look over at the doorway of my room, and she is leaning against the doorjamb. Before I can answer her, she continues. It's like she can see the answer written across my face. "I'm sorry, sweetheart." She pushes herself away from the wall and begins to walk toward me.

I suddenly feel uncomfortable. I don't want to be comforted because that means his absence means something. I don't want to feel anything for him. Standing up from the window seat, I start busying myself by unnecessarily moving things around my room. Aunt Violette must realize I don't want to talk about it, because she stops midstep and changes the subject. "So how was school today?"

This is something I'm willing to discuss. "It was pretty re-markable, actually. It seems I've already made a friend. Her name is Emme Fleming. She seems to be super sweet, and of course, you know there's Drake." I try to sound nonchalant when I say his name.

"Yes, I do—know Drake," she says, and I can hear something in her voice I can't put my finger on. I'm not sure what to think about that, but I choose to ignore it. "I also know Emme. The Flemings are a nice family. It's only the second day of school, and things are going well. That's wonderful."

Aunt Violette sits down on the bed. Quietly, she watches me. "You know, Selene, I've seen a difference in you lately. Don't get me wrong, I know you're hurting. I understand be-tween losing your mama and the difficult relationship with your daddy, it's hard. I'm aware the same untrusting little girl still lurks in there. The thing is, I see a difference when that boy is around..."

"No, I—" I begin to interrupt her, but she doesn't let me.

"Let me finish, please." She waits before continuing. "I see the difference, and while it may be tiny, I think you're letting him in. I've made my thoughts clear where Drake is concerned before. I don't want to go on and on about this, but I have to say it again. I'm happy. In fact, I'm delighted you're letting him in, letting him be your...friend. You need that—you deserve that—and so does he." She stands up and walks toward the door. Stopping next to me, she places her hand on my shoulder. "I love you, Selene."

Aunt Vi is the only person other than my mother to ever say those words to me.

When she is just beyond the door, I take a deep breath, and then I hear her shout, "I love you, but it's still your night to fix supper!"

I hear her tinkling of happiness drift through the door of my room and suddenly feel a warm, unexpected sense of joy. I fall back on my bed, unable to hold back a giggle of my own.

Drake

I made it home before my parents, although I was a little late. Now we're sitting around the table having dinner, each of them at opposite ends of our long mahogany table with me sitting alone halfway between them.

My mind drifts to the dinner I shared with Selene and Mrs. Durham nearly a month ago, and I can't help but notice the differences. Selene and Mrs. D were cheerful and making conversation. The atmosphere of that night filled me with comfort and joy.

Tonight is different, but typical for this house—for this family. I almost find the irony of this well-put-together and influential family sitting around the table with nothing but anger and tension floating between them hilarious. I'm only filled with coldness and loathing here.

"Drake!" My head snaps up when I hear her angry voice shout my name. I look at her with a blank stare, and she eases her voice into what she thinks sounds reasonable and motherly. I'm so used to her way of speaking that I'm surprised I haven't started to find it reasonable, also. "I was asking you a question. Quit daydreaming. How is school?"

My first thought is, *As if you care*, but I keep that to myself. "It's good. Pretty much the same as it is every year," I say, keeping my voice monotone out of fear of sounding either too excited or not excited enough.

"That's nice, dear," she responds, taking a bite of her steak, which she has cut into very small, precise, one-ounce pieces. My father remains silent at the other end of the table, checking his emails on his phone between bites.

I put my head down again and take a bite of potatoes, practically forcing myself to swallow. I can hardly ever eat when we're all at the dinner table together. I'm so consumed by thoughts of how to make it through dinner without any mishaps, my appetite is almost nonexistent.

I hear the clanking of a fork against a plate come from my father's end of the table, so I look out of the corner of my eye in that direction. I don't dare turn my head, in case I get caught in a conversation that has nowhere to go but bad. Tonight, though, my luck must have run out, because I can see his gaze is directed toward me, and he is glancing back and forth between his phone and my face. I keep my head down.

"Drake, what did you do?" My father's voice is full of uncommon emotion. I can feel the shivers run up my arm like a light breeze just blew through the dining room. I still keep my head down; I can't seem to move or respond, although I know whatever he is upset about is only being made worse by my silence. Moving is impossible.

Suddenly, he is standing and placing his hands on the table. "Look at me when I talk to you." I swallow the venom that fills my mouth when I feel his angry indifference push its way into me. I need to get control before I say something I will regret later, but it's too late.

I don't even know what he is angry about, but I can't seem to control the anger I feel over being treated like a piece of trash. *Bury it. Bury it deep down.* I can hear the memory of her voice whispering to me, reminding me what we have to do to survive. I close my eyes and inhale. I hold my breath and count to ten before looking into my father's angry face.

"Sir?" I say in a voice so calm I can feel the threads of my control trembling in my throat.

"Don't try to bullshit me, Drake. What are you doing?" His voice rises a little as he walks around the table. He is standing so close to me that if I tried to stand up, my body would be touching his.

"I received an email from Principal Barnes saying he is glad we agreed to the tribute planned in honor of your sister at the homecoming football game!" My body begins to shake as it does every time one of them brings up Lacey in any way. "I never... we never agreed to this! You did this behind our backs, knowing good and well we want to put this behind us. The embarrassment that this...the overwhelming loss of Lacey and..." He trails off, turning on his heel and leaving me clenching the arm of my chair as I try to remain still in my seat. *Coward.*

When I hear his office door slam, I slide the chair back and stand up, forgetting I'm not alone.

"Drake Thomas, you stop right there!" I can hear it in her voice—it's going to be one of those nights, one of those nights I knew I needed to draw the attention to me and away from Lacey because she was too fragile. Now it's only me, and I have no one to save, no one to protect. I hate myself for fearing her. I hate even more that I feel heartache over the lack of parental love her actions and voice reveal. It's full of hatred, a hatred that hurts.

I freeze but never look at her. It's coming, and after all these years, I want to crumble to the floor and beg her to love me. I can see her move out of the corner of my eye until she is standing in front of me.

"How dare you? Do you know what you do to your father? To this family? Will you ever stop embarrassing us?" I keep my head down like I do every time. I hear Lacey again whispering for me to block it all out. My mother doesn't really want an answer, which makes it easier to keep quiet.

I can feel her take a step closer. "I thought maybe this all could stop. You would get your football scholarship and make your father proud...make this family shine again after your sister tainted us with even greater shame than any of your immature shenanigans did over the years!"

As soon as she mentions Lacey, I lose all concentration. The whispers in my head are silenced. I can take her vitriol, but as soon as she brings Lacey up, it's all over.

My head whips up, and my vision is blurred by the hatred I feel for this woman in front of me. "DON'T EVER SPEAK OF HER AGAIN! LACEY WAS EVERYTHING GOOD!" My voice is quivering on every word. I see her confidence waver for only a moment before she pulls her hand back and slaps me across the face. This time I don't back down right away, although I never raise my hand to her. Next thing I know, she is repeatedly hitting me across the face.

She begins screaming, "Don't tell me about your sister!"

With each strike of her hand, I start to feel the sting then full-on pain as she uses her fist on my face. I feel the skin below my eye split open, and all I can think to do is drop to my knees. It's like she can't stop herself, and she doesn't until my father pulls her away. I can barely see through my tears, and he is say-ing something to her as he grabs her around the waist, lifting her in the air and pulling her away from me. I see her nod her head slowly, and then he sets her down. She stares right at me as she straightens her blouse then turns and leaves the room.

My father looks down at me. "Why do you do this, Drake? You know what you do to her. Get up and clean your face. Do you see what happens? I—I can't…I don't know how to stop it." He releases a defeated sigh and then leaves me standing in the dining room alone with my hands hanging at my sides.

The only thing going through my head is the thought that, for just this one moment in time, I'm glad Lacey isn't here. I look around at the half-eaten dinner set perfectly on a perfect table for an ideal family, except that kind of perfect doesn't ex-ist…nor ever has it ever existed. Suddenly, the chime of a text message breaks through the sad silence hanging in the room.

I walk slowly to the table and pick up my phone from where it's lying on the floor next to my chair. It must have fallen when I stood up from the table.

Instantly, my heart beats back into a rhythm. I feel a warm sense of calm, which should seem impossible in this moment of total hopelessness.

It's a text from Selene: *Because of you, this place doesn't totally suck…friend. See you tomorrow.*

In those two sentences, this girl just kicked hopelessness's ass, leaving me with an unfamiliar sensation in my chest.

chapter 15

Drake

I can tell she notices as soon as my eyes meet hers through the crowd of students in front of her locker. It's like a light switches on in her head, and it's not one of joy, but of panic. I tried my best to hide it. In fact, I thought I did a pretty good job because I already talked to Tommy on my way into the building this morning, and he didn't even notice. Of course, that's typical Tommy—completely oblivious to his surroundings.

She is standing directly in front of me now, and a tiny gasp slips past her lips. Slowly, she places her hand against the side of my face, and I see her lip quiver as she opens it to say something. I want to lean into the warmth of her hand. I want to open myself to the comfort she wants to offer, but I know it would be the end of me, the end of the last tether I have to my sanity. I'm begging her to remain silent with my eyes. I don't know how, but she seems to understand me. Biting her lip, she lowers her hand. I need to lift the tension fogging the air between us.

"Good morning, beautiful!" I say as I lean forward and place a kiss on her cheek.

Her cheek tenses under my lips, and I think I may have made a mistake. Pulling back, I see I'm wrong. On her face, I can see a little of the happiness I've seen flicker there before. She pushes against my chest and rolls her eyes.

"That is not a friend greeting, Mr. Thomas! Keep that up and I will make you pay!" she says, trying to sound tough, but I can still hear the lingering anxiety in her words.

I can't help but wonder if it's from the cuts and bruises I've tried covering up on my face or from the kiss I placed on her cheek. Either way, I'm going to ignore it if it means I can keep things normal for Selene and me. I need normal. She is my normal.

"Ooooooh, I'm scared. Big bad Selene Chandler is going to make me pay! Do you have any idea what it does to me when you talk like that?" I ask her with humor in my voice, but I'm actually dead serious. I love when she acts all tough.

We reach the doorway of her first class so she stops, once again facing me. "No, what does it do?"

I want to laugh at the look on her face; she looks sincerely confused by my statement. This girl has no idea what she is capable of doing to me. I continue past her, leaning in close to her ear as I go by, whispering, "I've always wondered about being dominated."

Pulling a lock of her hair, I continue down the hall, laughing the entire way. It feels good to laugh. The laughter, the smiles are all for her...only for her.

Selene

I've spent the entire day barely holding myself together. When I saw Drake this morning, I wanted to burst into tears and hold him tight. The makeup he carefully put on the cuts and bruises was well done, but the problem is, I've unwillingly memorized every angle of every feature of this boy's face, his perfect, heartbreakingly beautiful face.

Someone injured his perfection, but that isn't what I worry about; the physical wounds will heal. I'm concerned his face will heal but his heart won't. I saw something in his startling green eyes that stopped me from pushing the conversation, but he doesn't have to say what happened. I know it did—I know something happened.

Now, I'm sitting here on the bleachers waiting to watch him practice. Emme said she would meet me after cheerleading practice, and I'm glad for that, because I feel awkward sitting here alone. The sun is beating down on my back, and I'm questioning if I should've just gone home and then come back when his practice was supposed to be over. I was just worried I would miss him.

It's not like he's avoiding me. He still met me after every one of my classes, still made inappropriate more-than-a-friend comments. He is still Drake, but I can see in his eyes that he has lost a little piece of himself. It wasn't there yesterday. Yesterday, he still had that something that makes him who he is. I can't quite put my finger on it, but whatever it is, he can't lose it. I need him to be Drake. I need him to be the boy who is tearing down my walls.

I look at the field, and the team is running out to the center and breaking into groups, which I suppose is split between defense and offense. I finally spot Drake running across the field, and suddenly I can't breathe. He looks just as he has many times before in my mind—like a Greek god—but this time it's a little different because the pads and uniform make him look bigger.

I've lost complete track of why I'm here, and finally I feel the air filling my lungs again, but my heart rate has yet to slow down. This is Drake. Drake is my friend. I don't want more. He doesn't want more. I can't want more.

I hear the rumbling of footsteps on the bleachers below me, and I look down to see Emme climbing them toward me. As she approaches, I feel a little relief at the distraction she'll provide. When she reaches me, she looks up and beams at someone behind me, and I start to turn to see who it might be. "Hello, Mr. and Mrs. Thomas." I freeze mid-turn and slowly angle my body back toward the field. She doesn't even wait for them to say anything before she plops her bottom down next to me. They're behind me. Part of me wants to stand up and confront them about the pain they're causing Drake, but before I can do anything stupid, Emme nudges me in my arm with her shoulder.

"Hey! I have some news to share with you!" She sounds so excited I'm not sure how to react, although this is Emme, so she is pretty much in a constant state of excitement.

"Oh, yeah!" I say with as much enthusiasm as I can muster.

"I spoke with the cheerleading sponsor and the other cheerleaders, and they agreed we should give you the opportunity to join the squad! Isn't that fantastic?"

It takes a minute for what she said to register in my mind. I feel my throat starting to tighten, and panic fills my chest. I stare out in front of me toward the field, desperately searching for Drake. I need to see him to calm down. *Breathe, Selene, breathe,* I tell myself. Drake...where is he? There—I only catch glimpses of him as he moves among the other players, but it's enough.

"Selene—earth to Selene! Did you hear me?" Emme is looking at me like I jumped off into the deep end.

"Yeah? Great! Really, it's great! I'll talk to Aunt Violette about it."

She stares at me with a confused look on her face, and I pray she won't ask questions. She must've decided to not ask what's wrong with me because she doesn't say anything else about cheerleading.

"So, why did you want me to meet you here? I never really took you for the type to sit and watch your guy practice football," she says with a sunny expression on her face.

I lean toward her and whisper? "What? One, he isn't my guy, and two, I didn't ask you to meet me—you offered!" A hurt look crosses her face, so I quickly amend my response. "I'm glad you did though, because I would feel like a fool sitting here all alone. Plus, I sort of like you!" I lean into her in a friendly kind of half hug, which feels strange to me. I never even did this with Ryan, let along any of my other friends.

An elated look spreads across Emme's face. "I sort of like you too, and he is totally your guy. You just aren't ready to admit it...yet!" Then a burst of hilarity erupts from her lips, and I couldn't stop my own smile even if I wanted to.

Emme has no idea what she has done for me in the mere fifteen minutes she has been sitting with me. In fact, I don't think she knows what she has done for me in the few days she has known me. I look over at her, and she has a beaming smile on her face. I realize that as much as I'm beginning to want to connect with this girl, I'm not ready to tell her everything. I'm holding back, just like I do with everyone.

"It looks like they're getting done a little early," she says as she nods her head toward the field.

When I look over, I notice they're headed for the locker rooms. *Thank God.* I'm hanging too far out of my comfort zone, and with his parents sitting a few feet behind me, it's only getting worse.

"Let's go. I'm gonna meet Drake at his car," I whisper, worried they'll hear me. I stand up, and Emme follows behind me.

As we approach Drake's truck, Emme says, "I think I'm going to head home. I have a paper to write and need to get started on it."

I nod and tell her I'll see her tomorrow. I decide to sit in my car, which I parked next to his, until he comes out of the locker room. I just hope he's willing to talk because if he doesn't, I'm not sure how to handle this situation.

As I walk out of the locker room, I feel my nerves go into overdrive. During practice, I noticed Selene sitting in the bleachers with Emme at her side. At first, I felt a surge of excitement that she would stay to watch me, but then I saw my parents sitting just a few feet behind them.

Even at a distance, I saw my mother watching every move Selene made, and it made my blood turn to ice. I can't let her hurt Selene—I *won't* let her. Rounding the corner of the locker rooms, I nearly stumble as I come to an abrupt stop. My parents are standing next to my truck, and Selene's car is sitting just on the other side of it. A sudden urge to break into a full sprint and put myself between my mother and Selene fills me, but instead I keep calm and walk toward them as if everything were normal. I can see them, but Selene is still nowhere in sight.

As soon as I'm within reasonable hearing distance, my father addresses me. "Drake, excellent job out there, but I noticed your elbow slip a few times when you were going to make those long passes." I stare at him and try to imagine what it might have been like if he'd only said the positive part of his statement.

"Thank you, sir," I say instead of trying to pretend this means anything more than it does.

My eyes dart around, trying to find any sign of Selene. I'm

trying my best to cover the panic I feel when my mother says, "We saw Emme Fleming and that girl from the restaurant."

I hate the way she says *that girl* but hide it by placing a bored look on my face. "Yeah, that's interesting. Did you talk to Emme?"

My mother remains quiet a moment, and I can tell she's examining my response. "Of course. She said hello, and we acknowledged her. She was your sister's best friend." I swallow hard at the mention of Lacey but keep my face neutral. "I did find it peculiar that the girl and Emme seem to be close friends. Did you introduce them?" She is still trying to poke at me to see if I'll pop. *It's not going to work, Mother, so give up*, I think to myself.

I maintain the same bored look and my voice as steady as possible. "Mother, I'm reasonably confident Emme Fleming is capable of finding her own friends. I wouldn't be surprised if they actually have a class together. Selene is a nice girl too, so I'm sure they hit it off."

I shouldn't have added the last part about Selene because I see the flicker of interest burst into a full flame in her eyes. "I'm sure you're right," she says stiffly.

It almost worries me that she doesn't say more on the subject because it leaves me unsure of what she's thinking, but I just want them to leave so I can find Selene. My father finally looks up from his phone and turns his attention back to us.

"Well, we must be going because we have a council meeting tonight. See you later, Drake." They both turn and walk away without another word.

Once they get in their car and drive away, I run around to the passenger side of my truck, where Selene's car is parked. I peer into the car and begin to laugh uncontrollably. Selene is lying flat on the front seat, waving at me as I peek in. She is so fucking cute. I swing the door open as the humor subsides.

"What the hell?" I ask as I reach my hand into the car to

help her out.

She is still grinning from ear to ear. "You should have seen me totally dive down when I saw them coming." She sounds joyful, and the distinction is so sweet I want to grab hold of her and never let go. She is so damn beautiful, and I need a constant reminder that we're just friends. If she keeps looking and smiling at me like this, I'm going to need to set a reminder on my phone to go off every fifteen minutes just to keep my feelings in check.

"Drake, do you think they saw me? I mean, I don't want to cause you any problems. I just needed... I didn't realize they came to your practices."

Shaking my head, I close her door, walk around to the back of my truck, and pull my tailgate down for us to sit on. "They didn't see you, at least not over here. They saw you in the bleachers, and my mom brought you up. I think she's suspicious but can't put her finger on it, so no biggie—for now, anyway."

She hops up on the tailgate and swings her feet. "I just don't want to give her any more reasons to hurt you." She pauses and sighs. I can tell she is nervous about something. "Drake, I know this morning you didn't want to talk..."

"And I still don't. Selene, let it go," I say abruptly. I hop off down to put space between us and begin pacing. I just can't do this.

She looks up at me, tears rolling down her cheeks. *Oh God*, I've made her cry...again. I can't look at her.

"What am I supposed do, Drake? Don't you see? You're being hurt—how can I ignore that?" My back is to her, but the concern in her voice is nearly bringing me to my knees. Suddenly, I feel her standing behind me, so close I can practically feel the heat from her body. "I just don't know what to do." She sounds like she is going to shatter at any moment.

Slowly, I turn to face her. She is looking down at her feet, and her small frame seems even more fragile when I'm standing this close to her. I place my hand under her chin and tilt her head back so she is looking up at me. I never want to hurt this girl. She is my friend...my hope. "Please don't cry. I can't take it if you cry, especially over me. I don't deserve your tears." She blinks a few times, and I can still see the tears sparkling in her hazel green eyes.

Raising her hand, she caresses it over the bruises on my face. "Drake, it could be worse next time. I'm acting selfishly here. I need you around because I trust you. I need you around because you're my friend. I can't lose you too when I've lost everything else, so never ever tell me you don't deserve my tears, because you deserve more." I see conflicting emotions warring in her eyes before she guardedly puts her arms around me.

She's stiff at first, but when I put my arms around her and slowly pull her into me, I feel her relax. I think I even hear her sigh, as if she's finally attained something she's been waiting a lifetime for.

"I need to do this my way, Selene. You can't help me," I finally say after a few minutes. "I've been dealing with this for most of my life."

She pulls back and looks up at me again. "I'll keep your secret for now, but if I ever think you're in danger of...you know what I mean, I won't hesitate to tell someone, anyone to help you."

I nod and rub my thumbs across her cheeks to wipe away the tears. "Fuck. If I had known having a girl as a best friend felt this good, I would have done it a long time ago." I probably just made her uncomfortable.

"Fuck really isn't a nice word, you shithead!" she says, surprising me. She chuckles, punching me in the arm. We both start lose it as I rub my arm like she actually hurt me.

"Remind me not to make you mad—you have a mean right hook," I say, and then she hops in her car and sticks her tongue out at me before driving away.

As I watch her go, I say a little prayer that I can keep my word and never hurt her.

chapter 16

Selene

It's been three weeks since Emme told me everyone on the cheer squad agreed to let me try out. After a lengthy discussion with Aunt Violette, I decided to do it.

It felt good putting myself out there again, taking a chance on getting things back to a more normal routine, letting go of some of the guilt I have about continuing my life without Mama. The tryout was just a formality, according to Emme, because I was pretty much a shoo-in. I didn't care—I enjoyed every minute. It's one more step toward healing.

I missed one football game before I had my uniform and everything I needed to be ready to cheer with the squad.

Emme was beyond excited and let me know every chance she could for a week straight. Even Drake was particularly glad to have his own personal best-friend-slash-cheerleader at every game. He is such an ass, but he is the ass that has kept me together.

No one realizes most days are a struggle for me. Many

mornings, I wake up and just want to stay there. Then my phone will ding with a *Good morning* text from Drake, like he knows I need that extra push to go on with my day.

Nearly six months have passed, and all I can think most days is, *People lie.* It doesn't get easier. Maybe I can make it through the days, but not a moment goes by that I don't think of her...and that is not easy. Sure, it's different, and I'm learning thanks to Aunt Violette, Drake, and Emme—and maybe even Tommy—to go on with my day.

Two months have passed since Dad dropped me off in this little town without a second thought, and he has yet to return any of my calls. He did call Aunt Violette once while I was at school to make sure I wasn't causing her any trouble. I don't even know how to feel about this anymore.

This is what I do know: time keeps passing, even if we feel like we are at a standstill. I measure time by events. Some I wish I could undo, and some not so much. I think Drake is measuring time too—the time since he lost Lacey, the time that goes by in between bruises left by his mother. I think he may be measuring time from the moment we met; I know I am. It's what helps me keep my feelings in line. I tell myself we haven't known one another long enough to feel this way. Sufficient time hasn't gone by for me to love his smile or know his different laughs. Enough time hasn't passed by for me to miss him when he isn't around. Those things take years, right?

I don't know what it is exactly, but something is different with us, and maybe it doesn't take years. The one thing that is taking time is my ability to admit and accept all these feelings about my mama, my dad, and, most of all, Drake.

Leaning against his truck while I wait for him to come out of the locker room, I can't help but think we're linked tightly together in some fated way. Just as I'm about to push away from the truck, a pair of warm lips makes contact with my cheek and then is gone before I know it. I'm so startled, I let out a little yelp.

"Shit, Drake!" He's hysterical. "It isn't funny! You scared the shit out of me!"

In between his breaths, he manages to say, "You looked so serious. I had to do something." He continues for a few minutes, my heart still racing a little. When he is unguarded and looks so carefree, I realize this boy is everything. His smile only accentuates his good looks.

"What's up, Chandler? Are you ready for some serious grub?" he asks as he lets out one last laughing cough.

I can never stay irritated at him for long, but I don't have to let him know that. "Oh, my name is Drake Thomas, and I like to scare girls standing alone in the dark, crack up about it, and then talk about food like nothing happened," I say with sarcasm before pretending to laugh uncontrollably.

All at once, I'm grabbed around my knees and slung over his shoulder. "We don't have time for your sarcasm, Chandler! I just helped win a football game and need food! I'm a growing boy!" he shouts as he runs around to the passenger side of his truck, opens the door, and tosses me in the seat. I'm surprised he didn't beat on his chest like a gorilla. I giggle, because I adore him.

I will never get enough of this impossible guy—never. I may not understand what exactly I'm feeling at this moment, but I know it's real. As Drake pulls himself into the driver's seat, chuckling, I realize the only thing that really matters is the fact that I can't imagine not spending every moment possible with him. There isn't any doubt my time with Drake helps make all the other things in my life better.

Drake

I can't stop my levity as I pull myself up into the driver's seat of my truck. Selene is so ridiculous sometimes, which only makes her more adorable. I look over, and she is watching me with an expression I've noticed her directing my way before, but I can never quite put my finger on what it means.

"I really can't decide if I love you or hate you," she says as she releases a slight giggle, shaking her head. We both freeze at the word—*love*. I peek over at her from the corner of my eye. She is beginning to fidget, twisting her long golden hair around her finger.

I do the only thing I can to lighten the mood—I tease her. "Soooooo, you looooove me!" I sing in an exaggerated way, just to annoy her.

She swivels in the seat next to me. "You wish. I definitely hate you," she replies too quickly. "I thought you were hungry, Mr. Big Shot Quarterback. You need your strength, remember?" She says this all so quickly, it's as if she doesn't even take a breath.

I stare at her face, grinning, but on the inside I'm a little uneasy. Do I wish Selene loved me? I don't know the answer to that, and I'm not sure I want to.

So, once again, I ignore the way my heart clenches at the thought. "You finally get it. Let's get out of here." I start the truck and put it into drive. "Do you want to go to Fran's with everyone else or go somewhere different?"

Fran's Diner is about a twenty-five-minute drive outside of town, heading into Austin, and it's the post-Friday-night-football-game hangout for all the high school students of our town. I've spent many a Friday night there, but for some reason it just doesn't seem that important anymore. I no longer really

123

care about what others think or how to keep my popular social status. Eventually, none of it will matter anyway.

"Fran's is fine. I told Emme we would meet her there," she replies as she stares out the passenger window. Then she turns, looking at me. "Is that okay? I could always tell her we're going somewhere else if that's what you want to do."

I'm so tempted to say yes, but how do I explain why I feel reluctant about showing up at Fran's? I don't want to talk about the fact that it reminds me of who I was before, the person I'm scared I might truly be deep down.

Selene doesn't know that guy. She doesn't know the Drake who pushed the limits of right and wrong, the guy who chased girls, found humor at others' expense, and used his father's status as a reason and safety net to do as he pleased.

She also doesn't know why I did it all. No one knows why. No one knows I did it to create a distraction, that being that person was a way to protect the one right thing I had in my life. The only thing is, I still feel the need to not care and live recklessly. It's what scares me most.

There are two people who keep me from going completely over the edge. One is a memory, and the other is sitting next to me. I watch her from the corner of my eye as I pull into the parking lot. She begins fidgeting with her uniform skirt and draws my attention to her long tan legs. I snap my eyes back and take a deep breath. I can just hear what she would say if she knew I was having a hard time not thinking about running my hand over the smooth skin of her legs: *That is not how friends look at one another, Mr. Thomas!* I love when she gets an attitude and calls me Mr. Thomas.

"Drake, are we going to sit here all night, or are we actually going to get out?" Her question pulls me from my thoughts. I didn't even realize I had parked, but she is already hanging halfway out the door, looking back at me.

"Yeah...yeah, I'm coming," I say as I shut off the truck,

unbuckling my seatbelt. "Selene, let's sit in a back booth. Just you and me...Emme and Tommy, too," I say as I climb out of the truck. I barely hear her answer as I shut the door and walk toward the restaurant.

She's beside me, watching my face carefully as I reach for her hand. "Sure, Drake, just the four of us."

chapter 17

Selene

I strum my fingertips across the guitar strings. It's been a while since I picked it up and attempted any music; time has gotten away from me between school and cheerleading. Another three weeks have passed, and as much as things have changed, Drake seems to be the one person in my life that gets that I need to go slow.

I haven't wanted to burden Aunt Violette, so I've kept my feelings to myself. I'm still struggling with the loss of my mom and the loss of my home, although Aunt Violette has been amazing every moment since my dad left me nearly three months ago.

Looking out the window, I notice the sun beginning to set just beyond the trees. I've heard a melody play over and over in my head, on that gives me a sense of comfort and security. Closing my eyes, I let my mind clear and feel the music. I know the lyrics will come to me, just as they always have.

As I continue to play, his face comes to my mind...the way his eyes crinkle when he laughs, the way he says my name, even the comforting way he takes my hand without asking. It's like he can tell when I need to know someone is there and cares.

The last few months with Drake have been everything I've needed and the only thing that has kept me from drowning in the despair that threatens to consume me at every moment. Suddenly, lyrics appear in my mind, so I continue to play, singing from my heart while my mind pictures only one person.

You came into my life
When I didn't want anyone around
I feel so out of control
It's like I don't have a choice
in the direction my life is taking
Then you're there
I can feel I need you
And you're there
All I need is you
And you're there
I want you to be here with me
The beating of my heart tells me yes
My mind says no, so I say just friends
I can see you struggle, too
Keeping that smile on
So I can't see the truth
And you say just friends

There is a sense of relief as I write the last word and set my journal down. Leaning back against the pillows that line the window seat, I look out at the dark, star-filled sky. For the first time in a long time, I feel a little lighter and less burdened by my emotions. I may not be perfectly happy, but I'm definitely happy. This is the first time since Mama passed away when I don't feel guilty about feeling something other than sorrow. It's almost like Mama is connected to bringing me here, bringing me to

Drake. I just need to figure out how I can be honest about my feelings other than through my music.

I'm beginning to get nervous. Life has been a little too calm, even considering how I feel every time I'm around Selene. When she is around, I feel anything but relaxed. I'm comfortable and happy, yes, but far from being completely at ease with my feelings for her.

I glance over at the clock on the wall. There are thirty minutes left of this class, and as usual, I'm ready to come unglued. She'll be standing outside of her classroom. She'll be talking to that asshole, Jared. If I thought I could get away with murder, I would have killed him the first day I saw him speaking to her.

The worst part is he knows it bothers me. He knows I want her for my own. She just doesn't know I want her, and I'm pretty sure if she did, she would run the other way. I just can't let that happen. Friends are what we will stay for as long as she needs us to be, because being nothing at all is out of the question. For now, we'll just be complicated.

Before I know it, the bell is ringing, signaling the end of class. I practically jump out of my seat, stumbling in the process, and bolt toward the door. This is pathetic, the way I'm running to meet a girl, but I don't care. For the first time in my life, I've found something real.

Just as I'm about to round the corner, I feel a hand on my arm. I look down at the fingers that are wrapped tightly around my forearm before looking up at the face they belong to: Abby Donovan.

She is looking up at me, batting her eyelashes. I would swear on my life she practices this exact expression in front of a mirror every morning before school. "Drake Thomas, I've been waiting long enough for you to stop ignoring me. When are we going to pick up where we left off?"

I stare at her in disbelief, but really, can I blame her? If I'm really honest, she is talking to the old Drake, the only Drake I ever let anyone know. It isn't her fault I'm not that person any longer. She doesn't know me. She never did, but I never let her...or anyone.

Prying her hand off my arm, I say as gently as possible, "Abby, look, I'm really sorry for the way I treated you in the past. While it was fun for a time, I think I'm going to pass. You deserve someone who really cares about you." I feel good about what I just said, especially since I actually meant every word.

I realize that as good as I feel and as honest as I'm being, Abby doesn't give a shit. She looks pissed. *Fuck.* "Excuse me, how do you know what I deserve, you stupid asshole? You'll be sorry for tossing me aside." She disappears as quickly as she appeared.

I look around me, and most people are staring in my direction. The whole school will know about this little scene before I even make it to my next class. *Shit!* Speaking of the next class, Selene is probably waiting for me.

With Abby completely forgotten, I dash down the hall and around the corner when suddenly I stumble to a stop. Selene is giggling, and Jared is standing entirely too close to her. I have that sudden urge to pummel him into the floor again. They are looking at something, and I can see he is easing his way closer to her. She doesn't even realize it because she is so caught up in whatever they're looking at on her phone.

My body goes completely rigid, and I begin to count to ten to get my anger in check. She is not mine. I need to cool down. Plus, she wouldn't like it if I knocked this guy over. We're friends. Just as I finally begin to feel myself relax, Jared chooses to make a mistake. I watch as he takes another step closer to Selene and sets his arm over her shoulders. Instantly, I recognize the change in her body language, all humor gone. Stepping the last few feet forward, I quickly take her hand and pull her to me. She resists a little before she recognizes me, and then I feel her relax.

"Hey!" I say as a look of relief washes over her face. "We better get to class."

I glance over her head and notice Jared is standing with a fixed stare on his face. He is pissed at me for interrupting them again. I haven't figured out what his game is, but I will, and then I will make sure he understands he will never win Selene, will never hurt her the way he hurt Lacey. I'm not sure what it is about him that blinds girls, but he was the one thing Lacey and I never agreed on.

Looking down into Selene's green eyes again, they seem to have a lovingness in them that I'm unused to seeing. "Yeah, I think we better." Her voice is still a bit shaky, and I can't help but wonder what exactly changed between her laughing and Jared putting his arm around her. As much as I didn't like him touching her, that is all he did, and not even in an aggressive way. "See you later, Jared," she says calmly, giving him a friendly look.

I don't really get this girl sometimes. The more I get to know her, the more I realize I don't really know anything about her. Glancing at her out of the corner of my eye, I notice her face is a bit tight again, but her hand feels relaxed in mine. I squeeze it a little, and she looks up at me. I see something in her gaze and realize she trusts me, which makes me feel so good and so scared at the same time. She is so beautiful; I can't ruin her like I ruin everything else. I also can't let her go completely. The little voice in my head reminds me—*just friends*.

I need the reminder because she suddenly releases my hand

and loops her arm around mine, pulling me closer to her. I smell her sweet scent and listen for the voice again, but this time it's different. This time it whispers one simple word: *more.*

Selene

I don't really mind Jared. I can tell Drake doesn't like him, but I sort of enjoy his sense of humor. He definitely makes that hour of my life more interesting. Everything was fine; we were watching an amusing video he told me about while I waited for Drake. Then he stepped just a little too close and put his arm around me. I have never been comfortable with someone being in my space with the exception of my mama, Ryan, and now Drake.

It took me years to let Ryan even stand close to me. I just feel unsafe…uncomfortable. So, when Drake pulled me to him, my first reaction was to pull back. Then I saw it was him, and everything in me softened. Now, as we walk down the hall, I can tell he noticed. He won't ask, but he wants to know. I can tell he is struggling to stay quiet by the way he keeps looking at me.

I know everyone is looking at us as we walk down the hall, holding one another like we belong to just each other. In a way, I want to yell, *Yes! This is exactly what it looks like!* But I know it's not, and I wonder if it ever can be. I look up at him and he smiles at me, so I smile back. He is so beautiful it almost takes my breath away. I can't fathom how we got here. This relationship, whatever it is, has my emotions all over the place. I've never been more confused. I don't know what to think or feel, so I just stay quiet and lean into him. I only know I feel safe when I'm close to him.

Suddenly, Drake is bumped from his side, and we are both taken off guard, stumbling into some lockers. He pulls me to his side and turns our bodies so he is the one who makes contact with the locker.

"Tommy, I swear, dude—one day I'm going to kick your ass." Aggravation is apparent in his voice and on his face before he glances down at me. His voice is gentle as he says, "You okay?"

Before I can answer, I hear Tommy and say, "Dude, no wonder Abby is spitting fire! You two are practically groping one another in front of everyone!" he says, pointing at me and Drake, except I don't really care that he's talking so loud it's practically echoing through the hallway. I lost focus on everything after I heard the name Abby.

Who the hell is Abby? And why is she pissed? I gaze over at Drake's face and notice he has turned a bright shade of crimson and is staring at Tommy like he might kill him.

"Shut the fuck up!" he says under his breath, and I can feel his whole body is completely stiff now. "Abby Donovan and I had one little fling last year. It was nothing more, so she has no reason to be pissed." Drake glances at me, so I keep my face neutral as if I'm completely unaffected by the conversation. "And Selene and I aren't groping one another, we just...we're just friends."

Even though I know I've said we're just friends from the beginning, I can't help but feel like the wind has been knocked out of me. I pull away from Drake. I just can't help feeling hurt, and I know it's completely irrational of me.

"We need to get to class," I mutter before turning for the classroom door.

"Jackass!" I hear Drake say to Tommy before he catches up with me. "Selene, I'm sorry he said we're basically making out in front of everyone."

Really? Is that what he thinks I'm upset about? I stop as I near the row of desks I usually sit in and raise my eyes to meet his. They're so green, I can't help but think of springtime. I could get lost in his eyes without even realizing it.

"Is that—I'm not upset. The bell is about to ring, and I didn't want to be late. Speaking of, you should get to class yourself. I'll see you next period."

I take a seat and notice Drake has stopped at the door. He's looking straight at me, as if trying to figure me out. I put on my best smile and lift my hand in a wave. For the first time, there is an awkward tension between us. He raises his hand in return and gives me an unsure look. Drake is uneasy, and it's my fault. I reacted ridiculously—even if he does have something going on with this Abby girl, I have no right to say anything. I did say we're just friends.

I skip out on the rest of the school day. I try to pretend it's because we don't have football practice tonight, but in reality I didn't want to face Selene. I'm not sure exactly why, but she started pulling way the moment Tommy mentioned Abby.

Of course, I'm not sure I helped any because I felt completely guilty, and I couldn't hide the fact that I was uncomfortable myself. I'm probably making everything worse by avoiding her, but I just have to. I want more, although I know I shouldn't. It's harder and harder to deny as each day passes, so I need a timeout.

As I pull up to the cemetery, I'm almost instantly comforted. I swear each time I pull up here, Lacey knows exactly what I'm feeling, just like she did when she was alive. I know it's a little strange. We were connected just as most twins are thought to be, but there was an even tighter bond because of what we had to endure each day.

I turn off the truck and am starting to make my way to the gravesite when I hear the crunching of gravel and the soft rattle of an engine. I know it's her before I even turn around. How did she know where to find me? I swallow the lump that has formed in my throat. I can't make myself turn around, even when I hear the car come to a stop and the engine shut off, not even when the door opens and closes.

Frozen in place, I just wait. I'm not even sure what I'm waiting for, but I still can't make myself move. Her gentle touch to my shoulder causes a spark to run down my body.

"Drake?" she says softly, as if she is afraid. "I'm sorry."

Sorry? Her words confuse me. What is she sorry for? I can't imagine, but she has nothing to apologize for. I need to make her understand.

I whip around so fast it knocks her hand off my shoulder, and she takes a step back. I don't understand her. As soon as I look into her eyes, I know I'm making her nervous. She's on edge, and I want to be angry at her for that, but I push those feelings down. I want all of this to be easy between us. I hate that she still has moments of unease with me. "Selene, why are you sorry?"

She runs her hand through her long hair, which has more of a wave to it than it did this morning. I remember one time she said the humidity hated her hair, but I know at this moment her tousled locks are my favorite look. I'm suddenly picturing myself running my hands through her hair, pulling her toward me, meeting her rosy lips with mine...

"Because I made everything awkward between us when everything was going so perfect," she says, interrupting my thoughts. "I ruin—"

"No," I say, shaking my head. "You didn't ruin anything." I want to shout, but I stay quiet. "I'm sorry. I acted guilty when Tommy mentioned Abby, and you were only reacting to me."

Shaking her head, she takes a step toward me. "I acted crazy because of me, not you." She turns her back to me so I can no longer see her face. "I—shit!" I'm about to tease her when she continues. "I never have…"

I step closer to her. "You never what?" I ask her.

"Shit, Drake, I'm jealous, okay! I'm jealous out of my mind, and I have no right to be because we're just friends!" Selene blurts out.

She's jealous. I didn't see that coming. I mean, not really. I hoped, but I didn't think it was possible. I want everything to feel less awkward. I want everything to be just as it was before today so I do the only thing I could think to do. I reach down and take her hand in mine.

Leading her through the gates of the cemetery, we walk in silence. She doesn't resist me in the least, and she doesn't ask questions. Selene just let me take her hand and allowed me to guide our way around every headstone until we reached the one that means something, the one that means everything to me.

Tightening my grip on her small hand, I glance over at her and find her staring down at the name written in perfect script across the headstone, tears filling her eyes. Following her gaze, my lips tip up at one corner.

"Hey, Lace, uh…I brought someone very special with me today. You might remember her because you knew her before I did. This is Mrs. D's niece, Selene." I swallow before continuing. "You were right, there is something special about her."

It takes me a few seconds before I face Selene. She is standing wide-eyed, tears rolling down her cheeks as she stares at me. I feel an overwhelming urge to take her in my arms. My heart is pushing me in a direction I've been trying to avoid, and I'm not sure I can change its course. I'm pretty sure things just went from awkward to complicated.

Selene

He just introduced me to his sister…a sister I was once sort of friends with during the summers…a sister who is now dead. It isn't the fact that Drake introduced me to someone who isn't here that is making me freak out a little; it's the meaning of his actions, a meaning I'm not quite sure I get.

What does special mean? I don't know exactly what he meant, but I feel a warm sensation coursing through my body. I want to run away because I feel afraid, yet I want to stay because the thought of leaving makes me even more scared.

Before I have time to react either way, Drake makes my decision for me. He reaches out and wipes the tears from my cheeks with his slightly calloused thumbs. I can't do anything but stare back into his eyes. He reaches for my hand, and I don't say anything as he leads me once again.

Slowly he lowers himself to the ground and pulls me with him. Leaning his back against the headstone, Drake keeps his hand in mine while he reaches into his back pocket and pulls out a book. A book? Surely he isn't about to—

Before I can finish my thought, he gives me that crooked smile I love so much. "So, Lacey sort of loved romance novels, and I read to her when I come here." His cheeks seem to redden a little, and it tugs at my heart to see it. "I know it sounds crazy, but it helps me feel close to her."

Shaking my head, I whisper as I lean forward and place a kiss on his cheek. "No, not crazy at all. Actually, I completely get it." I don't want to ask, but I wonder if I might be intruding. "Are you sure you don't want me to leave?"

His look fades. "No, I want you here. Please don't go."

I lean into him, making myself comfortable. "Good, I didn't want to leave."

I can feel his relief before he places a kiss on top of my head. "Good, because I need someone to explain why the girls and guys in these books always have to let these silly miscommunications come between them," he says, and I want to laugh at the serious tone of his voice.

"Sorry, I've never been the kind of girl to believe in love, so you might be asking the wrong person," I say.

I feel him tense a little, but he doesn't say anything. Instead, he explains what has been happening so far so I know what is going on in the story, and then he begins where he left off. As he starts to read, I close my eyes and let the words float through my mind.

All uncomfortable feelings are gone, and now a new feeling begins to take over, a sense of security and comfort—two things I have only truly felt with one other person in my life, and she is no longer here.

chapter 18

Drake

Ever since that day in the cemetery, Selene and I have been more relaxed around one another. It's like the strange awkwardness of that day never happened. We haven't discussed Abby, Selene's confession, or our shared moment at Lacey's gravesite. We just continue on as if we never missed a step.

I'm okay with that, but I can feel whatever brought us together in the first place tugging hard on my emotions, and I'm not sure what I'm going to do about it. It's getting to be more of a struggle to ignore how I feel about her. It's so natural to touch her and be around her. Even Selene seems to be more at ease with me. She has only reminded me I'm not acting as a friend would act in certain situations a few times, and she has initiated handholding and affection nearly as much as I have—I think it's part of my inability to continue to put our relationship in the friend zone.

I look up when I hear the door open. Mrs. Durham is standing on the other side of the screen, smiling at me.

"Hello there. Have you come to take another piece of my niece's heart?"

A light expression spreads wide across my face. "No ma'am, I came to let her steal another piece of mine." Cheesy, I know, but I realize Mrs. Durham loves this kind of honesty. Plus, she was trying to take me off guard with her comment, and I can't let her think she wins.

An exuberant bubble escapes her lips. It's a rare sound coming from the older woman, who is usually full of quiet emotion. She opens the door and stands to the side, allowing me in. I wink at her as I pass. Of course, I should have known her sweetness wouldn't last too long, because she smacks me on the back of the head.

"That is just a reminder to not try to use that charm on me again. I've got your number, Drake Thomas." Her eyes sparkle before she heads toward the kitchen, leaving me standing in the entryway. "Selene, your friend is here." I hear another chortle escape her lips before she disappears behind the swinging kitchen door.

As I turn back to where I know Selene will be coming from, I realize I hear the sound of a guitar. I make my way toward the sound and quietly walk up the steps. Reaching the top of the landing, I stop in front of her room and listen. She must not have heard Mrs. D, because her door is only slightly open, and she is in the middle of playing something. I've never heard it before, so it must be a song she wrote.

I realize she is singing softly, and it takes me back to the first day I saw her beneath the trees along the river. I'm just as mesmerized by her voice today as I was then. I want to knock, but as I listen, I'm struck by the words and stop my fisted hand just before I interrupt. Her voice and words float around me.

But my mind says no, so I say just friends
I can see you struggle too
But you keep that smile on before I can see the real truth
And you say just friends
Yet we never really let go, and then you need me

I think my heart stops beating, or maybe it's beating so fast I can't feel it anymore—either way, I'm frozen by her words. Did she write this? Who is she singing about? Part of me wants it to be me, but another part of me is so scared it is, and that frightens me for us—for her. I also feel a slight burn of jealousy at the thought of it being about someone else.

I drop my hand and take a step back. I can't let her know I heard her playing, so I silently make my way back downstairs and into the kitchen. Mrs. D looks up with a smile, but it falters a bit.

"Drake, you look like you've seen a ghost." She walks toward me, and all I can think is, *Do I?* "There is not any ghost in my house—that is just a rumor, and you know it." She attempts to hide her delight at her own joke.

I try to mask the emotions on my face. "No…no, I'm fine. I just don't think Selene heard you." She gives me a strange look then pushes the door open and begins to shout. "Sel—oh, good, there you are. Drake is here waiting for you."

I freeze, keeping my back toward her until I can compose myself. I want to turn around and ask her if she means it. I want to ask her if she really wishes to be more than friends, but maybe I'm wrong. Maybe I misunderstood, so I just keep my mouth shut because frankly, I'm not sure what I would do about it. We're friends, and I don't want anything to ever taint or change that.

"I thought I heard you two down here." She walks up behind me and nudges me with her hip. "So what's on our agenda tonight, Sir Thomas?"

I look over at her, and she is smiling up at me. All nervousness leaves me because just being near her makes everything right.

"Sir Thomas?" I ask with mirth in my voice.

Her smile widens, and she changes her voice to her best British accent. "Yes, you are the knight in shining armor who is rescuing me from the utter despair of a lonely Saturday night, are you not?"

I can't help myself when I lean forward and place a kiss on her cheek. "You're ridiculous—you know that, right?"

I offer her my arm as she says, "I have no idea what you mean." Since I can't resist her when she is so adorable, I just smirk.

"Well, my fair lady, we are going to a movie. Is that to your liking?" I decide to join in on the act.

She looks up at me like I'm crazy. "Why are you talking like that, you weirdo?" Then she cracks up like she just said the funniest thing ever. I shake my head at her.

"Oh, yeah, I'm the weirdo. Let's go, Chandler."

I suddenly realize Mrs. D is still in the room with us and watching our entire interaction. We make eye contact, and she shakes her head at me for at least the fourth time since I walked through the door.

"I think you're both pretty strange."

Selene glances over at her, looking as if she just remembered she was there too. "I think we're leaving. I'll be back later, on time," she says as she leans in and gives the petite older woman a kiss on the cheek.

We leave Mrs. D in the kitchen and make our way to the truck. This isn't the first Saturday night I've picked Selene up, but something definitely feels different this time.

Selene

I t's an unusually cool night as we lie along the shore beneath
the cypress trees in the dark. I can feel my heart trying to
find a place for him as my mind tells me to keep my distance. If I could just let him in, I think it's possible I could still
feel safe. I'm trying to be brave and open up to him more than I
already have.

We came out here to our spot along the river after the movie
because neither of us wanted to go home. It was like neither of
us could bear to leave the other. Drake has done everything he
can to gain my trust. While I've let him in more than any other
person before him, I've still been holding back.

There is something about tonight, though. Something is different; things feel right. He feels exactly right. Drake trusts me,
and I trust him. I feel like this comfort and trust between us will
never change. Anything I knew before this moment is a distant
memory.

"I like it here," I whisper against his chest. I can feel the
rhythm of his heart in tune with my own, and this only solidifies
my feelings of trust.

"Yeah, this has always been my favorite spot," he says softly. I hear the peacefulness in his voice.

A breath escapes my lips. "No, I mean—yes, I like it here.
It's special for me too, but I meant here...in your arms." I can
feel my cheeks flush.

It's the first real confession like this I have spoken out loud.
Sure, I admitted to being jealous once, but this is different. Suddenly, it feels like Drake has stopped breathing.

Everything is quiet except for the crickets and the running
water of the river. I wonder if I made a mistake. *Shit. Shit. Shit.*
Just as I'm about to try to cover up my intimate confession, I feel
him relax.

"Thank you," he whispers in an unsteady rush of breath. "I like you being here too." His embrace tightens a little. I love the way it feels.

I can't help myself. I let a quiet smile spread across my face and bury myself farther into his side. I have a bad habit of letting honest affection make me uncomfortable, but not this time. I'm changing. I feel a laugh welling up inside me, though I can't even explain what I find so funny at a moment like this. I just feel so happy.

"Hey, why are you laughing? I'm serious!"

He is trying his hardest to sound offended but is failing miserably. He pulls me beneath his body and stares into my eyes. My laughter instantly stops when I see the look on his face.

"Selene, I'm serious. I've been waiting for you to let me in. It's been killing me, and I know how hard it is for you to say those words."

A tear slips down my cheek. He wipes my tear away, leans down, and kisses my cheek. Between brushes of his lips against my skin, he says, "Please—please don't cry. I'm sorry if I said too much."

I begin shaking my head. "No—no, you didn't say too much. It's just I have never felt so safe, so able to just be me. I only have that with you. I should be thanking you, Drake, not the other way around."

He leans down to kiss my cheek again. I'm not sure when this became so routine between the two of us. Friends—isn't that what we are? As his lips touch my skin, I feel that familiar tingle run up my spine. I have become a natural at hiding my reaction to his touch. I mean, it hasn't changed anything between us, after all. We are just friends...the kind of friends who spend nearly every waking moment together, who hold hands and occasionally give and accept kisses on the cheek. In the beginning, I would tense every time Drake touched me or showed any sort of affection. It was something I just wasn't used to, and he usually caught me off guard, but I've gradually relaxed. I've come to expect it and, to my surprise, enjoy it. If I'm truly honest, I crave it.

The only thing that hasn't changed is our friend status, but maybe it's time for that to change too. I just don't know if I'm brave enough to admit it out loud tonight. I think he feels the same, but I still can't bring myself to release us from the hold we have on allowing our feelings to move beyond the very confusing crossroads we have reached.

I look up into his beautiful green eyes, and I know I'm in trouble, because there is no denying it—I think I love him.

Drake

We took a step in a new direction. I can feel it, and I know she can too. She doesn't seem afraid though. She seems unsure, but not afraid. I'm a bit uncertain, too. This feeling is one I've felt deep down, and for longer than I'll ever admit to myself.

I'd be lying if I said I wasn't afraid—afraid of what will happen if I allow my real feelings for Selene out, afraid of what will happen if I don't. Jared still hasn't stopped with his incessant flirting, and Selene seems oblivious to his intentions. This only makes me more nervous and more aware of my emotions.

We finish putting everything in the back of my truck, and Selene gives me one of her devious smiles as she tosses the keys at me.

"Think fast!" She giggles as I fumble with the keys and they drop to the ground. "I guess I know better than to listen to rumors." I can tell she is holding back another bout of hysteria as she pushes her tongue into the side of her cheek.

"What is that supposed to mean?" I ask, already regretting acknowledging her statement, knowing she's baiting me for something.

She pats me on the shoulder as she leans up and whispers in my ear, "That you have the best hands in the state." She tries to run off before I can catch her, but I grip her belt loop and pull her back to me.

"You think you're funny, don't ya, Chandler?"

She finds this so funny that her whole body is shaking. I'm struck by the fact that I haven't seen her laugh this hard in all the time I've known her. I pull her against me tighter, and I can't help loving the way she feels when she's this close to my body. *Fuck.* I need to get a grip on myself. I'm going scare her away again.

"You have no idea how good I really am." Pushing her forward and giving her a swat on the butt, I smirk at the squeak that escapes her lips. "Now get your rear in the truck so I can get you home before Mrs. D sends out a search party." She shoots me a dirty look, but I can see the humor in her eyes.

As we pull away, she slips her shoes off and puts her feet up on the dashboard. She looks relaxed and comfortable sitting next to me.

"Hey, can we put the windows down? The night is so beautiful. I want to let the fresh air in." Selene pulls her cardigan off.

Without answering, I roll the windows down. She reaches over and switches the radio on.

"I love this song!" she shouts above the wind blowing through the truck. I love seeing her this way—so happy. I can't help but feel like I've had some part in making this happen. I can only watch her, fighting the urge to pull the car over and beg her to give me a chance at something more.

I watch her laughing and singing Bruno Mars from the passenger side of my truck. The wind is blowing through her hair and whipping gently against her cheeks. The grin on her face

145

makes her eyes sparkle. Even though it's dark outside and I can't see the color, I know them. They are in my every thought, my every dream. I suck in a sudden breath. I'm struck by the fact that I have never felt so...*happy*. I know then that I love her. Yeah, maybe she is my friend, but she is more too. She will always be more, and I love her.

Selene

I can see him watching me out of the corner of his eye as I reach over to turn the music up. It feels so natural being with him. It always has, but tonight something is definitely different. The longer the night goes on, the more confident I am about how I'm feeling.

I want to say something. I want to—I do—I guess it's just more of a question of whether I can work up enough nerve to do it. As I belt out the song playing on the radio, I notice a slow smile spread across Drake's face. He's happy, and my heart soars as we continue down the road.

When we're pulling into my driveway, I turn the music back down. I don't want to risk waking Aunt Violette up. I pick my shoes up as the truck pulls to a stop.

Before I lose my nerve, I say, "Drake, I had a nice time tonight. Do you think we can talk a minute?" I lift my eyes to his and find him staring back at me. We sit like this for what seems like an eternity before he answers me.

"Yeah, I'll walk you to the door." He seems as nervous as I feel.

He leans over me to open the door, and I inhale his scent. His smell is just one more thing I love about him. We both get out of the truck and meet in the middle. He takes my hand and links our fingers together. I look down at them and love how they look made to fit together.

As we come to the steps of the porch, I sit down on the middle step. Drake stays standing, watching me, not letting go of my hand. Then, slowly, he takes a seat next to me. I look out over the front lawn. The night is turning to twilight, and a breeze is blowing the leaves of the trees gently back and forth. I swallow the breath I've been holding and turn toward him. I'm startled a little by the intensity of his gaze.

"Drake, I...I think I finally realized something tonight, something I probably should've known all along," I admit with a little reluctance. "I think maybe I would like to see..."

Before I know what's happening, Drake has taken my face into his palms. "Shh," he whispers as he rubs his thumbs across my cheeks, back and forth. "I want to see it too," he says quickly.

We gaze into one another's eyes, neither of us moving or breathing. I've never been so scared in my life. There are so many what-ifs. What if this doesn't work out? What if he changes his mind? What if I do?

Shit! Who cares about the what-ifs, except for this one: what if I don't take this chance? Drake seems to be struggling with the same questions and realizations. We've tried to rationalize how we feel for one another, but the problem is, there isn't anything rational about it. He deliberately begins to lean toward me and places his lips to the tip of my nose, and then to one cheek, and now the other. Pulling back, he stares into my eyes one last time. I hope he sees the answer in my eyes to the question in his.

As soon as he moves forward, I know he does. At first, his lips move softly against mine as his hands slide down my cheeks, onto my shoulders, and then around me. As soon as I'm in his complete embrace, our kiss becomes more demanding, and I'm not sure if it's him or me who changes the tempo. All I know is my body and mind feel incredible. I wrap my arms around him, wanting him closer. He will never be close enough.

This is it. This is what I've been waiting for most of my life, and I didn't even know it. Drake Thomas just changed my world, my mind, my existence.

I never want to end this kiss, want it to go on forever. The tingling I felt as my lips met hers has now spread through my entire body. This first kiss between us is taking possession of my body and soul. I can't breathe, but I don't want air if I can't feel like I do right now with my lips pressed against hers.

I know now this kiss was inevitable, these feelings unavoidable.

As I sink deeper into her, I know a girl like her is impossible to resist. I knew it the moment I saw her. Selene just became the beat of my heart.

I slowly begin to pull back, and I can feel her resist ending our kiss too. It makes me want to pull her in tighter. I hold our bodies pressed together and rest my forehead against hers, our breathing heavy.

"Wow," she whispers breathlessly.

All I can do is grin. *Yeah, wow.* She has no idea just how *wow* that kiss really was.

This kiss, this girl—it's everything I never knew could be possible. It's love. This is what a life with love feels like, and it just changed everything.

chapter 19

Selene

When I open my eyes, the sunlight is streaming through the sheer curtains. Although I know it's well after breakfast time, I remain snuggled under the blankets of my bed. I curl up on one side then stretch my legs out before rolling onto my back and looking up at the ceiling. I feel good. Actually, I feel better than good. Elation spreads across my face at the thought, because honestly it has been so long since I genuinely felt like waking up had meaning.

Of course, it's something that has gradually been building since the day I literally ran into Drake Thomas. My bliss only grows as his name floats around in my mind and my thoughts drift to last night. It wasn't a dream—Drake kissed me, and not just on the cheek. The best part is, I don't want to run anywhere but directly into his arms. I've never felt this way—ever. I've never given anyone—not even Ryan—the opportunity to get this close to me. Making myself this vulnerable is new and scary, but the thought of not letting Drake in is even more terrifying. I think the whole incident with Abby Donovan is what prompted me to honestly evaluate if I was going to allow Drake to slip by, and I realized it's a risk I'm just not willing to take. A light knock on my door draws me back into the present.

"Selene, are you awake?" Aunt Violette's small, gentle voice drifts through the doorway.

Pushing myself up into a sitting position, I rub my eyes. "Yes, come in."

Slowly, the door opens, and I watch as Aunt Violette makes her way over to me.

"Good morning," I say, unable to hold back my smile as she takes a seat on the edge of the bed.

She looks at me for a long moment before she reaches her hand out and pushes a loose hair back from my face. "This looks good on you," she states, and I'm slightly confused by it as I glance down at my plain cotton tank top then back up to her face. "The smile, Selene. The smile looks good on you. You have a face meant for smiles."

A tear slips down her cheek. It isn't often Aunt Violette allows her vulnerability to show, and I feel a knot forming in my throat. *No. No. No.* I don't want any sadness creeping into this euphoric feeling I'm experiencing right now.

"Please don't cry, Aunt Vi."

Aunt Violette shakes her head slowly. "No, this isn't sadness. These are happy tears."

Leaning forward, I place my head on her shoulder and release a sigh. It feels so good to not hold back, and it's easy to let go of any possible sorrow.

"This isn't why I came up. I really wanted to see if you planned on going to the farmer's market with me today." She pauses only briefly before adding, "But I do want to restate that the glow, which I can only assume Mr. Thomas is responsible for, is exactly what I've been hoping for you." Standing up and placing a kiss on my cheek, she rubs her hand gently over mine.

"Be down in a half an hour if you're going with me. I love you, Selene."

I let those three words settle over me. I want to tell her I love her too, but I can't seem to make them come out. "Aunt Vi, I..."

She turns back to me with a look of understanding on her face. "I know, sweets. I know." Tears fill my eyes and threaten to spill over, but she leaves me alone, and I quickly brush them away.

As I swing my legs off the side of the bed, I reach over to my nightstand for my phone. The first message I see is from Emme, and it's filled with more emojis than I thought existed. As usual, she is extremely enthusiastic about asking me if I want to join the study group tomorrow night for our history exam. I can't help but roll my eyes at her over-the-top text that could've been a simple one-liner. The next message is from Drake, and I feel my heart speed up just at the sight of his name on my phone. He sent it when he got home last night, saying he had fun. I don't feel any panic, any sadness, any hesitation—that all changed last night with one amazing kiss.

Putting the phone against my chest, I let out a soft sigh. In the past, I would have rolled my eyes at such a sappy gesture, but that was before; that was another Selene. Now I'm embracing the over-the-top emotions. Now, I just need to vocalize them. Blushing, I think about how we got the feeling part down—we just need to say the words.

Drake

I splash water on my face and stare in the mirror. I can see the worry in my eyes. I'm worried that the decision my heart made last night is going to be a mistake. I'm open to what I've been fighting for months, and there is no going back. I'll just have to find a way to protect her. Protecting her is all that matters.

I close my eyes and lean forward with my hands pressed against the mirror in front of me. I picture the way she looked up at me, those incredible green eyes, soft lips, and the complete trust she handed to me with just one look, entwining our lives unconditionally. There isn't another choice for me now. I don't think there is another choice for either of us, or at least I hope there isn't because we didn't talk much. I just know we're going to need to talk this through because we'll have some things— some*one*—stacked against us.

I try to stay quiet when I hear the door down the hall open and close. I've been lucky to avoid her as much as possible the past few weeks, although I often wonder if I'm lucky or if it's her intention to avoid me until she feels me slipping away from her control. She often used Lacey to get what she wanted from me. It was like a thrill for her to feel she had power over me, and she knew I would do anything to take her attention off Lacey.

Walking out of the bathroom, I tiptoe toward my door. I wonder if I should wait in my room or slip out while I know where she is. Deciding to take the chance of leaving unnoticed, I grab my jacket and wallet. I take one last peek out into the hall-way before closing my door gently behind me and making my way to the stairs. Just as my foot hits the last step, I stop dead in my tracks at the sound of her ice-cold voice.

"Drake Thomas, I hope you didn't think you were going to

sneak out and avoid me again." A chill runs up my spine. Her words may not be threatening in nature, but I know the threat lies beneath.

Taking three deep breaths in, I finally answer her. "Uh, I didn't realize you were home."

I try to remain calm. I'm not sure if I fear a repeat of what happened a few weeks ago or if I know she's guessed Selene is something more than what I've been trying to let on.

"Don't try to pull that innocence with me. I know better," she states calmly, although her voice is dripping with venom.

I remain with my back to her, not moving. After a moment, I hear her footsteps making their way toward me. I stiffen my shoulders, bracing myself for what's to come. To my surprise, that moment never arrives. She brushes past me and makes one last statement just as I'm about to release a breath.

"Oh, and Drake? I know exactly what you're doing. I know there's something going on with that girl, and it will only be a matter of time before I know for sure." With that, she opens the front door and disappears.

It takes me a minute before I slowly lower myself to sit on the stairway. I feel a fear I've been trying to avoid since I met Selene. Maybe telling her the truth about exactly what I feel for her isn't a good idea after all.

Selene

As I wander through the farmer's market, I swing the bag of fruits and vegetables Aunt Vi and I have picked out so far. I watch people smiling and chatting with their neighbors, and I realize my dad did me a favor by leaving me with Aunt Vi. He knew it, even if I didn't understand at the time how he could do it. I look over at Aunt Violette, the fall sunlight shining on her face, and for the first time, I notice her eyes are the same shade of green as mine and Mama's.

Suddenly, Aunt Violette's hand tightens on my arm, and I can feel her pull me closer. The happy expression is gone from her face, replaced with one I've never seen before. She stops walking, pulling me to a stop with her.

In a voice I don't recognize, she says, "Hello, Claire. You're looking well."

I glance back to find Drake's mother standing before us, a leer stretched across her face. She is looking directly at me as she replies, "Hello, Violette. Won't you introduce me to this niece of yours I've heard so much about? It seems my son is a bit smitten with her."

The idea that she has heard about me makes me nervous. I can tell she is used to being intimidating and looked upon with envy for her beauty and wealth, but I only see a cruel and hateful woman. I can hardly hide the disgust and hatred I feel for her from my expression. She is still watching me, and I notice a curiosity in her eyes that sends a chill up my spine.

"Selene, this is Claire Thomas. Claire, this is my niece, Selene Chandler."

As my name leaves Aunt Vi's lips, I notice Mrs. Thomas stiffen, and a new kind of malice replaces the hostility that already lies beneath. I wonder what that is about. She quickly recovers and once again eyeballs me as she reaches her hand out for me to take. I hesitate a moment, not wanting to touch the hand I know has caused Drake so much harm. However, since I don't wish to cause a scene, I reluctantly shake her hand.

"It's nice to finally meet you, Selene. Drake has told me so much about you." A hint of coldness still lingers in her tone. I try to keep my face neutral because I know Drake has done no such thing.

"Really? That's strange. I hardly know him at all," I reply, adding a slight chill to my sugary sweet southern accent. Two can play at this game. I will not let her intimidate me.

We stare at one another, and I can't read what she is thinking at this moment. A slight panic fills me as I wonder if I've made things worse for Drake. I can feel Aunt Vi's confused expression staring at me before she recovers and turns back to Mrs. Thomas. I have an urge to be overly friendly, but Aunt Violette interrupts before I can react.

"We really should be going," she says in a voice that is still unrecognizable to me. "It was very nice seeing you, Claire." Aunt Vi begins to pull me away.

I quickly add, "Yes, nice meeting you, Mrs. Thomas."

Even with our backs to her, I hear her response. "Yes, it's been very intriguing."

I'm not sure what that means, and even though I tried to not let her intimidate me, I feel a little fear. I have so many questions. Claire Thomas definitely had a strange reaction to me, one I'm positive is about more than just me knowing her son. I'll ask Aunt Violette as soon as we get home. I need to see Drake, too.

As for seeing Claire Thomas again, I would like to hope it doesn't happen, but I know that's more than I can hope for because there was an alarming threat behind her words.

chapter 20

Drake

W hen I pull up to the light-yellow Victorian, the first thing I notice is someone sitting on the porch I don't recognize. The second thing I notice is Mrs. D's car is gone, and a truck sits in its place.

As I pull into my usual spot, I can see the person on the porch more clearly. It's a guy about my age with dark hair. I wonder who it could be and why he is just sitting on the porch like he has a right to be here. I turn off the ignition and step down from the cab. As I round the side of the truck, I notice the dark-haired guy is standing up and watching me approach. I go on the offensive immediately because, for some reason, I just don't like him, even though I have no idea who he is.

"Hey there. Can I help you?" I ask, putting an authoritative air to my voice.

He runs a hand through his hair, and another uneasy sensation runs through me. Even I can admit he is handsome, which doesn't give me a good feeling.

"Uh, well, maybe. I'm looking for Selene Chandler. This is her aunt's house, right?" The knot I hadn't realized was forming in my stomach tightens. Who is this guy, and why is he looking for Selene? I feel compelled to shout that she's mine.

"Who's asking?" I say instead as I stop at the bottom of the steps with my hands on my hips. He is standing on the top of the steps above me, but I can easily see he is few inches shorter.

He takes a step down off the porch. "Look, man. If I have the wrong house, I'm sorry. I'll go now, but could you possibly point me in the right direction?"

He is almost directly in front of me now, and as ridiculous as I know I'm being about this, I can't help feeling territorial. *Fuck!* Selene and I just—well, I don't know what we just, but that's why I'm here. I want to know why this guy is here. I glare at him. He is looking at me with confusion, and I realize I need to let this go. I have nothing to worry about. Although I have no idea who he is or what he wants from her, I relax a little.

"You have the right house," I say warily as I walk past him and up the steps.

Once I'm on the porch, I turn and find him staring at me. I can't actually read his expression, but can tell he is no longer feeling apologetic for trespassing. He walks back up onto the porch.

"So if I have the right house, who are you?" he asks when he is directly in front of me again.

I hesitate, giving him another onceover. Slowly, I extend my hand toward him.

"Drake Thomas," I state plainly as he looks down at my hand then back up to my face. I lower my hand and move to one of the rockers on the porch, making myself at home. The guy didn't want to shake my hand; I don't give a fuck. As I rock back and forth, a sneer spreads across my face. "Looks like we'll be waiting for Selene and Mrs. D together." Throwing daggers at me with his eyes, the guy leans against the side one of the pillars.

I'm not sure how long we remain silent before I notice the ruby red convertible coming up the road and see Selene's hair blowing in the wind. I glance over at the nameless asshole, and he is still leaning against the pillar with his eyes closed. I gradually stand up and make my way down the steps. As I reach the bottom of the steps, Selene gets out of the car, smiling one of her beautiful smiles I've always felt were reserved just for me. She comes toward me and throws her arms around my shoulders, so I lift her slightly in an embrace.

"Hey, Chandler! Did ya miss me?" I ask teasingly.

I can hear the playfulness in her voice when she says, "Maybe a little, Mr. Thomas, but don't get cocky." She releases a light, airy sound, and it warms me to my core. The asshole is forgotten until I feel her body go rigid in my arms.

From behind me, I hear him on the porch. "Hello, Selene."

I want to tighten my hold on her at the possessive way her name leaves his lips, but before I have a chance, she is pushing at me to put her down. When I let her go, I turn but keep her hand in mine. The look on her face is one I never want to see again. It's the same look she had the first day I saw her, one of hurt and sadness. I watch them as they stare at one another. I take a step forward, wanting to fucking pummel this guy for hurting her. He hurt Selene, but how? Did she love him? He obviously loves her, and this only makes things worse. I wanted to be the first guy to fall in love with her.

As I move, her hand tightens on mine. "Drake, no," she whispers. I look back at her, and I can see the plea in her eyes. Her eyes leave mine, returning to him. "Hello, Ryan," she says, and it's as if those two words wedge their way between us.

Selene

When his name leaves my lips, I want to shout at him, but everything comes out in a whisper. Drake looks ready to kill him. They were here alone. Why is Ryan here? As I watch the boy I've known my whole life, I realize he never really knew me at all. Maybe it's my fault, but maybe he never actually tried to see anyone but who he wanted me to be. The happiness I felt when I saw Drake standing at the top of the steps has vanished, and I'm reminded of another time—a time when I didn't trust, a time when no one saw me...a time when I had my mother.

Ryan starts walking toward me, and I can't move. I'm not even sure why I'm not moving or saying something to him...something like *go home*. I just can't form the words. When he is standing directly in front of me, I feel a sudden tug on my hand. It startles me, and I pull away and step closer to Ryan. When I glance behind me, Drake is standing there with hurt in his eyes. His hand is still suspended in midair toward me. *Shit!* I was so lost in thought, I forgot he was there, holding my hand. I just stare at him, unable to form any words. This entire moment has sent me spiraling on an uncomfortable trajectory. I feel so out of control.

Breaking my thoughts, I hear Ryan say my name again. "Selene?" I look over at him. "Are you all right?"

I glance at the face that is supposed to be familiar and comforting, but there's nothing. He puts his hand on my shoulder, and I immediately look over at Drake. He has a grim look on his face, and I can see the slight quiver of his lip. He's angry. I brush Ryan's hand away from my shoulder and face him.

"Selene, I'm going to take these things in the house," Aunt Violette says from somewhere behind me. "If you need me, I'll be in the kitchen." She walks past me, leaving me alone, stuck between my present and my past. One of Aunt Vi's greatest qualities is keeping her nose in her own business. I can only nod before turning my attention back to the boy in front of me.

"What are you doing here, Ryan?" I ask in a harsh tone. Before he can answer, I continue, "I mean, you walked away months ago and never looked back."

He shakes his head. "No—no, I looked back, but you were gone. You're the one who never looked back." He tries to step closer and raises a hand, letting it linger in the air close to my cheek. I can see he wants to touch me, and I freeze. Ryan glances over at Drake. "Are we really going to do this with him here?"

Again, I peek out of the corner of my eye at Drake. He's watching me, and I can see he wants me to say something. I just can't find the right words to make him understand.

Shaking his head, Drake turns and walks away. I step toward him, and I'm almost positive I see a tear slip down his cheek. I start to say his name, but no words come out. He doesn't turn around, and I don't stop him. This isn't the way I imagined this day going. I planned on telling Drake how I felt, how I trust him. I was going to tell him I'm his no matter what anyone says or does to come between us. Looking back at Ryan, I know this is the first test. I'm always being tested, and when I take one last look at Drake as his truck disappears down the road, I know this is one I can't and won't fail.

With tears in my eyes, I face Ryan. "I'm going to ask you again: why are you here?"

I watch the expression change on his face. He isn't used to me using this tone of voice with him. I'm mad at him—angry about the way he feels about me, the way he tried to make me feel guilty for not feeling the same, and the way he walked away and let this come between our friendship.

Ryan closes his eyes and sighs. "I came because I miss you. I had to see you and see if you were all right. I came because my feelings haven't changed."

I take a step back. Shaking my head, I turn and walk to the porch, taking a seat on the steps. Ryan doesn't move at first, just watches me. I know he's waiting for me to say something, wants to hear me say something has changed. My heart speeds up. Something has changed, but it isn't what he wants to hear.

"Some days, I missed you too, especially in the beginning. You've been my best friend since we were five years old, but you left me when I needed you most." I look up at him. He is now kneeling in front of me, his hand touching mine. "You asked the impossible. I love you, but not like that, and you knew it. You were selfish. She left me, but it wasn't her choice. I needed time. You were supposed to be there, but you left me. You were the only two people I had in my life, and you chose to walk away." I wipe the tears from my cheeks. It feels good to let that out. I feel like a weight has been lifted.

"Selene, I was wrong. I—I'm sorry, but I just couldn't deal with you slipping away." He stands up again and starts pacing. "I needed you to open your eyes and realize you had me."

I swiftly stand up. "Are you kidding me? Have you always been so selfish, and I didn't see it?" I want to scream. "You made your choice and...and you need to leave! I need to go find Drake."

Ryan takes hold of my arm as I whip around and head toward the house. "You can't be serious! You're going to walk away from me to find him? You barely know him, and you've known me practically your whole life!"

I can feel the desperation in his grip. I look at him, feeling only a dull sadness for the boy I once knew. "I know him, and he knows me. I'm sorry if this hurts you. You'll always be special to me, but things are different now. You made that choice." I hug him while he just stands there with his arms at his side.

Turning back to the house, I run up the steps, never looking back. This time I'm the one who walks away, but it doesn't hurt so much. This time I don't feel like I lost everything; I feel like I finally found myself.

Drake

66"There's someone else," I whisper to her.

Leaning my head back, I try to grasp what just happened. I thought my life was changing, but I should've known something good could never come to someone so bad. Deplorable—that is exactly what my mother has called me over and over for years. Destructive was what I strived to be on a daily basis for most of my life, bad until the only good I knew died. After that, something in me changed, and I couldn't pretend any longer. The problem with not being bad anymore is it's already too late. I did too much to ever come back from. That's why Lacey was taken from me and why Selene can never be mine, no matter how much I want her.

"I don't deserve her anyway."

"Drake?" I hear my name, and although I know it's impossible, for a moment I hope it's Lacey. I lift my head instantly, looking around for her smiling face. Lacey's face is not the one I see though; it's Selene. Her eyes are puffy and red from crying. I'm on my feet so fast, walking toward her before I even realize what I'm doing.

"Did he hurt you? I will kill him if he hurt you." I reach her, pulling her against my chest. She pulls back and looks up at me, shaking her head.

"No, Ryan is..." she says with tears in her eyes. I pull her back to me, holding tight like she might disappear if I don't keep her close.

"Selene, I don't care who he is. I just wouldn't forgive myself if something happened to you." God, she feels so good against me. She isn't mine though; she belongs to someone else.

"Drake, Ryan would never hurt me. We've been friends since we were five years old. Plus, he says he loves me." I burn with jealousy at those words. She continues, "He ruined that though. Ryan couldn't accept the fact that I didn't return his feelings, and then he turned his back on me when I needed a friend most."

I'm not sure I heard her right. "He was only your friend... you don't love Ryan?" I'm not even sure I mean to say it out loud. Her words flood me with relief.

She pushes away from me and turns her back. "Drake, I'm sorry I didn't stop you from leaving, or if I gave you the wrong impression about me and Ryan. I just needed to speak with him—alone." She faces me, and I can see the lingering hurt in her eyes.

"Selene, don't—"

"No, I need you to understand. I need you to know you mean more to me than that. You deserve more than how I treated you. You've given me so much since I came here, and I trust you completely. I've never trusted anyone the way I trust you, except for my mama."

At first I'm not sure I heard her right. She trusts me. I mean something to her. It's like she knew every doubt I'd been feeling. If I didn't know better, I would swear I can hear Lacey laughing like she did when she was right about something.

Before another doubt can enter my mind, I reach out for Selene and grab her hand. "You have nothing to apologize for, and I need you to know I trust you more than anyone too." I place my hands on the sides of her face and wipe the one tear that escaped with my thumb. "I need you to know—"

Before I can say another word, her mouth is covering mine. Kissing her is something I may never get used to.

chapter 21

Selene

It looks and feels like any other Monday morning in the crowded hallways of Montgomery High. Football is over and, therefore, my cheerleading days have ended.

I make my way toward my locker as usual, my eyes darting in every direction, eager to make contact with the dark green eyes I've grown so accustomed to seeing each morning. My heart speeds up a little. From the very first day of school, this has been my routine. There is only one thing different about this day: Drake and I have moved past the simple pecks on the cheek and handholding, completely away from the friend zone I so comfortably enjoyed for months. We're now in the one place I safely tucked my heart, previously utterly incapable of opening it up to the possibilities of more.

I should've known I didn't stand a chance the moment I found myself flat on my butt looking up into his unreasonably handsome face. I gave it a good fight, but in the end, my heart knew better. I have to trust him. He's been the only person capable of keeping me on solid ground. I felt the connection that first day, and it has only grown stronger.

Suddenly, there is a strange sensation running up and down my arms—I can feel him even before I see him. I'm not sure how, but Drake has brought out a side of life that defies all reason. All the walls I put up around myself have slowly begun to crumble, and there isn't anything I can do about it. The moment my eyes meet his, I know it's about more than what I can see on the outside. It's undeniably about the vulnerability and understanding I see when I truly look at him. He gets me, and if I'm honest, that is what scares me most.

A smile spreads across his face as he pushes his way toward me. When we're only inches apart, he takes my hand, pulls me into him, and brushes his lips across my forehead. "Good morning." He breathes against my skin.

Typically, this kind of affection would make me uncomfortable and send my defenses into high alert, but today everything is different. Drake quickly turns and leads me through the crowd to my locker. As soon as we squeeze past the last group of students, I notice Emme leaning against the wall with an all-knowing expression. It's like she's been waiting for this moment.

Pushing away from the wall, Emme turns in the direction of our class. "'Bout time. See you in class." She says all of this over her shoulder as she walks away from us. I stare at her in disbelief until I can't hold back my amusement anymore. I don't even know how I became friends with her.

Shaking my head, I look over at Drake and realize he's been watching me. Suddenly, I feel the heat in my cheeks, and there is no doubt they are a deep shade of crimson. I'm sure I'll never get used to him looking at me as if I'm the only other person on earth.

Without thinking, I quickly lean in and give him a light peck on the cheek. "See you in class," I whisper as I pull back and dash away from him before he can even react. As I look back over my shoulder, I notice he is still watching me, his lips turned up in one corner.

Drake

I feel free. No…that isn't the right word. I feel *lighter*. The weight that has been pressing down on me has finally lifted, and it's all because of her. Her name plays through my thoughts as I round the corner, and my eyes land directly on her sweet face. It's as if she senses me, because her gaze rises from the conversation she's having with Emme and lands directly on mine, a look of contentment on her face. I'm positive it's a reflection of my own, and I feel elated.

Before I even know what is happening, I trip over something and lose my balance, flying forward and landing flat on my face. "Have a nice trip, Drake?" Jared's voice echoes through the now silent hallway. The silence means two things. One, the entire student body is staring at me. Two, they're all waiting to see how I'll react.

I look up and see Selene making her way over to me, and she comes to a sliding stop when she notices my facial expression. I slowly rise to my feet and turn to face that piece of shit.

"What's your fucking problem, Jared?" I move toward him, but before I can act, I feel a light touch on my shoulder.

"He isn't worth it, Drake. Just let it go. Please." I stop. Closing my eyes, I take a deep breath, allowing her gentle touch to settle the nervous energy running through my body. I've wanted to beat the shit out of Jared from the moment Lacey came home and told me he was her boyfriend, but I never have.

"I should beat your ass, you coward. I should do it for all

the shit you pulled with Lacey over the years. Dammit!" He continues to smirk at me.

"He isn't worth it. Please," she whispers behind me as her
hand moves down my arm and into mine.

She gives it a light tug, causing me to open my eyes and
turn. Feeling the anger still moving beneath my skin, I keep my
eyes averted from hers. I'll never look at her in anger. The crowd
around us instantly dissipates and there are several moans of disappointment because the fight didn't happen. Fights in the halls
of Montgomery High were a phenomenon in this small, quiet
town.

I keep my eyes focused straight ahead, although I can feel
her gaze trained on my face. "Are you mad at me for stopping
you?" she quietly asks.

I stop suddenly, all anger I felt toward Jared draining instantly at the uncertainty I hear in her voice. Turning toward her,
I place my hands on either side of her face. The skin is so soft
under my calloused hands.

"God, no, Selene. I just fucking hate that guy. This feud between us is something that has been going on since long before
you ever came into the picture. I'm mad at him, not you. I don't
think I could ever be angry with you." Slowly, I place my lips
against hers.

Usually, I would worry about her reaction to me showing
this kind of affection in front of people, but I just can't bring myself to care right now.

Selene

For once, I don't resist Drake's affections or pull away at
his insistence on public displays of affection. It feels natural, nice. I close my eyes, savoring the way his lips feel

against mine. It's like I'm flying. Just when he begins to pull back, my feet touch the ground again, firmly in place.

The buzzing of voices surrounds us, and still we are the only ones who matter. "Thank you," he says as he places one last peck against my forehead. Taking my hand again, he pulls me along with him to where Emme and Tommy are talking near my locker.

"Dude! Why the fuck didn't you punch that worthless piece of shit?" Tommy asks once we reach them. I can feel his eyes on me with a knowing look, as if I ruined all his fun.

Drake shakes his head. "Just let it go, Tommy. Punching Jared isn't worth getting suspended, especially because I'd be stuck at home all day with my mother."

My body automatically reacts at the thought of what would have happened if I hadn't stopped him. Tommy makes some typical teenager response about being stuck at home all day with a parent. I don't think he has any idea Drake's situation is anything but normal. Looking over at Drake, I can see his thoughts are the same as mine.

"Let's get to class and get this day over with," Emme chimes in, tugging at Tommy's arm.

I look over at Drake, shrug my shoulders, and pull him in the same direction our friends went. He closes his eyes and follows willingly, but I don't miss the demons that creep into the depths of his gaze. If he wants to hide his fears, I'm definitely not the person to judge or force them to the surface.

I quietly walk through the back door, into the kitchen. She's home, and I'm hoping to avoid running into her before I make it up to my bedroom. This is my life.

Tiptoeing my way through the hall, toward the stairway, I can hear movement in the study. I practically hold my breath as my foot touches the first step.

I'm only on the third step when I hear someone behind me. I know it's her. "Why didn't you tell me your little friend is a Chandler?" Her voice sounds cold and hard when Selene's last name leaves her lips. I don't even need to turn around to know the facial expression that is undoubtedly placed on her face.

Slowly, I pivot to face her. "What do you mean by that?" I ask her, trying to hide the tremble in my hands. Something feels off, wrong. Why would it matter what Selene's last name is?

"I know the name, and that's all you need to know—that and the fact that you will no longer remain friends with that girl." The venom in her tone almost has me cowering back from her. It's like she slapped her hand across my cheek. Before I can respond, she continues, "I'm surprised Violette has let…never mind, just keep away from that girl. If you don't, I can promise you it will be your biggest regret." With that, she turns on her heel and returns to the study.

My mind is racing with thoughts, trying to make sense of what just happened. I'm not surprised by her need to control who I'm friends with since it's something she has always done; I'm more confused by her apparent disdain for Selene in particular. What did she mean she knows the name? And why did she mention Mrs. Durham?

I lower myself onto the steps, my head falling into my hands. One step forward, three steps back. Just when I think everything is clear between Selene and me, another obstacle is put in front of us. This isn't just my mother being controlling; it's more, deeper, and I need to figure out what it is before everything is ruined.

Selene

The bell rang nearly twenty minutes ago, signaling the end of the day, yet Drake still hasn't made it to our usual meeting spot. I'm worried—this isn't like him. When I think about it, he has been acting strangely since I spoke to him Monday night on the phone. Everything had been wonderful that day—minus the almost fight with Jared—but Tuesday morning, I sensed something was different. He was holding back a little, and as the week has gone on, it's only gotten worse.

I've played the week over and over in my head, trying to figure out what could have caused him to act this way. I even asked him if something happened between him and his mother, but he denied anything was wrong.

I look around, wondering if I should wait, but then I see him. He is walking slowly toward me with his head down. I feel the urge to run to him and wrap my arms around his waist, giving him the comfort he appears to desperately need. I push those thoughts back as he looks up, his gaze locking with mine. Unable to turn away from the intense way he's staring at me, I begin to walk toward him.

Once we're standing face to face, Drake reaches for my hand, pulling me against him. We stare at one another for a moment; I can see he is hurting and worried. "Dra—"

Before I can finish, his lips crash against mine. I can feel every bit of sadness pour from him in that kiss, and I gladly accept it. I want to take away all of his heartache, every disappointment, every worry. He wraps his arms tighter around me and moves his lips to my cheek, my neck, and then back to my mouth. It feels as if we've been here for an eternity, and I still don't want it to end.

He holds me hard against his chest, his face pressed into my hair. "I'm sorry. I'm so sorry."

I don't understand—why is he apologizing to me? I try to push against him so I can see his face, but he just holds tighter.

"Don't. Just listen," he whispers. "My mother questioned me about you, wanting to know why I didn't tell her your last name is Chandler. I asked her why, and she said I didn't need to know, but she made it clear she wanted me to stay away from you. I've spent this entire week trying to figure out why and how I can protect us from whatever issue she has, but I haven't been able to figure anything out. I know I've been acting—"

I push against him. There is no way I'm letting him do this to himself. "No, Drake. Stop," I say as his embrace loosens. "Stop doing this. I don't care about your mother. We're fine. There isn't anything she can say or do that will change this. Do you believe that?"

He looks at me for a long time. "Yes. Okay. I just don't want you to get hurt." He hugs me again then says, "I'm just afraid of what she meant. You didn't hear her voice. It was as if she knows something that will change everything."

Even as a chill runs up my spine, I say, "Nothing will change what I feel for you."

I look over at Selene as I drive her home and see a smile play across her lips as she sings a Miley Cyrus song playing on the radio. Looking at her makes it easier to ignore the unsettled feeling in my stomach. It still lingers, but I push it down. She is so fucking cute I don't even make fun of her for singing Hannah Montana at the top of her lungs.

"I know everyone says how crazy and gross she is acting now, but I love this song," she says, her gaze never leaving the passing landscape. I grin, watching her out of the corner of my eye. Suddenly, she bursts into the chorus again. "I came in like a wrecking ball…" Then she dissolves into a fit of giggles. "Love it!" She beams as she looks over at me. When she sings, the happiness I see is how I always want her. I smile back, but a nagging feeling is punching me right in the gut.

As we pull into her driveway, I notice Mrs. D on the porch. She is rocking back and forth, lifting her hand in a wave. We roll to a stop, and Selene leans across to kiss my cheek. Looking up at me, she puts a mask on her face to hide her real emotions. It dawns on me that she's feeling my anxiety and trying to help me focus on something other than what my mother might be up to.

"Wanna come in?" I know I shouldn't draw any attention to the fact that I continue to spend time with Selene, but when I look into her eyes, I can't resist her request. I can see she needs this. She needs reassurance that I won't let my mother keep us apart. I can get out right now, but I'm not sure I can guarantee she won't come between us in the future. It's the one thing that actually frightens me about my mother—she always wins.

"Sure, for a bit," I say, noticing the light in her eyes brighten.

As we get out, Mrs. D stands up, making her way toward us.

"Hello, you two. How was school? Are you hungry?"

Selene reaches the top of the steps and places a kiss on her aunt's cheek. "School was school," she answers, and then she turns to me as I step up onto the porch next to her. "Are you hungry?"

"Have you ever known me to turn down food?" I ask as I nudge her in the shoulder. She laughs, and the sound pushes more of the worry out of me. She has a way of making me forget anyone else exists. Grabbing my hand, Selene pulls me toward the screen door.

"There are some cranberry scones I made this morning on top of the fridge," Mrs. Durham calls after us. I hear her shuffling about on the porch. I think about the fact that my mother said something about Mrs. Durham. I wonder if she knows what my mom's issue is with Selene.

When we head to the kitchen, I take a seat on one of the barstools at the counter while Selene pulls the scones down. As usual, I'm overwhelmed by the comfort I get simply by being in this house. I think Lacey must have felt it too, and it's why she loved coming here. This house embodies everything mine lacks.

The beep of the microwave pulls me from my thoughts, and the smell of the warm scone makes my mouth water. My stomach releases a little rumble. Selene looks up from spreading butter over the top crust of the scone.

"I heard that," she says.

Walking over to me, she places the pastry in front of me. As hungry as I am, my hunger for her is stronger. I reach across the bar for her hand and guide her around until she is standing in front of me. I reach up behind her neck and pull her mouth to mine. When our lips meet, the scone, my mother, and her threats are forgotten. It's only the two of us, and an undeniable feeling that all is right with the world when we're together envelops me.

This is all that should matter, and that's why I need to discover whatever threatens to ruin it and destroy it.

Selene

D rake doesn't think I know he is still worried. As his lips touch mine and he deepens the kiss, I can't help wanting to put everything I feel for him into it, even though I can't quite come to terms with exactly what that is. I mean, I know I have never felt these feelings before, and I can't even begin to imagine giving my trust to any other person. I'm unsure if I'm ready to think beyond where I am at this point. I do know without a doubt I need to hold on tight and not let him worry about whatever his mother's issues are with me or let that come between us. We need one another, and there isn't anything that can change the way I feel about him or my need to have him in my life.

"Okay, okay!" I chuckle, trying to push away from him, even though I love the way his lips feel on mine. "The scones are much better warm, and I'm hungry!" I playfully slap his hand away as he tries to pull me back. He gives me that Drake Thomas smile, the one that stole my heart the moment I saw him. "Drake, stop it right now!" He puts his hands in the air and begins to back away.

"All right, whatever you say," he says, still giving me a look that tells me if I don't move back to the other side of the bar, his hands and lips will soon be on me again.

Shaking my head, I pour us each a glass of milk. How did this impossibly handsome guy end up kissing me like I'm the only girl in the world? The thought of us being together is one I will probably never get used to. It defies all logic in my mind.

I take a seat across from him and we eat our scones together quietly, only exchanging lingering looks. He seems more re-laxed, but I still feel this strange sensation, like something could change at any moment. I can't let that happen. I've come too far from the girl I was when I arrived here nearly six months ago, and I never want to be her again.

I look at him, and I can tell his mind has drifted off to a place that isn't good. A crinkle has formed between his eye-brows, and he is staring down at the crumbs left on his plate.

I reach my hand across the bar and lay it over his. "Drake." I wait for him to look at me, and when he doesn't, I say his name again. "Drake." This time his gaze rises to meet mine. I can tell he's trying to hide the worry that lies beneath the green hue of his eyes. "Drake, I need you to promise me something." He just stares at me then nods. "I need you to promise me you will never let anything or anyone come between us. I need you to fight for us, to protect us, because no one has ever done that before." I don't know why I'm saying this. Maybe it's the look in his eyes. Maybe it's the fact that the anxiety I see surrounding him seems so high, and the people I care about are always taken from me. "Can you promise me that?"

He stands up and moves to the other side of the counter. Placing his hands on my shoulders, he lifts me up until we're standing face to face and he is looking down into my eyes.

"I promise to protect you and whatever this is between us. I may not know exactly what it all means yet, but I can tell you that you're the most important person in my life. Do you under-stand? I will never let anyone hurt you, Selene, and my mother —"

I place my fingertip over his lips and shake my head. "Shh, you've said enough. I don't know what this is either, but it's im-portant to me. I don't care about your mother and her schemes or cruelty. I just care about this—about us."

As he pulls me against him, I can feel his breath coming quickly against my ear. "This is all I care about too. I gotta go."

Letting me go, he takes a step back and turns away quickly. I barely catch a glimpse of his face, but I would swear he looks scared. I want to reach out to him, but I realize that isn't what he wants or needs. "See you tomorrow," is all he says as he leaves the room.

I listen to the rush of his boots across the wood floors, the slamming of the screen door, and his polite goodbye to Aunt Vi. I lower myself back onto the stool and begin rubbing my finger-tips in small circles over my chest, trying to extinguish the flutter of anxiety I feel there. I'm not sure why I feel so nervous. We'll be okay. Why can't I just let things be and enjoy them while they're good? I need to put this feeling aside because Drake promised things would be okay, and if there is one thing I'm confident about, it's the fact that he would never break a prom-ise.

chapter 23

Drake

I'm scared. I'm so afraid I just lied to the one person I feel I can be honest with. It wasn't intentional. In fact, I believe with every fiber of my body I'll fight for us, but I'm not so sure I can keep anything from trying to come between us, and I'm definitely not sure I can win a fight with my mother.

As usual, I hold my breath when I enter the house, hoping I can make it to my room, my sanctuary. For some reason, she never actually comes in there. I've never questioned why because I've always been too afraid it might change. I make it to the top of the stairs then she comes out of her bedroom at the end of the hall. Her gaze is so cold it freezes me midstride, and I know this isn't good. A sick feeling settles in the pit of my stomach as she stalks toward me. The muscles in her shoulders are so tight, she reminds me of a captain in the army who's about to dole out a punishment to his subordinate.

Before I can move, she reaches me, and her hand swings

back. "You little idiot!" Her hand connects with my cheek so hard a vibration of pain runs through my jaw into every bone, sending me into the wall. "I promised you would regret this, and you will."

She begins pacing in front of me. I can't do anything but stare at her, unable to understand what this all means.

She continues, "For some reason, you and your father can't seem to control yourselves around those Durham women. I thought I was finally rid of that family and then this…this girl shows up and falls all over you."

I'm trying to follow the direction of her words, but she is rambling, and I can't exactly connect her thoughts. She's saying something about Selene's family…she said Durham though… and something about my father. The nervous feeling in my stomach I've had for a week just intensified. I remain silent, because maybe she will continue talking and I'll learn more. It may be the only way I can find out what she has against Selene.

She stops in front of me again as a look of contempt spreads across her face. "Do you know what is so funny about this whole situation? You both are such fools, giving your hearts to two women you've inadvertently hurt so badly they can never forgive you. You ruined your chances with that girl before you even met her—a simple mistake because you're a selfish fool. She'll never forgive you when she finds out." She practically spits in my face.

My heart stops at her words, my mind racing, grabbing at any memory of what I may have done that Selene cannot forgive me for, something I did before I knew her.

"I guess that will be punishment enough. She's not worth it anyway, especially being Elizabeth Durham Chandler's daughter."

She steps around me. My eyes don't even follow her. I don't move until I hear the front door close, and then I slide down the wall to the floor.

I pull my knees up and rest my head on my folded arms. I can't lose her. I promised I would fight for her, and the only way to do that is to know exactly what I'm up against. I'll never get a straight answer from my mother. Maybe my dad, perhaps Mrs. D—and maybe I'll need both. Either way, I need to find out before Selene does.

Selene

S omething is wrong…off. Drake hasn't answered his phone for over three hours. Maybe it's nothing. I'm not sure what it is, but the uneasy feeling is strong. Sitting out on the porch in the cool night air, legs folded under me, I shiver from the breeze coming in from the north. Winter is in full effect, but the cold weather has rarely made an appearance. As usual, the Texas weather cannot make up its mind, and multiple seasons in a week are not unheard of.

Staring out over the back lawn, my mind wanders to the first day we met. I remember watching him cross the lawn, effortlessly carrying old boxes for Aunt Vi to put in the shed.

Even from my window, I could see his eyes held something special, something that was going to change me. God, how I wanted to avoid this feeling. It felt wrong then because I had never experienced this kind of feeling before that day, and I wonder now if I will be strong enough to handle the way I feel today.

The tapping of my fingers on the wooden arm of the chair grows more rapid as I begin to open up to those feelings. The way my heart races when he is near. The way I fall asleep thinking of him. The fact that he is still on my mind when I open my eyes. He consumes my every thought. Just imagining being away from him hurts. *Oh, shit. Shitty shit shit!* My fingers freeze mid-tap.

Abruptly, I stand up and cover my heart with my hand as if it will protect me from what I'm only just now realizing, something I'm sure my heart knew long before my mind ever did. *I...I...oh, shit. I need to go.* I rush into the house to grab my coat and the keys to the car. As I rush back out the door, I yell out to Aunt Vi, "I'm running out for a bit. I won't be back late."

I'm out the front door before she even answers and get in the car to head to the one place I can think clearly, the one place I can trust my feelings are safe until I can figure out just exactly what to do about them. Maybe Drake not picking up his phone is for the best.

"You were in love with Selene's mom?" I repeat the words in my head, even though they just left my mouth. "I thought you and Mom got married when you were eighteen." It's a statement more than a question since I already know the answer.

He stares out the window of his office, a distant look in his eyes. "Elizabeth Durham was my world from the moment I laid eyes on her." He pauses, but I can tell he isn't finished, so I remain quiet. I'm not sure what I would say anyway. "We met at the Fourth of July parade the summer I turned sixteen. She had just moved here to live with her Aunt Violette, and I knew it was meant to be. We were inseparable."

I sit down in one of the armchairs in front of his desk, laying my head on the back of the chair with my eyes closed. I'm not sure what to say or feel, so I continue to wait for the rest of his story. Maybe then I'll know what this means for Selene and me.

"I'm sorry, Drake. I failed you as a parent—not just you, but Lacey too." He turns to face me, and I see tears in his eyes. "I ruined all of our lives." He stops long enough to clear his throat, now clogged with tears. I can only stare at the man who typically seems so in control and unemotional. "It's my fault your mother is the way she is…" This is the first time he has ever acknowledged my mom is anything but the perfect mother she always portrays herself to be in the public eye. In fact, when I really think about it, it is the first time he has ever actually acknowledged my mother.

He continues, "You see, Elizabeth left to visit NYU in New York City over winter break of our senior year. I didn't want her to go, so we argued, and she told me it wouldn't change anything between us, but I told her it changed everything. I told her not to go, and she left anyway. There was a party while she was gone, and…I was angry and drunk. I slept with your mother. I betrayed Elizabeth. I betrayed myself."

Shaking his head, he lowers himself into his chair behind his desk. I sit staring at him, struck by the fact that I've never thought of my dad as anything other than my father and the mayor of Montgomery. It's weird picturing him as an average teenage boy in love.

"When she came back, we told one another how foolish we were for arguing. She said she realized she could never leave me. I was expected to go to UT in Austin. Anyway, we were more stable than ever, or so we thought. Your mother kept quiet about our tryst, and I tried everything I could to forget, but a month or so later, your mother told me she was pregnant. Once our parents found out, they forced us together. My father said I had to break things off with Elizabeth. I broke her heart, Drake. I broke mine in the process, but I broke her heart so badly she had Violette take her out of school. I tried to make her understand, but how could I when I couldn't understand myself?"

The more he says, the more sadness I feel. I have a whole new perspective on my parents' lives. My father stands up and walks around the desk, kneeling in front of me.

"I know I seem cold and distant. I've never been the loving father you deserve. I know I haven't protected you, and I never protected your sister. I'm so sorry. I not only ruined Elizabeth, but your mother lost all of her dreams. She knows if I had a choice... Drake, I've never regretted you or your sister. So, you see now, right? Your mom has tried to make me happy, but it's me. Every time I saw Elizabeth as the years went by, my feelings... She died that night and..." I look up at him, and I now feel numb. He isn't scary or strong. He is weak.

Abruptly, I stand, and he leans back as I look down at him. "No! Don't you dare try to make me feel sorry for Mom! Don't ever attempt to make the things she has done to me and Lacey over the years not her fault. She made choices too. People's lives don't always go the way they want, but that gives them no right to hurt others." I swallow the knot in my throat. "As for you, I can't even look at you anymore. You were supposed to be our father. You stood by and watched us die a little more inside each day. You were allowing her to drag us down with you both!" My whole body is trembling. "I...I gotta get out of here."

Reaching the door, I throw it open, leaving Mayor Gregory Thomas sitting stunned on the floor of his office. I can understand the way he felt for Selene's mother and his heartache. I even know why my mom said my father and I were alike when it came to the Durham women. That isn't what scares me. The thing that scares me is her being right about the last part, about me having done something so irrevocable, Selene will never forgive me—but what could it be?

chapter 24

Selene

If I'm honest, I was hoping he would be here. Instead, I'm sitting all alone against his sister's headstone, talking to myself. There is something about sitting here though, a sort of peace I typically only have when I'm with Drake. Her presence surrounds me, encircling me in a blanket of understanding that seems to be nudging me to open up.

I close my eyes, taking a deep breath. "I'm not sure why I'm really here or what I was expecting." My mouth curves at the corners, and a small laugh escapes. I've spoken to my mama many times, but for some reason, for one tiny second, I feel silly. "Sorry, I've never felt this before, and I most definitely have never admitted to this kind of feeling. It's just…I trust him, I do, but I needed to come here first." I stop talking, letting the silence settle over me. "Maybe I came to tell you first because it's easier for me to say to someone who is not really here than it is to say it to someone who can reject me. Plus, you were the closest person to him, so I feel almost as if I'm saying what I want to say to Drake."

Shaking my head, I release a frustrated sigh. Why can't I just say what I feel? I'm tired of being afraid…afraid to live, afraid to be happy. I want those things, and I finally see that I deserve those things, thanks to Drake. Picturing the way his face lights up the moment our eyes meet makes my heart skip a beat. How can I deny this any longer?

"I love him, you know. I do." As soon as the words leave my mouth, I feel relief but also a sudden worry. I've admitted it to myself before, but it almost seems like now that I've said it out loud, it makes me more defenseless against Drake's mom. It makes me more at risk of being hurt, the one thing I've always been afraid of the most.

The relief I feel at finally realizing what my feelings are for him has disappeared. I understand that I asked him to fight for us and never let anything come between us—what if I can't return that promise? The only thing that will help push these feelings aside is if I talk to him. I need to find Drake and speak to him. Looking down at my phone, I find two things. One, it's really late, and two, Drake still hasn't called me back.

Picking up my phone, I only just realize I left it sitting on my dresser. When I got home the night before from my dad's office, I immediately crawled into bed. Selene called half a dozen times, and my heart tugs at the thought of her looking for me. I hope she isn't worried. She left one message, so I play it back. The sound of her voice is happy yet timid as it echoes back to me through the phone. God, I hope she'll be as happy once this mess is over.

Without thinking, I dial the one person who can help me finish piecing this all together and put this behind us—hopefully. "Good morning, Mrs. D. Oh, Selene isn't home?" Even though I didn't call to talk to her, I wonder where she could be. Maybe this is the perfect opportunity to talk to her aunt without her around. "Actually, I called to speak to you." She gives me her usual playful remark. "Will you be home? Because I'd like to do this in person."

Her voice turns a little more serious, and I can tell she knows this is more than a casual request. "I would really like to talk to you face to face if that's okay. Great, I'll see you in a few minutes." We hang up, and I hurry down the stairs. Once I get this over with, I can find Selene.

Selene

My early morning run did very little for my nerves. I slept last night, my mind racing with thoughts of Drake. Also, I had a hard time pushing away these negative feelings that seem to keep creeping into my thoughts. It's typical Selene, but I won't let my insecurities ruin this for me.

For once, I've decided to take control and follow my heart. Sitting in front of Drake's house, I debate if it's a mistake to show up here this early. Actually, I wonder if it's a mistake to come here at all. Nope, not happening—I will not allow myself to sabotage this relationship.

Stepping out into the cold, I race across the street and up the walkway. The weather continues to change, and I can smell the rain in the air. Another storm is coming, and with it being cold, that won't be pleasant to get caught in.

Standing in front of the door, I count to three. Then I count to three again, trying to work up the nerve to knock. What if he doesn't answer the door? What if he's still asleep? So many questions and what-ifs, but I'm determined to do it. I've waited long enough, and the feeling of racing against time to tell him how I really feel seems to be weighing on me.

I lift my hand and knock hard three times. I knock so hard my hand is the same scarlet color as the door. After a few minutes, it opens swiftly. To my disappointment, Drake isn't the one to answer the door, although I see a resemblance. His father is an older version of Drake—the same color eyes as the ones I love so much, the same hair, just slightly graying at the temples, which only makes him more attractive. I realize neither of us has said anything yet. We're both staring at one another, lost in our own thoughts. I begin to fidget under the intensity of his stare.

Finally, I clear my throat. "Uh, hello, Mr. Thomas. Is Drake available?" I hold my hand out. "I'm Selene Chandler."

I see something spark in his eyes, but it's gone before I can figure out what it is.

My hand is still hanging between us when he finally speaks. "Ah, yes." He takes my hand in his for a moment then releases it. "Drake isn't home. I'm not sure where he went so early, but he left about fifteen minutes ago." His voice is surprisingly kind. He is still gazing at me with an expression I can't quite pinpoint. "I can tell him you stopped by."

I realize I've been staring at him too. "Oh, uh…yes, please. I'll try calling him too." He just continues to stare. Pushing a strand of loose hair behind my ear, I give him my brightest smile. "So, I guess I'll be going. It was…uh…very nice meeting you, sir." I turn, leaving him standing in the doorway, and head back down the walkway.

I barely hear him when he says, "You look exactly like she did at your age." The statement, so ordinary and innocent, stops me midstride. "It was nice meeting you too, Selene."

I quickly turn before he can shut the door. "Who?" I ask loudly. "I look just like who?" I say again.

When I look at him, there are tears in his eyes. "Your mother, of course," he says matter-of-factly before closing the door.

"You knew my mama..." I finally say as more of a statement than a question, and to no one in particular since I'm completely alone.

I watch the door for another few minutes before walking back to the car in a confused daze. Drake's dad knew my mother. I don't know what this means, but that uneasy feeling has returned to the pit of my stomach.

Drake

We stand facing one another in the kitchen, anguish and sorrow written across Mrs. Durham's face. "Yes, Elizabeth was in love with your father. They were inseparable for more than two years. Everything your father told you is true."

I swallow hard and turn away from her pitying eyes. Then I feel a hand on my shoulder. "Drake, that shouldn't change anything between you and Selene," she says gently, but I can hear the *but* lingering in her voice.

"There's something more, isn't there?" I say, almost so quietly I'm not even sure I said it out loud.

Her hand leaves my shoulder, and she steps around the counter. When I face her again, she's pouring a cup of hot tea, the steam rising and the scent of lemon filling the air. I remain silent, just watching her, because I can tell she is gathering her thoughts.

"You know that day you showed up on my doorstep, I

wasn't sure I could look at you. I may be tough, but I'm a south-ern lady, and we're always polite." I can see her mind drift to that day for a moment before she continues, "Then I looked into those eyes, and I could see something familiar." She blows into her cup and takes a tiny sip.

My eyes begin to tear. "Lacey?" I croak.

Giving her head a slight shake, she sets her cup down again. "No, loss and pain, maybe even guilt. I saw everything I've felt since the day they were taken away from me, so I knew I could look at you—if I couldn't, how did I look into a mirror each morning? I knew you were sent to me so we could help one an-other heal."

There is so much I want to say to her, but I can't seem to form the words. I can't make complete sense of what she's say-ing.

"Everything appeared to be working out nicely until Mike brought Selene and practically left her on my doorstep. Then you two met, and I thought to tell you then, but I couldn't. I knew from the moment you knocked her on her butt and she began that girlish stuttering, you were going to save one another." A tear slips down her cheek. "I knew I would need to tell you both at some point, especially after we ran into your mother at the mar-ket. She had that look in her eye, especially when she realized who Selene was. I just wanted to be sure you both could see this all has nothing to do with you. I wanted you to know this love and friendship between you is worth fighting for. I especially wanted to be sure Selene knew because, although you both have a tendency to hide that side of you, she tends to hold back more."

She looks up at me, and I'm more confused. I was right. This is more than just the fact that our parents were in love.

"Drake, the other car...the other driver in that accident with Lacey...it was Elizabeth. It was Selene's mother."

I feel like I've just been punched in the stomach and the breath has been knocked out of me. I take a staggering step backward and hit the wall. Mrs. Durham steps around the bar and moves toward me, a gentle, understanding look on her face.

Shaking my head, my voice trembles. "No—I—Lacey had been drinking…I left her alone, and I was mean to her. I was trying to protect her from being hurt by Jared…by our mother. I left her. She never drinks, but she did that night." A sob escapes me, but I continue. I've never said any of this out loud. "I hurt her anyway. Then she got in the car and came after me. She knew I had been heading to a party out on Mill Road. She just wanted to be with me, and I left her. I wanted to protect her, but I didn't. I allowed her to feel unloved and alone. She got in that car to look for me, and she died! She died, and she killed Selene's mother, too, and the worst part is, it's all my fault!" I shout through the sobs leaving my body.

Through my screaming and crying confession, I never heard the front door open or her footsteps in the hall. I only hear her gasp from behind me. Mrs. D's eyes go wide, and she reaches her hand toward Selene, saying her name. I turn and find Selene staring at me, her tears and heartbreak reflecting my own. I can't move; I only watch her. Mrs. Durham freezes too as Selene shakes her head. I hear my mother's words echoing in my head. *They can never forgive you.* This is the one thing that is unforgivable.

chapter 25

Selene

I stumble to the car and get in without thinking. I don't even want to think about what I just heard, but it's on repeat in my mind. I'm trying not to think about what this all means. There are two people I've felt I can't live without. One is dead, and the other... *Oh God, this can't be happening.*

I fumble with the keys in my hands before sticking them in the ignition and throwing the car into drive. As I speed out of the driveway, I see Drake run out the front door and jump off the porch. Aunt Vi is close behind him and calling my name. They are both shouting for me to stop, Drake's voice begging for a chance to explain. I keep going.

I can barely see through all the tears, and I'm gripping the steering wheel hard, as if it's the only thing holding me together.

The convertible top is down, and it's starting to pour down rain, but I don't care. I can't stop. If I stop, I'll have to face what I heard. The tormented look I saw on Drake's face makes me want to turn around, but what would I say? He would want to

191

explain, but what could he say that would change any of this? What could he say that would bring her back? Nothing. He can't tell me or do anything to change what happened. He can't change the fact that he is indirectly responsible for her being taken from me.

The windshield wipers are barely helping now, and I'm soaking wet. My hair is sticking to my face, and my clothes are clinging to my body. I know it must be cold, but I'm so numb it doesn't even matter to me. All I care about is getting away. I know I'm going too fast, especially since it's raining so hard. I may know it, but it doesn't change anything. If I slow down, I'll start to feel again, and that can't happen.

Suddenly, my phone rings, and without thinking, I look at it lying next to me in the seat. I see Drake's name light up on the screen. I put the phone up to my ear as I steer the car with one hand. "Leave me alone, Drake!"

"Selene, please, Selene—please stop the car!" I can hear the panic in his voice. "Please, you're driving too fast, and the rain—I need to explain, I—please just stop the car."

I begin shaking. Hearing his voice makes me feel like I might crumble into a million pieces.

"How—"

Before I can finish, the car hydroplanes. Without warning, I'm sliding back and forth across the two-lane highway. As I scream, the phone flies out of my hand. I can't stop it.

I can hear the muffled sound of Drake yelling my name into the phone, which is now somewhere on the floorboard.

All at once, I come to a stop, my head slamming against the steering wheel. The last thing I remember is thinking, *How can I forgive you?*

Then everything goes black.

Drake

I can barely see three feet in front of me, and Selene's tail-lights are the only indication I'm heading in the right direction. I'm scared because she is driving too fast. I beg her to slow down. I beg her to let me explain. My voice is trembling, and the knot of utter despair I've felt since I turned around and saw her standing in the doorway is only tightening. Suddenly, I realize she isn't going to forgive me—she isn't hearing me.

"How—" This is the last word she says before I hear her frantic screams and see the faint lights in front of me make volatile movements across the road.

She's losing control. "Selene!" I shout into the phone, knowing my words are futile in helping her. "Selene!" My foot pushes the gas a little harder as I grasp the fact that she is no longer on the road in front of me.

The rain only seems to be coming down harder when I notice her car slammed into a tree on the side of the road. *I did it again.*

Pushing against the brakes, I come to a sliding stop on the shoulder. I don't even turn off the car as I swing the door open and jump out. As I dash around the front of the truck, I put my hand up to block out the blinding headlights and the rain. I slip and fall to the ground, practically bouncing off the asphalt and immediately back on my feet again. I need to get to her.

"Selene!" I call out to her, although I know she isn't going to call back to me. The dread of the situation is coursing its way through every part of my body. My limbs feel heavy, like I'm running in place. I feel like I will never reach Selene. Seconds seem like minutes before I finally reach the passenger side of the car.

The car spun around until it was facing completely away

from the street. The driver side is pushed against the tree, and I can see blood coming from the side of her head. I stand frozen, looking at this girl who holds my heart in her palm. I can see her slipping away before my eyes. Suddenly, I snap out of the shock and jump over the side of the car and into the front seat.

"Selene...oh, God, baby." My throat is clogged with worry and tears as I speak to her.

I gently run my hand along the side of her face, moving the hair away. I bring my fingers to her neck and feel for a pulse, a rush of emotion hitting me as I feel the beat of her heart playing against my fingertips—a chance. *Thank you.*

Leaning forward, I place a kiss on her cheek. "Please hold on. I can't live without you. I can't live with you hating me... stay with me," I whisper in her ear. "God, don't let her leave me too."

Pulling out my phone, I dial 9-1-1. I stay on the phone with the operator, holding on to Selene's small, delicate hand until I hear the sound of the sirens. Overcome with relief because help is here, I kiss her again. "They're here, baby. Everything is going to be okay."

I keep my fingers on her pulse to remind me that every beat of her heart is a sign that this time will be different. I can't help touching my lips to her cold cheek. "You're going to be fine," I whisper, wondering if our love has the same chance.

chapter 26

Gregory Thomas

Ten months earlier

L ights are flashing all around us. Claire is her usual emo-
tionless self. We were called and told Lacey was in an
accident and…nothing. No emotions at all. Claire just
looked at me and said, "I'll get my purse." There were no tears. I
don't even know who she is.

As for me, I've gotten good at hiding my emotions. I know
I'm not a good man. I'm selfish. I ignore my children. I ignore
their pain. I've allowed Claire to hurt our family, and that makes
me just as guilty.

I look down at Lacey's lifeless form. I feel a crack splinter
across my heart. *My beautiful baby girl.* Leaning down, I place a
kiss on her already cold cheek. *My God, why can't I cry?* Have I
actually lost all my humanity?

As they cover her face, my thoughts drift to Drake. This
will destroy him. I have no right to shed a tear, but thinking of

him makes me feel like crying all the tears I've held back over the years.

"Mayor?" I hear Terry Gilbert say from next to me. I slowly turn to face him, a dazed look on my face. He clears his throat, and I stare at him. I have no words. We have known one another our whole lives. "Greg...uh, the other car...the driver didn't make it."

I had almost forgotten they said another car was in the collision. I wonder who it could be. Will I have to look into the eyes of a grieving mother? I wonder what that would look like as I notice Claire standing a few feet away from us, her expression still cold and bored.

"Greg...did you hear me?" My eyes gradually focus on his face. "I think you need to come confirm the identity, but I should warn—"

Before he can finish his sentence, the EMTs wheel up the stretcher with the other driver on it, the face already covered. They come to a stop in front of me and pull back the sheet. I hear Claire gasp behind from behind me.

My body begins to shake, and I reach my trembling hand out toward her face. Even with the cuts, blood, and bruises, she stills looks as beautiful as the first day I saw her.

I brush back the hair sticking to her face. *Oh, God.* Can I bear this? My daughter...the woman I've always loved. I want to scream at the cruel joke God has played on me.

Without caring who's around me, watching, I place my lips against hers for only a moment. It isn't long enough.

Turning to Terry, I say her name. "Elizabeth Durham." The splinter Lacey's death caused to my heart has just cracked open completely. I feel exposed, and I feel lost in my thoughts until Claire comes to stand next to me.

Coldly, she says, "You mean Elizabeth Chandler. Right, dear?"

Terry's eyes lock with mine. Pity clouds them. "Yes, Elizabeth Chandler," I whisper.

He nods. "One more thing, Lacey had been drinking." I can see the regret in his eyes.

I begin to say something, but Claire beats me to it.

Without looking at me, she firmly states, "You better make this go away. We can't have our name dragged through the mud. It was an accident, and no one will believe Lacey was drinking. You make this go away." She walks away and gets back into the car without so much as a last glance at our daughter.

Terry and I stare at one another for a long time.

He speaks first. "There's no sense in dragging that poor girl's name through this small town's mud. It's not going to hurt anyone, but you need to speak to—"

I know what he's going to say so I beat him to it. "I'll speak to Violette. She didn't just love..." I have a hard time saying her name. "She didn't just love Elizabeth. Violette loved Lacey, too." *And so did I.*

Violette

I'm not usually up this late, but Elizabeth left later than planned. She usually came to check on me once a month. Selene often came with her, but this time she came alone. When I asked why, Elizabeth only said Selene had school obligations and she wanted to talk alone.

From the moment that girl came to live with me, she became my world. I've only wanted happiness for her. While I think she found it with Mike, I know a part of her has always been with someone else. If it weren't for Selene, I'm not sure what her life would be.

We spent the day talking. Elizabeth confessed her worries for Selene and for herself, and I comforted her just as I always have through her life. I'm not sure if I helped her work through anything, but she left appearing less weary than she had when arrived.

Exhausted, I decide to head upstairs to bed. When my foot hits the bottom step of the staircase, I hear the quiet sound of an engine outside pulling to a stop in the driveway. I wonder who it could be at this time of night.

As I open the front door, I'm startled by the figure standing before me, only the screen door separating us.

"Violette." His voice sounds hollow when he says my name.

I haven't seen him on my front porch in a long time. The years have been good to him. He still looks like the boy Elizabeth loved so much, but there is one difference. Even in the dim porch light, I can see a troubled, sad soul in his eyes. The same eyes visit me nearly daily, but in the form of a sweet young girl.

"Gregory Thomas. It's been ages," I say to him, only because I am confused as to why he's standing on my doorstep after so long. "Would you like to come in?"

He shakes his head. "Uh, can...could we possibly talk for a moment out here?"

Still confused, but curious, I nod my head. Pushing the screen door open, I walk to join him in one of the rockers that line my porch.

Clearing his throat, he sighs and runs his hand through his hair and over his face.

"Gregory—"

"I always loved sitting out here on this porch." He chokes on the last word, and I know something is terribly wrong.

Lacey. Although it has never been formally acknowledged, everyone knows she spends a lot of time over here with me. Surely he isn't here because of Elizabeth—they've kept their distance for nearly eighteen years.

"Gregory, why are you here? If it's to tell me Claire will no longer tolerate Lacey's visits, after all these years, I will fight you on it." I swallow the uneasiness I'm feeling. "I love that girl, and no thanks to either of you, she is so good."

He looks over at me, tears in his eyes. One finally breaks free.

"Violette, there was an accident. Lacey…Lacey…is…"

My brittle hands cover my mouth, trying to contain the immediate heartbreak I feel inside.

Oh, no. Sweet Lacey. He's still looking at me, heartache in his eyes. I reach my hand over to cover his, to show him some comfort. He takes my hand in his and holds tight, almost too tight.

"I'm so sorry for your loss. The pain of losing someone you love is unspeakable." His grasp tightens a little more, but I ignore the pain; the ache in his eyes and in my heart are more prominent.

"Violette, you don't understand. It wasn't just Lacey." He almost sounds like he's begging me for something I just can't understand.

I'm almost afraid to ask, but I need to know what's going on. "What do you mean? Gregory, why are you here? If this isn't just about Lacey, what is it?"

Shaking his head, he whispers, "Eli…Elizabeth. Elizabeth was in…"

"No." He doesn't even need to finish. I see it now. He has lost someone he loves—two people he loves—but so have I. "Oh, dear God, no."

We sit quietly, holding one another's hands for a while before either of us speaks again. Our broken hearts try to make sense of what all of this means. What can all of it mean?

"Violette, there's more, and I need you to hear me out. I'm not even sure how I'm going to say this…ask this." He isn't making a lot of sense, but this whole situation doesn't make sense.

"What is it, Greg?" I ask sorrowfully.

"I'm not sure why or how, but Lacey had been drinking. She lost control and hit Elizabeth head on. They both died on impact." He chokes on his words.

I can only stare at him. *Lacey, drinking?*

"Are you sure?" I ask. "Lacey wouldn't…"

When he looks at me, I can see he thought the same thing. I feel so tired and old right now. My mind and body ache all over.

I look out over the front lawn, the moonlight shining down through the trees. Somberly, I ask, "What is it you wanted to ask me, Gregory?"

I can feel his gaze burning into my cheek. "I don't want to have this ruin Lacey's reputation…her name. Terry said we could keep names out of this, could keep the alcohol out of this, and I'm wondering if you would be willing to go along with this story."

He sounds sick asking me. I feel sick hearing it, but what justice would it actually serve Elizabeth for any of this to come out? I wonder if he is worried about Lacey's name or his own. I want to ask him how he could ask such a thing of me. At this moment, without time to process what has happened, I want to be upset with him.

Then I look back at Greg and into his eyes. He returns my gaze, and I recognize that he is just as broken over this as I am.

"Yes," I say, and I can see the shock in his eyes. "Yes, because I loved Lacey, and I know the girl she is…was…yes, because Elizabeth would want me to say yes." I see something come alive in his eyes, a question. "Were you aware Elizabeth knew Lacey? They met many years ago, here at my home. Lacey would play with Selene when Selene and Elizabeth visited me. She was very fond of Lacey." I watch his face as the words leave my mouth. First I see shock, and then I see a sort of bittersweet acknowledgment. "I often wondered how Elizabeth could be so kind to the one reminder of what led to a great unhappiness.

Then one day I asked her."

I pause and wait for him to catch up to what I am saying.

"Elizabeth told me she could never look upon Lacey with anything but kindness because she was a part of you. So, yes...yes, because I know it's what Elizabeth would do." I squeeze his hand in mine. "We will keep this secret, because keeping it won't hurt anyone, and telling it will hurt people we love."

He just nods then sits with me while we both quietly shed tears for two people we loved.

chapter 27

Drake

Present day

I watch the bluish green line of her heartbeat move across the monitor, the sound of the beep the only thing keeping me sane. How did this happen? It's been six days—six days since everything changed, since I watched her heart break, since mine broke right along with it—and now I sit next to her bed, waiting for her to wake up, waiting to see if our hearts can be mended.

My heart clenches tight as I think about how when she opens her eyes, I'll only see hatred. My eyes roam over her battered face, the cuts and greenish purple bruises that have begun to fade. She is so beautiful, everything about her. Why didn't I make sure she knew how I feel about her? About how she made me feel about myself? I'll always regret being too afraid to tell her. I should've learned my lesson when I lost Lacey. I always hold back, too scared to let those who mean something to me know for fear it will only hurt them in the long run, but I was wrong then with Lacey, and again now with Selene.

I watch her face, so peaceful and quiet. Some of the nurses say she can hear me, although she isn't awake. I'm unsure if I believe it's true or not, but I know I can't hold back any longer. I lean forward, pressing my lips to hers and allowing them to linger there, savoring the moment because I may never have the chance to do it again. When I pull away, I whisper the three words I should have told her long before this day, the words I should've voiced when she was awake and looking back into my eyes. I should've said them when she could say something back, even if it were to only tell me to never speak to her again. Instead, I now whisper, "I love you, Selene. Please wake up."

When I pull completely back, I continue to stare down at her. I guess I'm pathetic for hoping that one simple declaration would miraculously wake her up like some fairytale. I smooth my hand gently over her hair. I wonder if she will want me here when she wakes up. Will she even remember what happened? Will she remember me? There are so many questions, and I'm not sure what is worse—not knowing the answers or the fact that I probably won't like the answers.

The door creaks open behind me. Without looking, I know it's one of the two people: Emme or Mrs. Durham. We've all been taking turns sitting by her side. Mrs. Durham has been so kind and understanding. She feels just as responsible as I do for Selene almost losing her life; I'm not sure which of us feels more guilty. In fact, I wouldn't blame Selene for one second if she wakes up and tells me to never come near her again.

A soft hand settles over my forearm. "She isn't going to forgive me, is she?" I hear the words come out of my mouth, and immediately I feel the crack in my heart splinter a little more. I pick up Selene's favorite lip balm and rub it over her dry lips. "I know I don't deserve it, but I can't help but hope." I feel the tears threatening to spill over my lids.

"Drake." I realize now it's Emme. "I don't know what Selene will want when she wakes up. I don't know most things—I can barely pass calculus—but I know that girl is crazy about you. I know this accident wasn't your fault, Drake, the same way Lacey's accident wasn't—"

"Don't even go there, Emme!" I shout, facing her tiny frame and knocking her hand away, unable to control my emotions.

She keeps her body straight and doesn't back away. "No, Drake! *You* don't go there. This is ridiculous. Lacey made a choice, her own choice, and so did Selene." She pauses but then keeps going. Just talking about this makes me sick to my stomach. "Selene chose to drive too fast in the rain instead of listening to you. She wouldn't want you to beat yourself up over this."

I turn back to Selene as the tears I've been holding in begin to flow. "She blames me. I could see it in her eyes when I realized she was listening to me and Mrs. D, Emme. I may not have been driving the car that night, but Lacey was. I wasn't there to help Lacey. I wasn't there to stop her drinking or to make her realize Jared and I weren't worth risking her life over. She ended up driving that car, which not only killed her, but Selene's mom too. It's my fault Lacey was in that car searching for me, and it's my fault Selene's entire world came crashing down around her."

I practically fall into the chair beside the bed, taking her warm, motionless hand in mine. "She told me to fight for us no matter what tried to come between us, but I'm pretty sure she didn't realize exactly what we would be fighting against." Standing up, I lean down again and cover her lips once more. I linger there, moving from one cheek to the other. Once again, I speak in a low voice. "Please know I never wanted to hurt you. I'm yours forever. I love you, Selene. You deserve this life, so it's time to wake up."

I kiss her one more time, straighten, and walk past Emme to the door. As I turn the knob, I pause and take a deep breath. "If she asks for me, I'll come, but not before. Thanks, Emme. Please tell Mrs. Durham to quit blaming herself. See you around."

I've barely made it through the door when I hear Emme say, "She'll ask for you." I'm not even sure she meant for me to hear her.

I look over my shoulder. "Thanks. I won't come back in, but I can't leave either. I'll just wait out here until she wakes up. She doesn't need to see me first thing, but I can't leave her." Emme just nods, and I watch as she takes a seat next to Selene.

chapter 28

Selene

My eyes are closed, but I can feel a hand wrapped around mine. *Drake.* He is my first thought, just like any other morning. His vibrant green eyes, that charismatic smile that always looks as if it holds a secret, and the gentle way he always holds my hand. *Drake, I love...*

I feel a squeeze on my hand. "Selene, open your eyes. He isn't here, but I can get him."

I hear the words and realize it isn't Drake but Aunt Vi. I must have called for Drake out loud—how embarrassing.

"Selene, open your eyes!" Her voice sounds a little more panicked. I can't understand why. Am I going to be late for school?

Slowly, I begin to open my eyes, but it's hard for some reason. It almost feels as if my eyes have been glued closed. My whole body feels a little achy; maybe I've been sick. I try to think really hard. I don't remember being sick. Suddenly, I open my eyes and see white all around me. Aunt Vi is standing over

206

me, her face etched with worry.

"Selene, praise God. Drake isn't here, but I can get him. They'll be so happy you woke up. Emme and Drake are in the hall."

Just then, I hear the door open, and I look over. Emme walks in and immediately bursts into tears, covering her mouth as if she might scream.

Aunt Vi...white room...Emme...crying—I suddenly realize I'm in the hospital and the memories begin rushing back. My unspoken confession. What I heard Aunt Vi and Drake discussing. Drake seeing me, the look in his eyes. Running to the car and him chasing me. The rain. The begging. The tree. My mama. Lacey. Drake. *Oh God.* I wrap my hands around my head, trying to keep the memories out.

I feel a sob erupting from me as all the pain and anguish I had forgotten fills me. I can hear Aunt Vi and Emme panicking around me, Aunt Vi calling for the doctor, trying to decide how to help me. I continue to squeeze my eyes shut and hold my head to block the memories out, but it isn't working. I can still feel it, all the pain, my heart breaking. I want to go back to sleep. I don't want this pain. I want someone to take the pain away, but no one can.

I hear Aunt Vi talking loudly, asking the doctor to help me as his hands cover mine, trying to pry them away from my head.

"Selene, tell me where it hurts. Is it a sharp pain? This isn't uncommon with a head injury." His voice is deep and soothing, but I can't be soothed—don't they understand that? Pushing his hands away, I look up at them with wide eyes, the burn of un- shed tears behind them.

"No! You can't help! I—I hurt everywhere!" I can see the confusion written all over his face. He doesn't understand.

I look over at Aunt Vi, pleading with her to understand what I'm saying because I can't say it out loud—I'll break completely if I do.

With an unsteady voice, she asks, "Do you want me to get Dra—"

I put my hands over my ears. "No! Don't say his name! I can't. I can't see him! I can't think about him! I can't love him!" Looking up at her, I say with an eerie calm, "I don't ever want to talk about him again."

Turning over and curling into myself as tight as I can, I stare at the heartbeat scrolling on the monitor. I watch it and am surprised it hasn't flatlined, because I can't feel my heart anymore. I'm pretty sure it stopped beating the moment I remembered I can't love him anymore.

We both stand the moment we hear Mrs. D saying Selene's name and talking to her. I rush to the window of the room and watch as she pleads with Selene's stirring form.

"She's waking up," I say to Emme, who's now standing beside me. We can't actually hear everything Mrs. D is saying, and now we hear Selene's quiet voice. I think I hear my name, and a small gleam of hope lights inside me. I put my hand against the glass.

I feel Emme move beside me and realize she's headed toward the door. She looks back over at me. "Aren't you coming?"

She has an exultant look on her face and tears glistening in her eyes. I can't form the words, so I just shake my head. She starts to say something but just nods her head and goes into the room.

I watch everything that is going on, and then suddenly, Selene covers her head and begins crying out like she is in unbearable pain. On instinct, I start to move toward the door to protect her, but then I notice the doctor rushing into the room and know I would only be in the way. So, I watch from the window. Every howling sound she releases, I feel a piercing my soul.

I can't take it any longer and rush the door. Just as I open it, I hear her say my name. She's shouting at Mrs. Durham and the doctor, saying she can't see me, can't think about me. I swallow hard. She can't love me. I'm nearly brought to my knees. I feel them buckle, and I put my hand on the wall to steady myself. She never wants to talk about me again.

I've lost her. I've really and truly lost her. She won't ask for me. She doesn't want me to fight for her. The tiny bit of hope I had left has been extinguished. I slowly make my way down the cold, empty hallway of the hospital, feeling colder and colder the farther away I get from the brightest, warmest part of my life. I'm not sure how I'll make it through this loss, but I guess I'll just have to try.

Selene

Silence. It's been three days since I woke up in this nightmare, a place so full of lost dreams, broken hearts, and utter despair, all things I don't want to face. I keep my eyes closed in hopes they will all leave me alone. If I could escape it by sleeping, I would, but even in my sleep, I dream of them...all of them. I dream of Mama and her sweet face. I dream of a girl I only knew briefly, a girl who changed my life forever, and most of all, I dream of a boy, a boy with a devilish grin and a gentle touch, a boy who holds my heart.

"Selene." I hear Aunt Vi say my name, but just as I've done every morning, I keep my eyes closed. "Selene, I know you're awake." She pauses, and I hear her sigh deeply. "Selene, you need to open your eyes. You get to go home today. The doctor will be in soon to check you over and sign the release papers."

Maybe if I keep my eyes closed, he'll let me stay. As shitty as I feel here, the memories are easier to deal with in this cold white room. This space doesn't come with old memories I've yet to think about. I don't have to get in a car and drive a familiar road reminding me of things I want to forget. Forgetting is the only way I'll survive—if I can actually survive.

Reluctantly, I open my eyes and watch as Aunt Vi pulls the blinds closed over the glass. She turns, faces me, and our eyes meet. I resist the urge to close them again as the need to shut everyone out pulses through me. "Aren't you excited about leaving this room today? You get to go outside." She pauses and watches me. I can see she is waiting to see if I'll respond. I don't. "Winter is definitely here, so I brought you warm clothes. I'll leave them here at the end of the bed, unless you need me—"

"No!" She looks startled and a little hurt by my reaction. I feel bad for hurting her. "I mean, no thank you. I can do it myself."

She nods and walks to the door. Before she leaves, Aunt Vi pauses in the doorway. "She wouldn't want this for you, Selene."

Confused, I can't help but ask. "Who? What do you mean?"

She still doesn't face me. "Your mama. She wouldn't want you to close yourself off and throw away an opportunity for love." Without waiting for a response, she leaves me alone.

I lie back again and cover my head with the pillow.

Closing my eyes, I just want the darkness to swallow me. I can't think of what Mama would want, because it doesn't matter now. She is gone, and as for love, I don't really believe it exists. Maybe the thought of real love exists, but falling in love only hurts. I know, because I'm hurting, so I just want to stay in this darkness. I don't want to get up. I don't want to open my eyes until I can let them go...until I can let him go.

chapter 29

Drake

aking myself move through the days since I left the
hospital has been nearly impossible. I've gone to
school, but I haven't really been present. Emme and
Tommy have tried to pull me back into life, failing each time.
Now they look at me as if I might break at any moment. The
thing is, they don't realize I'm already broken.

It scares me, this feeling of hopelessness taking the place of
every thought I've ever had. I'm spiraling—again, except this
time I don't know if I'll ever be able to pull myself out. The
things that normally scare me or make me think twice have no
effect on me now. Put simply, I don't care anymore. Crossing
my mother's path doesn't even faze me as it once did. Nothing
fazes me. I'm a shell of who I once was.

Barely able to lift my head, I look toward Tommy, who's
calling my name. I raise my eyes to meet his, and he winces
when he gets a good look at my face. He can't even hide his re-

action.

"Dude, what the fuck?"

I just keep walking until I reach the locker room door and enter. He finally talked me into meeting him up at the school to work out a little. I don't really want to be here, but I knew I couldn't keep avoiding him.

"It doesn't matter." He watches me as if waiting for more of an explanation, but I don't give him one.

After a moment, he follows me into the building. I breathe a sigh of relief, knowing I don't have to lie. I just don't think I have it in me.

I'm wrong though. He isn't going to let this go. "Uh, man... I thought this shit stopped." His comment catches me by surprise. Looking up at him, I see he is looking straight at me. His facial expression changes once he catches the look I'm giving him. "It just seems...umm, well I thought maybe things mellowed after Lacey."

He knows. Tommy knows, and apparently he has known for a while. The most self-centered, unobservant person I know actually noticed something other than what was right in front of him.

"Sorry I brought it up like that, but fuck—you didn't cover it up this time, so I thought maybe you wanted to talk about it." Shaking his head, Tommy takes a seat next to me.

Not knowing what to say, I remain quiet, staring at a speck of red paint on the gray lockers in front of me. We sit in silence until it almost becomes suffocating.

"I don't think I realized what Selene meant to you until the last few weeks." Just hearing her name makes me feel like I'm breaking to pieces. Turning toward me on the bench, Tommy watches me. "You changed after Lacey, but you opened up when Selene moved here."

I still can't seem to focus on anything other than that red paint. I hear him. I know he wants me to say something.

Suddenly, he stands up and hits the locker. "Fuck, Drake! Say something! Anything! Do you know what it's like to watch your best friend hang on by a thread? I know I'm an asshole, but I see things. Just because I don't know what to say or do about these things doesn't mean I don't see them." Seeing this side of Tommy catches me off guard.

"I'm sorry," I say without the emotion I'm actually feeling on the inside. "I don't know what to do anymore. I have been in survival mode my whole life, Tommy." Standing, I begin pacing, feeling alive for the first time in weeks. "And I'm not sure I have anything to survive for any longer. My parents hate me. Lacey is gone. Selene blames me for—"

He puts his hand up to stop me, and his voice is loud with anger. "Bullshit! Snap out of this shit. You're a fighter. Dammit, Drake, you've fought your whole life, and to give up now would be fucking stupid. You fought against your bitch mother, your pathetic father, and you've fought for everything you ever wanted. You survived. Do you want Selene?"

I keep my eyes focused on my feet, remaining silent when I know he wants an answer.

"I said, do you want Selene?" I look up at him and nod my head. "Then fucking fight for her. If you can't win this time, you'll survive." His voice softens again, and he puts his arm around me. "But I think you'll win. Drake Thomas doesn't give up." He doesn't wait for me to answer. Smiling, he says, "Glad we could have this talk." Patting me on the back, he keeps smiling at me, and something resembling happiness makes an appearance on my face for the first time in weeks.

I never thought I would say this, but Tommy is right—I can't give up. I won't give up because I want and need her, and—whether she realizes it or not—she wants and needs me. Maybe this will just take time and persistence.

Looking over at Tommy, I push him off me against the lockers. "Dude, get the fuck off me." I open my locker and take out my track shoes. "And, seriously, don't ever get emotional like that again. It freaks my shit out." Just like that, thanks to my typically insensitive friend, I feel a glimmer of hope. I might be able to get Selene back. I just need to figure out how.

Selene

The last time I went weeks without speaking to Drake, I felt lost. This time seems a thousand times worse. I haven't figured out if it's because I'm feeling the loss of him and my mama all over again or if it's just him. Physically, this is nearly unbearable. I can't see him. I can't forgive him.

Forgive what? a tiny voice in my head whispers. I push it out of my mind.

The conversation I overheard that day replays in my head over and over. When I saw his truck in the driveway that morning, I couldn't wait to wrap my arms around him and tell him I was ready—ready for love, ready to be happy. I couldn't hold back all the feelings only he had ever been able to reach for one second longer. For once, I was soaring high with the possibility of what my future could be. I finally thought I deserved something good.

I shouldn't have been listening. I should've let them know I was there as soon as I heard their muffled voices. Then, when I got closer to the entry of the kitchen, I heard his words.

She just wanted to be with me, and I left her. I wanted to protect her, but I didn't. I allowed her to feel unloved and alone. She got in that car to look for me, and she died! She died, and she killed Selene's mother, too, and the worst part is, it's all my fault!

It's all my fault keeps repeating in my mind. I can't see past that, and when he looked at me with all the guilt in his eyes, it was like he knew I could never forgive him. It was like he didn't think I *should* ever forgive him. Now, I don't know what to do or say. I don't know how I'll ever get past this. I shouldn't have been so stupid to ever think I deserved to love and be loved.

Aunt Vi says Mama wouldn't want me to live this way. I don't want to live this way either, but I just don't know how to move forward. How do I understand? How do I forget?

I glance across my room to where my guitar leans against the wall. I guess to find the answers to any of those questions, I'll need to believe I can first, and I'm not sure I believe in that kind of possibility.

Drake

Even after my conversation with Tommy, I still feel myself falling apart. Broken, I still hold on. Sometimes, it all seems pointless now that I don't have Lacey—or Selene. I loved them both more than my life, and somehow everything I did to protect them only hurt them more in the end.

I've tried calling Selene four times in the last few days. She never answers, and I never leave a message. I want to say the things I'm feeling to her, not some message. I would rather it be face to face, but I haven't worked up the nerve to risk rejection in person. It's been hard enough letting my mind go crazy, thinking she could be sitting there next to her phone, watching my name light up the screen and still not wanting to answer. This is torture. I won't let myself give up though.

It's killing me as I lie here thinking of her, of the mistakes I made. I feel like I'm in a dream where I want to run but can't move. Tommy said I can win her back; I'm not sure. Is it even possible for me to win? I take a deep breath and close my eyes. I think of when I last saw her. I remember how kissing her felt. It didn't feel right—well, the kiss felt good, and holding her felt good. All of those things with Selene have felt real since the first time our lips met, but the last time, the air around us was clouded with doubts and fears neither of us could explain but knew were out there. I could even see it in her eyes, although she tried to play it off like she wasn't afraid. Everything between us was coming to an end. I clench my fist into the blanket. There was something pushing us apart even as she kissed me and I held her.

I look at my cell phone again and push the talk button. It rings and rings until finally I hear her voice pick up—voicemail again. This time I listen. She sounds so happy, such a change from the girl who first came here, and even more of a change from the girl I saw a few days ago. When the phone indicates it's time to leave a message, the words rush out of me.

"God, Selene. I wish you would pick up. Talk to me... something. I...I don't know. I promised myself I wouldn't call or go to you, but I have things to say. I need you to listen." I plead desperately. I didn't realize how badly I needed to say these things. "I just want to say...when you came here, I had an enormous hole in my heart that needed to be filled up, and you did that, Selene. You made it whole again." Taking a slow breath, I say one last thing: "I can't let you go...I won't."

Hanging up the phone, I grab my keys and head out the door. There is someone else I need to visit. It's been too long, and I need to make sure she knows I haven't forgotten her either.

Selene

Looking up, I realize Emme is standing in the doorway, staring at me. I give her a half-heartedly pleasant look and put my phone under my pillow. She isn't impressed.

"You know, you should answer that call." Walking toward me, Emme sits next to me on the bed.

I widen my smile, hoping she doesn't see through it. "And please tell me why I should answer a telemarketer's phone call."

Reaching for the glass of water on my end table, I take a sip. I don't know why I just lied. I guess it feels like if I don't acknowledge his call, then it didn't happen. Rolling her eyes, she picks up the new People magazine and starts flipping through it.

"I know you're lying, Selene. It was Drake, and I can see in your eyes you're as miserable avoiding him as he is trying to get you to forgive him for something that really isn't his fault."

I feel like someone punches me in the stomach as the words leave her mouth. She continues, not even concerned by the idea that I may not want to talk about this.

"He has always felt the need to protect those he loves by taking on everything, even things he has no control over. It drove Lacey crazy. He hurt himself trying to keep her safe." Shaking her head, she lets out a long, drawn-out sigh. "We all knew, but no one said anything. We knew what she did to him—what kind of mother does that? Drake did everything to take the attention away from Lacey. That night, Lacey decided she wasn't going to let Drake be the only one who was bad, so she drank." Emme goes quiet, tossing the magazine aside. She gets up and walks over to the window.

Her shoulders seem stiff, like she's angry. I begin to feel uncomfortable and debate whether I should get up to comfort her or wait in this awkward silence. I prefer silence since I've never been good at this kind of thing. How can I give support to someone when I can barely handle these emotions myself?

I should get up. Just as I'm about to go to her, she begins to speak again. "It isn't his fault, Selene. She found out Jared was out at a party. Drake wouldn't let her go because he was afraid of her getting hurt. Lacey called me that night, drunk and upset. I just laughed. I bitched about Jared and told her what a piece of shit he is. She said she was going to show up at the party and give him a piece of her mind. Again, all I did was laugh." Facing me, there is a sad look on her face. I can't move; I only stare. "If you'd known Lacey, you'd know anyone would think it was hilarious to hear her say that because she was the most gentle person I've ever known. But, you see, I didn't take her seriously...I did nothing. I laughed it off, and she got in that car and died. She died, and so did your mama."

Falling to her knees, Emme takes my hands into her own. I stare down at her and realize she is trying to blame herself. Wrapping my arms around her, for the first time in my life, I attempt to give solace while feeling my own at the same time.

After we've both found the comfort we're seeking, I whisper, "It wasn't your fault, Emme."

She exhales, is quiet for a moment, and then says, "It wasn't Drake's fault either."

I feel a tight clenching around my heart, but I don't say anything.

chapter 30

Drake

D
arkness covers the cemetery like a blanket, but it doesn't bother me. I've lived in darkness most of my life. I always thought Lacey was my light, but she was struggling like a flame endeavoring to stay lit. I just never realized it until now.

When I finally reach her grave, I sit down in my usual spot and lean up against the stone. If I try really hard, I can imagine sitting side by side as we did when we were kids, reading out loud to one another, finding everything funny. It's her; I've always been able to feel Lacey.

Closing my eyes, I let out a deep sigh. "Hey, sorry it's been a while. I've been a little lost, or at least I thought I was for a while." I sigh wistfully. "I need your help, Lacey. I need to make Selene see we can get through this. I know she blames me—hell, I blame myself—but I need her. I love her, and she needs to listen." Just saying this makes me feel better.

"I want to ask you why. I want to know why you chose to get in the car that night and drive. I know you would be devastated by the chain of events caused by that decision. I should have been there to stop you." I blow out a long breath. The what-ifs are pointless.

Opening my eyes, I lift the book in my hand. "I brought it. I'm sure you've been dying to know how it ends. Do you think Sky forgives Holder? He just wanted to protect her." A cold breeze whips across my face. "Okay, okay, I'll just read it." I pull out the flashlight I brought with me.

Flipping the pages of the book, I begin to read out loud into the night air. I can picture Lacey snuggling in next to me, anticipating what her romantic heart already knows. Sky will forgive Holder. It's silly, but this damn girly book gives me hope. *Ha, hope.*

I read until the end. It didn't take me too long once I get started since we were almost done. She did forgive him, but she needed a little help figuring it out.

Standing up, I know what I need to do. I can still feel Lacey's presence around me. "Yeah, I'll admit it, I loved that damn book—sucked me right in." I feel good. "Thanks for everything. Thanks for being a good sister, for always understanding me, for loving me. I hope you forgive me. In the end, I couldn't save you because I needed saving too. I'm so sorry. I know you wouldn't blame me. I recognize now you were trying to tell me for years I couldn't always be the hero. I know you would have attempted to save me if I had let you."

My mind drifts to Selene and everything that's happened over the time since she stumbled into my life. I think about who I was then and who I am now. "The thing is, Lacey, I've finally been saved. She did that. Selene saved me, and now I need to save us."

I press my fingertips to my lips then touch the top of the headstone. "See you soon." Turning, I head away from her spirit, back into the darkness. This time, I know where to find the light.

Selene

About an hour after Emme leaves, I decide to head downstairs for the first time in days. When I enter the kitchen, I find Aunt Vi making dinner. It smells good. It's been weeks since I've actually eaten a meal. She doesn't even look up. I haven't been talking to her much either, so I don't blame her for not acknowledging me.

Taking a seat on the stool across from her, I softly say, "Hey." She still doesn't look up. I watch her as she chops the carrots with practiced precision.

Finally, she raises her gaze away from the carrots. I can see her grip flexing around the handle in nervousness.

"Selene, I'm sorry I didn't tell you about Drake's connection to your mother's death. I thought about it often, especially as you two grew closer."

She sighs and releases the knife, walking around the counter to stand next to me. I feel the bile rise in my throat at her words. It makes me sick every time someone mentions my mama. I thought I was over this feeling, but everything that happened over the last several weeks took me backward. She waits for me to look at her.

Looking up, I see the tears in her eyes. I don't want her to feel guilty.

"I wanted you to be able to see Drake the way I saw him that first day he showed up on my doorstep. I thought you would recognize the boy he tries to hide. I thought once you actually saw him, none of this would matter."

I put my hand over hers on the bar. "But it doesn't matter if I saw him. He…" I stop because I'm not sure I'm convinced what I'm about to say is true. I imagine Drake now, with all the pain and hurt he has endured over his life. It's so much more anguish compared to mine, really.

She sits next to me. "The thing is, Selene, I believe it would have made all the difference in the world if I had just said something…if you had heard it in a different way, at a different time."

Shaking my head, I don't want to believe that to be true. "You need to listen to me—" Aunt Vi is cut off by the sound of a slamming car door outside. We both look at one another, and she shakes her head, indicating she has no idea who it could be.

Standing and walking to the window, she pulls the sheer curtain aside and peers out into the dark. Slowly, she turns and faces me. There's a guarded look on her face, and it shakes my nerves a bit.

"Who is it?" I ask, a quiver in my voice.

Coming toward me, she places her hand gently on my shoulder. "Selene, just remember you'll have many regrets in your lifetime. Don't let this be one of them."

With that, she walks out of the room. I listen to her footsteps fade down the hall and up the steps, and it takes me only a moment to realize who's here. *Drake.*

I hear the screen door squeak open and a knocking sound against the back glass. I freeze, a knot forming in my chest. Am I ready to face him? I don't know, but somewhere deep inside I can feel the yearning of my heart urging me to open my eyes. Gradually, I lift myself off the stool, leaving my doubts behind me. As I turn the knob, I try to prepare myself to see his face. I have no idea what my reaction will be or how I'll feel; I only know there is a part of me that desperately wants to feel the security he has always given me.

There he is, and my heart speeds into a new rhythm. I lose my breath. Just this one look does it. I see him. I actually see him. Drake, the one person who makes me feel this way. Even with the distance everything has put between us, I see what I failed to realize before: there is love there. Finally, I recognize what I should've seen all along: Drake fixed me. For the first time, I feel unbroken.

At first, I think I'm imagining her standing in front of me. The beauty of her face and those sparkling green eyes set me on fire, just as they've done time and time again. A rush of emotions plays across her features so quickly I can't decipher what they mean.

Does she want me to leave? Is she happy to see me? Am I hurting her more by showing up? All my doubts and fears are swirling in my stomach, making me feel nauseous. I'm afraid to speak first, so I wait, anxious to not scare her off. Seconds begin to feel like hours, my palms feel sweaty, and my heart is nearly beating out of my chest. Maybe she's waiting for me. My mouth is only barely able to form her name.

"Selene…"

It rushes out of me like I'm gasping for my last breath. I feel paralyzed by the nearness of her.

Slowly, she reaches out her hand, pushing gently against my chest until I take a step back. My heart stops, thinking she is about to close the door in my face, but instead she steps out into the cold with me. She looks into my eyes, and I see something I can't explain.

"Can we go for a walk and talk?" she asks, her voice shaking.

I'm not sure if it's nerves or the chilly breeze that blows around us, but my voice squeaks out, "Sure."

She moves past me. I must be mistaken, but I think I catch a small glimpse of hope in her expression. Could it be? I don't say anything, watching her for a minute.

As she reaches the middle of the back yard under the huge oak trees, the winter moonlight illuminating her, Selene looks over her shoulder. "Are you coming or not?"

She just keeps walking, and I have to run to catch up with her. This isn't what I was expecting. I have my doubts, but I feel resilience trying to push its way through them.

I stop jogging once I'm a few feet behind her. I feel like I need to give her some space, and maybe I need my own, too.

She continues walking along the riverbank as we've done before. I follow her in silence. It's obvious to me she has some things she wants to say, and I'll wait until she is ready to say them, even if it's forever, as long as I can be near her. I don't even realize it, but we're at our spot, and she has suddenly come to a stop. Her back is still toward me.

For the first time, I notice her clothes are hanging on her a little more loosely than when I saw her last, nearly a month ago. She shivers when the wind blows off the water.

Stopping a few feet behind her, I wait, even though my hands are itching to touch her. Slowly, she turns around. I'm not sure what I expect, but it definitely isn't the smile I see spread across her face.

Even though I'm confused, I can't help my lips turning up at the corners too. She moves toward me, her eyes never leaving mine. She looks like a ghost with the reflection of moonlight on the water behind her, and I really hope I'm not dreaming.

When she is standing directly in front of me, she stops. Looking down at her, I watch her face…her impressive, beautiful, soft face. Placing one hand on mine, she moves the other to my face and lightly rubs her thumb over the bruise under my eye, her lips turning down in a frown.

"Drake, I'm so, so sorry. I regret not stopping and listening to you that day. I regret not trusting you enough to allow myself to hear the truth. I regret you living in fear I'll never understand." Tears are flowing from her eyes now, and I'm pretty sure mine are doing the same. She rises up on her tiptoes and places a gentle kiss to the mark beneath my eye. "I hope you can forgive me for not listening and causing you more pain. I want to hear you now. I want to listen to whatever you need to tell me because…" She swallows hard. "Because I love you, Drake, and I don't want you to be one of my regrets."

Did I hear her right? My brain is having a hard time wrapping itself around the fact that she said she loved me. I cover her hands with mine and pull them down between us. I interlock our fingers, staring at how small her hands are in mine before I look up at her. My heart is drumming against my ribcage at a pace I never thought possible.

"God, Selene, I lo—"

She gently pulls her hand from mine and presses her fingertip against my lips. Shaking her head, she says, "No, I want you to wait until you tell me why you think the accident is your fault. Then I want you to only say what you feel, and not in response to what I just said to you."

My lips spread wide under her finger, lightly kissing it before I nod my head. Only then does she put her hand down and lock it with mine again.

I thought it would be easier to explain that night to her than to earn her forgiveness. Apparently, I was wrong. It's hard to look at this girl and tell her things I've never said to anyone. Part of me is scared she will see me as weak and pathetic. Most of all, I don't want to relive one instant of the life that drove me to be the Drake I was before Lacey died.

I feel a tiny squeeze of my hand. Clearing my throat, I begin.

"I don't even know what I would've said that day, Selene. When your Aunt Violette told me the other car involved in the accident with Lacey was your mother, it broke me. I knew the boy I once was hurt you. I knew this was what my mother meant when she said I had done something to you that you would never forgive me for. She said it's my fault because it was my alcohol, and because I left Lacey at home that night when she wanted to go."

Pulling my hand from hers, I leave her standing alone while I walk to the edge of the river.

"It was mine, and I did leave Lacey there alone. I spent my whole life doing everything I could to draw attention to myself so she wouldn't have a reason to notice Lacey. Most of the time it worked, especially the older we got. I caused trouble and made sure Lacey stayed out of it. I just wanted to keep her safe."

Turning back to face her, I hold back the tears that threaten to fall.

"I was so disgusting, Selene. I used girls, people, and drugs. I numbed myself to the fear of my mother and in the process, made sure she had reason to only want to punish me. So, that night I could see Lacey didn't want me to leave. She had confronted me about hurting myself to help her. I didn't listen. I couldn't listen. I said things I didn't mean, and I left. I left her when she begged me not to. I blame myself because I'm still protecting her. It's my fault because it can't be hers. I need you to see it that way too because I don't want you to hate her. She was my sister. She was the good twin, and she doesn't deserve to be hated."

I'm practically begging now, standing before her, hoping she can understand what I mean and forgive me at the same time.

"She was good, and I'm not. I deserve to be hated, but I pray and plead for you to forgive me."

I fall to my knees in front of her, wrapping my arms around her waist and leaning into her. I don't care if I appear pathetic. I need her, and I'll do anything. Her hands brush over the top of my head.

"Drake, I don't know if I …"

My stomach drops because I'm sure she's about to tell me she can't forgive me.

"I've lived in darkness for most of my life, but that day I heard your voice and saw you, I knew you were here to finally show me the way out. I've loved you since that first moment and every moment since then. I hope—I need you to forgive me."

I'm still hugging her against me with my face in her middle. She reaches back and pulls my arms apart to loosen my grip. My heart stops. She can't forgive me.

"Drake, please look at me." Her voice is full of tears. "I can't forgive you because there is nothing to forgive you for. It wasn't your fault. I guess I've always known that, but I couldn't see beyond my pain to realize it. Please stop blaming yourself." She leans down and presses her lips to mine, and then she pulls back, looking in my eyes. "I could never hate Lacey either. I do forgive her—my mama would want it that way—but you have to stop trying to save everyone, okay?" Her eyes are searching my face. "Drake, say okay."

At first, all I can do is look into her eyes, trying to comprehend what she said. She forgives me and doesn't blame Lacey. It's everything I hoped. I don't deserve this, but I'm not going to question it any longer. I pull her down into my lap and then onto her back, cradling her in my arms.

"Okay." I give her a quick peck on the lips. "Okay," I say again.

I look into her eyes again, and I finally recognize what I saw when she opened the door earlier—it's love. I laugh a little, and it echoes through the cold night air.

"I love you, Selene Chandler. Fuck, it feels good to finally say that!"

She slaps my arm. "You say fuck too much!"

I waggle my eyebrows at her and then kiss her so hard she can't do anything but return it as I think, *So this is what living in the light feels like.*

chapter 31

Drake

Waking up to a little more than an inch of snow with promises of more can't dampen my mood. It never snows here, but a freakish winter storm moved in from the north, so I plan on taking advantage of it. Most likely, it will all be gone within a day, but this means we get a snow day.

It's been three days since Selene took me for a walk and changed my life.

She forgave me. She listened. She kissed me. The greatest part of all is that she said she loved me. I could see it was hard for her to open herself up like that and trust me; I could tell because I felt the exact same thing. She changed me. I changed her. We only need each other to get through anything, and it feels good to be confident in that.

I traipse my way through the snow to Selene's front door. The doctor finally released her to do normal activity, so I thought we would have a little fun—we both need it. The last month has been trying; fuck, our whole lives have been trying, but now we have each other. We can move on, finish school, and the thought of doing it together only makes it better.

When I reach the door, I give it a hard, loud knock and flinch a little from the pain shooting through my knuckles and into my fingers. *Fuck, it's cold.* The door opens just as I'm about to knock again, and Mrs. D smiles brightly behind the screen door.

Swinging the door open, she reaches out and pulls me by the arm. "Get your hiney in here and out of the cold, young man!" I remove my hat as she begins dusting the snow from my jacket. Just as I'm about to say something about her mothering, Selene comes bouncing down the stairs.

With each day that passes, she seems more relaxed and happy than I've ever seen her. I never asked her what changed her mind and made her listen to me. Frankly, I don't even think it matters. What matters is that she did.

I can't take my eyes off of her. She is in slim jeans, a pair of ankle boots, and a tight-fitting sweater that matches her green eyes. Coming to a stop directly in front of me, Selene looks up. She is so beautiful and has no idea. I know my desire for her is showing in my eyes, but I don't care. I don't even care that her Aunt Vi is standing behind me. I want her more than anyone I have ever known, and it isn't just for now; I want her forever.

She begins fidgeting under my stare. "What?" She starts wiping at her face. "Do I have something on my face?" she asks, and I hear Mrs. Durham laugh as her footsteps echo down the hall. She shouldn't have left us alone. I just keep staring at every inch of her face, my gaze caressing every feature.

"Seriously, Drake, why are you looking at me like that?" The tip of her tongue darts out and swipes across her lips nervously, breaking every bit of control I have. I reach behind her and pull her into me. My lips crash against hers, a startled gasp releasing from between our lips. I don't stop—I can't. It seems like an eternity before she gives in, but in reality it's only seconds. I feel her relax into me, both of us oblivious to our surroundings, neither of us caring.

Reality squeezes its way into my consciousness. Reluctantly, I take a step back. Her lashes flutter open, and this time I see the desire burning in every part of me reflected in her eyes. This isn't the time, and I know it. Her lips part, and the flame ignites again. I need to put it out now. "We need to go. There's snow, and it's cold. I—we need to go." I sound a bit frantic, which seems silly and out of place.

I leave her staring at me as I walk to the antique metal hooks lining the wall where her coat hangs. I hear her giggle behind me. She turns and watches me, her fingertips resting against her swollen lips. She giggles again.

"Yes, snow is definitely a good way to cool off." Her eyes light up, and I can't help the laugh that escapes as she takes her coat from me. "Bye, Aunt Vi. See you later," she calls out so Mrs. D will hear her in the kitchen.

"Have fun, you two," Mrs. Durham calls back.

Selene looks at me and shakes her head again as she walks past me. I guess I did react to that kiss in a funny way, and I'm glad she appears calm because it means I didn't scare her. I wish I could say the same for me.

Selene

I still feel the tingling sensation deep in the pit of my stomach.

I feel unsteady on my feet. There was something different in that kiss than any other we have shared before. I saw it in his eyes, and I'm pretty sure after I got over the shock, it was mirrored in my own eyes. I wanted him. Who am I kidding? I still want him now. I watch him trudge his way to his truck, oblivious to the fact that he has caused a storm to brew within me—one I'm not sure I can weather much longer.

Just as I reach the truck, Drake opens the door. Stepping up to the front, I slip on the edge and fall back, releasing a loud yelp. Drake catches me, but the surprise of my fall leaves him off balance, and we both fall to the ground. He lands first, and I land on him, knocking a rush of air from his lungs. Neither of us moves. Then just when I think about moving, a big, cold handful of snow crunches against my face. Suddenly, I'm sliding off his chest and to the ground with a thud as a roar of laughter fills the air. Stunned, I lie there for a moment before gathering a fistful of snow. Listening to Drake, I relish the sound. Slowly, I inch my hand up and smash it swiftly into his face. I jump up and try to run but end up slipping and falling again.

Drake is up, spitting snow out of his mouth as he darts toward me. I'm scrambling to get back up, unsure if it's the ice beneath my feet or my laughter hindering my ability to stand.

"You are in serious trouble, Chandler!" Drake shouts between snorts. He wraps his arms around me when I finally stand.

Barely able to speak, I manage to get out, "You started it!" just before I taste cold, wet ice in my mouth. Again, we both fall to the ground, soaking our clothes to the bone, neither of us caring.

I'm not even sure how long we've been out here, but we never make it out of the driveway. We both get in hits, Drake more often than I. We spend hours just enjoying our time together. For once, time doesn't matter. Nothing else matters.

Drake

I laugh, watching Selene wiggle her toes after pulling her boots off. I'm pretty sure snow found its way inside them by the look of uncomfortable disgust on her face. She looks up, glaring at me. "Oh, so you think it's funny that I may lose some toes?"

A boot zips past my head and hits the wall. My happiness only gets louder, and I can faintly hear Mrs. D singing to herself upstairs.

"You're a shithead, Drake Thomas! This hurts!" Selene exclaims as a laugh escapes between her lips.

I slowly stalk toward her while she tries to continue giving me the ultimate death stare. "You say shit too much," I state simply, keeping my face straight. She begins to say something, but I reach her before the words can leave her mouth, sweeping her up into my arms out of the chair.

She squeals and stiffens her body, nearly making us both fall to the floor. "Put me down, you nut! You're going to drop me!"

Looking into her eyes, we both abruptly stop. We stop moving altogether. I gently tighten my hold. "No, I don't think it's possible for me to ever let you go."

Leaning in, Selene presses her lips softly to mine. They taste sweet from her lip balm. "That's okay. I don't really want you to let me go, anyway."

Our light, fun moment turns into something more. Every day that has passed since the accident, we've had many moments of something more. Today seems even more significant, even more telling of the bond we've created between us, of the life we want together.

chapter 32

Selene

As I open my eyes, the morning sunlight pours over every corner of my room. It's a peaceful image, one that has my lips tipping up at the corners. For the first time, I feel lighter. I feel full of hope, full of love for a life I never thought I would experience.

It's April, a year since everything in my world changed, a year without Mama.

Life was so full of irreversible despair, I wasn't sure anything could change it. My heart was so broken and shattered, it was impossible to believe it would ever be whole again.

Never believe in the impossibility of anything, because possibility comes swooping into your life when you least expect. You may try to fight it—don't, it's pointless.

My possibility is Drake.

I tried fighting it, fighting our connection, our meant to be. It was futile. You can't win against these kinds of odds. I'm thankful for the perseverance of possibility.

It's April, and I'm not afraid of what this year will bring. How can I be afraid when I have Drake?

I roll over, reaching my hand out to search the nightstand for my phone, the darkness in my room making it impossible to know what time it is. Our whole house is kept dark and cold. It's always been this way, as if it wants to stamp out any light in my life.

Except it isn't the house. It's my mother.

As I find my phone and touch the screen, it illuminates a small space around me. Nine thirty. The phone also reminds me of the date. April.

Lacey left me in April. She left, and the point of my existence left too—or so I thought.

I was wrong. God, was I wrong, because I, Drake Thomas, had never even existed until I wandered upon a girl finding her own solace in my sanctuary. I was a shadow in a dark world before I met her, before Selene.

Rolling off the bed and onto my feet, I push open the heavy curtains. My eyes try to shut to block out the brightness of the day, but I hold them open. I only ever want to see light again when my eyes are open.

Selene did that, and no matter what happens, our lives are forever bonded—bonded by happenstance, bonded by love.

How can I not exist when I have that?

Selene

When Drake called, he told me to be ready. Ready for what? He hung up before I could ask—of course. I get the feeling he wouldn't tell me anyway. Whatever it is, he sounded excited.

Drake's excitement reminds me again of the possibilities of life I spent the morning contemplating. We both have found new possibilities. We both have found the missing part of ourselves. It feels good.

Peeking out the window, I'm feeling impatient. Just as I'm about to step away, I see Drake's truck pull into the driveway. My heart speeds up, and I stand there watching, waiting to catch a glimpse of him when he doesn't know I can see him.

Maybe that's a little strange, but Drake is his most handsome when he doesn't know he has an audience.

He doesn't get out right away, and I wonder what he's doing. If I didn't know better, I would almost think he was thinking about leaving instead of getting out of his truck. Then, before I can take another breath, Drake is lowering himself out from the driver's side door. I always love the initial feeling I get when I see him; it's like the first time every time.

From the moment I saw him all those months ago, Drake's beauty has left me speechless. It really isn't fair. I feel intoxicated by him. I don't know how or why, but he is mine, and there isn't a better feeling than this.

Drake

Before I knock on the door, I rub my palms against my pants to wipe the sweat from them. My nerves are shot. Selene is going to think I'm trying to forget them. I'm not, I just want us to move forward. I want us to embrace what we've found because life is so precious. This may upset her, and that scares me most of all.

I don't want her to hurt ever again.

The door swings open, pulling me from my thoughts. She's grinning ear to ear, and it's the most perfect smile ever. My worries melt away. I can't be afraid when she looks at me this way.

She throws her arms around my neck. "Where are we going?" I can hear the excitement in her voice.

Squeezing her tight, I let go. "It's a surprise. There's something we need to do."

One eyebrow quirks up. "We need to do?" She grabs my hand. "Now I'm even more intrigued."

"Let's go. I want as much time with you as I can get, and I promised Mrs. D I'd have you home by midnight."

We walk hand in hand back to my truck. I help lift her up into the cab and walk around the front to the driver's side, my eyes never leaving hers. It's April. Life has changed. It's becoming what it was always meant to be.

Selene

Drake takes us to our place along the river. As we walk along the path, closer to the riverbank, I feel a new kind of intimacy between us. Actually, it has been building

237

for some time. I'm completely aware of every breath he takes. I feel the beats of our hearts from my fingertips all the way to my center.

When we reach the river's edge, Drake has set everything up. It looks romantic and beautiful.

There are small lanterns hanging from the cypress tree branches, blankets spread out on the ground, and a picnic laid partway beneath the branches and under the open night sky. I'm speechless for a moment before turning to him and firmly planting my lips on his. I can tell I take him off guard at first because he doesn't move, but I'm just overwhelmed by my love for him, and I keep my lips where they are until finally he takes control. Running my hands up his back, I pull myself against him, wanting to be closer. I'm not sure how long we stay connected like this, but it takes Drake gently pushing me back to break the spell.

"We need to stop. I had a plan." He sounds like he hates himself for stopping. I want to laugh at the annoyance in the tone of his voice while at the same time fighting the urge to ignore him and force my own plans on him.

He kisses me on the cheek so I just nod, deciding to give him his way since it's clear he worked so hard. "Drake, it looks so beautiful out here. I love it."

He takes my hand, and we walk toward the water's edge. Silently, we watch the river move swiftly over the rocks. The sun is just setting behind the hills, a warm glow reflecting off the water from the last bit of sunlight. It's so peaceful.

"It's April." His low voice rouses me from my thoughts.

Turning my head slightly, I watch his face. He's still looking out over the water. I want to ask him so many questions, but I remain silent.

"Selene, I woke up this morning, and for the first time, I felt completely happy, worry-free." Turning, he faces me, taking both of my hands in his. Only a moment passes. "For the first time, I don't feel like I'm waiting for everything to crumble apart."

Rising up on my toes, I wrap my arms around his neck. Slowly, I place a soft kiss on his lips.

"It's April, and I don't feel the overwhelming sadness I expected to feel, the sadness I thought I would feel for the rest of my life."

Keeping my arms around him, I stare into his worried eyes. "Drake, I felt the same this morning, and I feel the same way now. Don't look so sad about it. We don't have to punish ourselves any longer for their deaths. It wasn't our fault." His gaze drifts away from mine. "No, look at me." His eyes meet mine again. "We deserve to be happy. It's what they would have wanted."

Pulling me tight against him, he releases the breath he seemed to be holding. "I was so worried you would be upset with me for feeling so happy when—"

"I could never be mad about that, especially when I feel the same." I kiss him lightly again. "It's our time. We'll always remember them. We'll always miss them. We'll also go on." I pause as I let the words sink in before continuing. "You made me realize we can have it all."

He lifts me off the ground and holds me tight against him.

Whispering, he says, "Thank you for loving me."

I can't help myself when a chuckle escapes my lips. "Is that what this is all about? Were you afraid I'd be mad at you?"

Placing me on my feet, he grins down at me. "No, but I was trying to make you happy too."

"Oh, Drake, you didn't need to do all this. I'm happy— happier than I've ever been in my whole life."

Drake

What a relief. It's amazing what a few words can do to a person. I should've known, but I guess sometimes our old worries still linger.

Taking Selene's tiny hand in mine, I lead her to the blanket I laid out for us.

The picnic by the river, although a nice idea, is completely insignificant at the moment. I can only think about how our lives are moving forward. My mind is consumed by one thing: Selene. She is mine, and we are happy.

My heart begins to pound inside my chest—not out of fear, but in anticipation.

Neither of us says a word as we reach the blanket. I pull her into the curve of my body and she touches her lips to mine. I move to the edge of her mouth and onto her cheek, pressing light, delicate kisses along her skin. I continue to make my way down to the curve of her neck and back up again.

My body is on fire with each touch of my lips, scorching me to the very depths of my soul. This is love. With the way she is pulling me closer, the soft sounds leaving her, I know she feels it too. I feel every part of our love tangling together until it is impossible to determine whose love is more.

We've never allowed ourselves to lose this control. I've always wanted her. From the very moment I saw her, I wanted to touch her sun-kissed skin and every part of her body. We just never went this far, although lately it has been harder to resist. Is she ready? Am I ready? I need to be sure now, before it's too late.

Pulling back, I look down into her eyes.

"Selene, baby, do you want to stop?" I ask, wanting her answer to be no, yet being perfectly okay with yes.

I want her to always trust me and feel safe. The darkness surrounds us, but the weak lantern light reflects the answer I'm hoping for in her eyes. The slight nod of her head gives me final confirmation. This is happening.

She gently tugs my shirt, her small hands fisted into it so she can bring my lips back to hers.

Our lips meet, at first soft and slow, and then she becomes almost urgent. I feel her hands clumsily roam over my back, reaching for the bottom of my shirt to pull it up over my head. Gently, I pull her hands away. I need this to be unhurried and deliberate.

Brushing her hair back, I stare down into her eyes, cupping her cheek. Slowly, I run my hand along the curve of her cheek, gently down her neck to the delicate skin at the top of her breast. I savor every touch and whimper that escapes her lips. Her beauty is mesmerizing.

She reaches up and touches my face, her eyes begging me for more. "I want this. I want you," she whispers.

We begin undressing one another, kissing and caressing as we free ourselves from the confines of our clothing. Finally bare, I cover her. The vulnerability I feel is reflected in her gaze as she stares up at me. Looping her hands around my neck, Selene gently pulls my head down so our lips are mere inches apart. Just before they touch, our eyes never breaking their connection, I confess, "I want you too."

Once our lips meet, our movements become more desperate, our need building to the breaking point. Through the fog of my need, I tenderly make sure Selene is ready. Her eyes closed, lips slightly parted, I watch her face for a brief moment. She is so beautiful.

"Selene, look at me," I tell her. "I need you to tell me to stop if I'm hurting you. Do you understand?" She gives a slight nod, her eyes glassed over with desire. "I love you."

My gaze never leave hers as I ease into her until we inti-

mately become one. I wait for her, although my body is screaming for me to take what it needs. This isn't about me; this is
about us. Selene closes her eyes briefly before opening them
again. Without saying a word, she gradually begins to move beneath me, letting me know she wants more. Soon we find our
rhythm, and all my wants become entwined with hers.

I want her to know she owns every part of me. I need her to
know she is everything, my everything.

Selene

We hold on to one another for so long. Although my
arms tingle from exhaustion, I can't let go. His arms
wrap around me tighter, pulling me close. Releasing
a heavy sigh, I relax further. This is all I need, just me and
Drake, together.

"I love you," he whispers. I feel myself smile.

"I love you, too," I whisper back, closing my eyes.

Only the sounds of the night surround us, and I can feel
our hearts beating to the same rhythm. It strikes me that
I've always been intended for this—for her. I believe it
more than I believe in anything else.

In a quiet, sleepy voice, she asks, "Drake, do you think it's
possible there are two people in the world who could love each
other the way we do?"

The idea seems a bit silly, but Selene is being serious. Humor creeps slowly across my face.

"I don't know," I say quietly. "I would like to think so."

Silence lingers between us before she clears her throat. Her voice is a little wobbly when she speaks again. "I don't know either, Drake, but I do know I can only love you. It hasn't been easy getting here, but you're worth it—all the pain, heartache, and confusion, every frustration, every mistake, every setback. You're worth every moment that has led me to loving you."

"I don't know the future, but I do know I want you in mine. I don't know what other people feel, I only know the way I love you."

I bury my face into the side of her neck, placing a soft kiss against her skin. At a loss for words, I place another tender kiss on her shoulder.

The future I want feels possible. We feel possible, and together, we can have anything we want.

chapter 33

Drake

I stare at it…the white envelope sitting on top of my desk, my name typed neatly across the front. It holds the fate of where my future begins. Selene received hers a week ago. We were both excited, rushed to find mine, and concluded that one had not come. She was accepted to the University of Texas, and she'll attend no matter what. She'll go, begin there, even if it's without me. I made her promise. I've already been accepted to my second and third choices, and I'll go to one of them if it comes to that. She made me promise.

When I first noticed the envelope, I thought about calling her so she could be here to open it with me. Then I realized I didn't want to see the look in her eyes if the letter doesn't contain the response we're looking for.

Trembling, I pick up the envelope and slowly tear it open. Unfolding the letter, my eyes begin to run across the words: *Dear Mr. Thomas, Congratulations! I'm pleased to inform you that you've been accepted to the University of Texas at Austin...*

The breath I was holding comes out in a rush. The relief and happiness feel so good.

Picking up the phone, I dial her number. It rings until her voicemail picks up. "Selene, I don't know where you are, but I'm headed to your house!" I say, unable to hide the excitement in my voice. "Your cute little ass better be there and ready to celebrate!" Hanging up the phone, I grab my coat and dash down the stairs.

Just as my hand covers the knob, I hear her cold voice behind me. As usual, it's filled with a hostility that leaves me paralyzed. It's been months since we had a real confrontation. In fact, both of my parents have left me alone for the most part. My dad only inquires about my days and, occasionally, Selene. It seems like he's trying, which is more than he has ever done in the past. Mom has just stayed away, or maybe I've been better at avoiding her. How does she do it? She always knows when I'm at my happiest and hunts me down to take it all away.

"Don't be an idiot if you think I'll pay for school just so you can be with her," she states so calmly I'm almost fooled into feeling safe. I don't move, don't say a word. "I know you got an acceptance letter. I know you've been waiting just so you can go chase that girl. You're pathetic!" she hisses at me.

Her heels click as she walks toward me, stopping just behind me. Slowly, I turn to face her. My face is hard and neutral, although I'm not sure I can hide the hatred I feel for her behind the mask I've perfected over the years any longer.

"Pathetic!" she yells again, and I try not to flinch. Seeing the look on her face, I recognize her next move. I close my eyes and wait.

When nothing happens, only the sound of a tiny whimper, I gradually open my eyes one at a time. I'll never forget this moment for as long as I live: my father is standing next to my mother, her small wrist caught in his broad grasp, slightly twisted, a look of pain on both of their faces.

"Claire, you will never touch our son in anger or violence again."

Her eyes are wide with shock. For the first time in my life, my dad has interfered in my mother's wrath.

"This has never been about Drake or Lacey. The way your life turned out was never their fault. I've stood by for years, pretending to not see what you've been doing to them, making excuses, being a coward—no more!" His face is red now. "I will not hesitate to have you arrested if you so much as look at him wrong. It's time to stop this. I'll no longer ignore your abuse. Drake deserves to be happy, to have whatever future he wants, with whomever he wants." I'm still frozen in place, watching my mother's face crumble and my father's hold steady. "This is over. Drake, go tell Selene your good news." I only nod. There are no words for what I'm feeling, but I know I want to be with Selene. "Oh, and Drake...I'm proud of you. Congratulations," he adds.

This is all too much. I need to leave. There is life in my dad, after all, and it's a good feeling. This moment is something I've always wanted, have always needed—someone to stand up for me so I could walk away.

When I get out of my truck, I look up at the house to see Selene running toward me. As she reaches me, she jumps and throws her arms around me. I catch her quickly and laugh as I twirl her around. Sure, we may look silly, but I don't care. Loving her doesn't feel silly, and I'm happy. Selene is happy, and this is something so rare, we deserve our cheesy love-story moment. I don't even care if my guy card is revoked because, *fuck, I love this girl!* I need her more than I need my next breath, and the best part is that she loves me, too. There isn't anything standing in our way.

As I twirl her, she pulls back and shouts, "You got in, didn't you!" I see tears in her eyes, and for once I'm not worried they are tears of hurt. I nod and press my lips against hers. I'm not sure how long I hold her in my arms while we kiss, but when I finally set her down, we are both laughing again.

I love seeing this look on her face, and it's one I'm confident she only shares with me. "See, we had nothing to worry about!" I tell her, although if I'm honest, I was never as sure as I let her believe I was. Selene and I aren't known for things going right or being easy for us. I'm not sure if it's the letter, what happened with my parents, or both, but I think things may go our way for the first time.

Selene takes my hand, pulls it up to her mouth, and places a kiss on my palm. "You were right. I'm so glad you were right." Again, I'm overcome by the love I feel for this girl standing before me.

We slowly walk hand in hand to the porch and sit together, talking and sharing our dreams of what is beyond graduation for us. I don't think about what happened at my house before; I'll tell her another day. Right now, I just want to be with her, because she is the only thing that actually matters when I think beyond tomorrow.

It's late when I quietly open the door and tiptoe into the kitchen. Flipping the light on, I'm startled to find my dad sitting at the bar in the dark. His head is tilted down as he holds a mug to his lips. It's strange for me to see him sitting here alone, almost as if he were waiting for me, which he has never done before.

He looks up at me, and again a sad look is in place on his

face.

"Hey," I whisper, unable to make direct eye contact with him. I go to the refrigerator and take out a bottle of water.

Finally, he says, "I—I've been waiting for you."

I pause mid-drink and look over at him. I think this might be the first time I've really looked at him: the crow's feet around his eyes, the shadows under them, the slight graying at his temples. For the first time, I'm noticing the sadness and broken look in my father, a man who holds power and respect in our sleepy little town. I frown. No one knows him. It isn't just me who doesn't know the man sitting before me; it's his own wife, his parents, and every individual who voted for him in every election for the last ten years. It's sad.

Don't get me wrong, I don't feel sorry for him—he was a father who sat by and ignored his children being abused and hurt. I don't feel sorry for the man who allowed people to cover up family secrets to protect his name at the expense of others. He was wrong for so many reasons, for so long, but I do find myself wanting to get to know him. I feel a desire rising in me to learn about what made him finally stand between my mother and me. When I look at him, yeah, I realize I don't know him, but I know I want to give him a chance to make things right in the future. The past is impossible to make right for so many reasons, but that's just it—the past is in the past. I need to move forward, to forgive completely, if I ever want to give Selene the kind of future she deserves. It always comes back to Selene; it always will.

Slowly, I walk over and take a seat on the stool next to him. "Thank you," I say after a moment. I don't look at him, but I can feel his gaze shift to me.

"You're thanking me?" He sounds surprised. I can tell he is actually confused by my words.

Looking up, I repeat myself. "Yeah, thank you."

Shaking his head, he stutters, "I-I don't understand why you're thanking me. I failed you. I've never done one thing for you or your sister in all of your life." I watch as a tear slips down his unshaven cheek.

"Dad, I can't argue with you there, but it doesn't matter now." I reach over and lay my hand on his where it rests on the counter. "But you did stop her tonight, and that matters. So, thank you for finally waking up and caring enough to interfere."

Before I know what is happening, he takes my hand and pulls me toward him in a hard embrace. At first, I'm stiff and awkward. I can't remember a time he has ever hugged me, not even when I was a little kid. Finally, I relax a little and hug him back. I didn't even realize I needed this too. I've missed this, which is funny to think about because how can you miss something you never had?

With his voice clouded by emotion, he says, "I promise to try. I promise you, Drake, I'll try harder in the future."

When we pull apart, I look at him. His smile doesn't seem so sad anymore, and the shadows appear a little lighter.

"I'd really like that, Dad," I say, and I truly mean it. I can see the relief in his eyes. "I think I'm going to head to bed."

The emotions surrounding me right now are beginning to feel suffocating. I'm not used to this with him, and it's uncomfortable. Standing up, I turn to leave. Just as I reach the entryway, he says my name.

"Drake?" I pause and turn back to him. He is standing now too. "She's gone. Your mother, I asked her to leave. I told her to never contact you, that if you wanted to ever talk to her, you'd call her." I stare at him, unbelieving. "I just wanted you to be aware so you know I mean what I said. I know it's late, but I'll do whatever it takes to protect you from here on out." I don't know what to say, so I just nod my head and leave him standing in the kitchen alone.

I walk up the stairs as quietly as possible. Halfway up, I realize I have no reason to be worried she might hear me. She isn't here. She is *gone*. I start taking the stairs two at a time and run into my room then flop down on my bed. I woke up today without any knowledge that this was the day my life would change. The rush of relief and lack of fear fills me. I can finally breathe, and I know nothing can hold me back any longer. The future and Selene are the only things I have to think about now. My eyes close, and I sleep soundly for the first time I can remember.

chapter 34

Selene

It's been four months since Drake's mother left, weeks of moving on, days filled with comfort and ease. The changes in him have been everything I could have ever wished for him, and Drake and his dad have also begun to mend. The idea that everything will turn out all right is so promising, I have to remind myself I'm not dreaming, especially now as I hold this unopened envelope to my chest.

The beat of my heart is knocking so hard against my ribcage, I'm sure it can be heard miles away. Sitting here on the window seat in my bedroom, I stare down at all the cypress trees lining the river, trying to work up the courage to open it.

When I found it lying on the small table in the foyer, I had to put my hand out against the wall to steady myself. There has been very infrequent communication from my dad, not a word to me directly since he dropped me off that day last summer. In fact, I can't even remember the last time we spoke. I left him messages every once in a while, but there was never a return call.

I really didn't expect one, if I'm honest with myself. I know how he feels about me, even if I don't understand why, and there it is—the why part is the reason I hesitate to open this envelope.

Although it's small, I'm nervous what it holds is bigger than I will be able to handle.

I let the curtain fall back into place. Drawing in a deep breath, my trembling hands hold the envelope as I slowly slide the letter opener to break the seal. Unfolding the page, I immediately recognize his handwriting. I always thought it was so elegant for a man.

Dear Selene,

I'm not really sure where to begin. The only way is probably to just get right to the point. I'd like to say I'm sorry for leaving you at Vi's that day during a time a father should be there for his daughter, but I've never been a father.

It has taken too much time for me to see I've always blamed you. I just loved your mom so much. I loved her from the first moment I saw her, and I think she loved me, but I just never believed it was enough. I knew she was in love with someone else, too. I thought I could make her forget about him. I tried. I tried so damn hard. I wanted her all for myself. Then she got pregnant with you. The day she told me, I was shocked but happy. I saw this as my opportunity to win her completely. She would love only me.

I could tell her heart broke a little when the realization hit her—us having a baby together meant her chance with him was gone. We were young and both so conflicted. She disappeared for two weeks after that, and finally Vi confessed she was there and just needed time to get things in order. She needed to clear up some loose ends. I knew what she meant, so I waited. Your mother came back, and everything seemed to come together for us. She wasn't distant. In fact, things were better than ever. We grew closer as you grew inside her. It all seemed per-

fect...magical. I had all her attention and love, and that was all I'd ever wanted.

When you were born and I walked into the room, I watched as your mother held you. Her eyes never left your face, and I could see you were her world now, and she loved you more than her own life. She never even noticed me walk in. In that moment, something changed in me. I realized I'd lost her again. She was no longer mine and mine alone. God, I know this sounds selfish, but I couldn't look at you. You stole her from me, and I only wanted her. I'm not sure why I'm telling you all of this. I guess I want you to know why I never opened up to you.

One night a few weeks ago, I had a dream about your mother. She was angry with me because I let you go, because I never showed you one ounce of affection. Just before I woke up, she whispered, "She is a part of me...and you. She isn't what came between us, but what brought us together." I woke in a cold sweat, crying. I cried for the first time since your mother died, but I wasn't crying for her—I was crying for you. I was crying for all the years I made you feel unloved and unwanted. I cried for all the time lost. I cried for every moment I should've been your father.

I know you may not ever forgive me. I know you may hate me, but I needed you to know what I was thinking, and I'm so, so sorry. I hope one day you can give me the chance to know you and to love you.

−Dad

I reread the last sentence over and over as the tears stream down my face, until my vision blurs and I can't hold my head up any longer. Releasing the letter, I let it float to the floor as I curl up into a ball on the window seat, brokenhearted and aching, until I cry myself to sleep.

When I open my eyes, I'm surrounded by darkness, only the dim glow of the moonlight shining through the window. I blink a few times to focus, feeling a little disoriented. Wondering what time it is, I search for my cell phone. Finally finding it on the floor next to me, I check the time: seven forty-five. I notice I have several missed calls from Drake, and the last one was only five minutes ago.

I stand up, and something crumbles beneath my bare feet—the letter. My heart starts aching again as I remember the words written to me. I'm not sure how I'm supposed to feel...happy? I don't know. I've waited years to understand my dad's coldness toward me and have longed for him to show any sort of affection to let me know he might love me, even a little. This contains everything I always thought I wanted, and yet I feel numb. I'm not sure what to think or feel, maybe it's because when it comes down to it, his reason is a bunch of shit—major shit—and I don't need this kind of shit. I have love, I am loved, but do I need his love too?

Walking to my dresser, I open my top drawer and place the letter inside. I'll decide what to do later, will choose how to feel later. The only thing I'm sure about right now is Aunt Vi loves me, Drake loves me, and for the first time, I trust to give my love to someone other than my mom. I never thought I was capable, but Drake Thomas has proved me wrong. I intend to hold on tight and not think about how to accept the love of someone who should have loved me from the start.

I make my way downstairs and into the kitchen. Without turning around, Aunt Vi begins speaking. "I was starting to wonder if you were ever going to wake up. Drake called at least three times. He really is becoming..." She trails off as she turns around and makes eye contact with me.

I must look bad. I didn't even consider that my eyes were probably red and puffy from all the crying I did. *Shitty shit shit!* I wanted to avoid the look of concern that has clearly settled on her face.

Rushing toward me, Aunt Vi places both her hands around my shoulders. "Dear God, Selene, what is it? Have you been crying? Did you and Drake have a fight? Is this why he is calling incessantly?" Her words are rushed and full of concern.

Taking a deep breath, I shake my head. How do I explain something I'm not even sure I understand? This is Aunt Vi, though. She will understand my need for time, my inability to know if I forgive him. I try to stop it, but a tear sneaks down my cheek. "No, Drake and I are fine—more than fine." I release a deep sigh. "It's my dad."

She immediately pulls me to her chest. "Oh, honey. Did you try calling again?" She pushes me away from her so she can look me in the eyes.

"No, he wrote me," I state plainly. I see anger cross her features before she can smooth them back out. It may seem odd, but I smile. I can't help the bit of comfort I feel at knowing she is ready to fight against any threat to my happiness. She remains silent, so I continue. "He apologized. He tried explaining the last eighteen years. He told me he loved me and asked my forgiveness." Again, a Mama Bear look quickly passes over her face.

"What a crock of shit!" she shouts as she releases my arms. "The nerve. If I—"

I place a hand gently on her back. "Aunt Vi, I'm all right. It's just a shock, and I'm not sure how to feel. I don't know if I can give him what he wants. He hurt me, but the thing is, I'm not hurting anymore. I have you, I have Drake, and at this moment, that's all I need. Because of you, he can't hurt me anymore."

She faces me again, her eyes glistening. "Oh, sweet girl. Your mama would be so proud." With that, she wraps me in the cocoon of her love.

Before Aunt Vi and I can wipe away our tears, a loud bang sounds on the back door. We pull back and look at one another.

Shaking her head, she whispers, "Poor girl, I'm not sure if this is love or obsession." She then walks to the door and puts a scowl on her face.

"Mr. Thomas, if you break my door, I will break your neck." Her face remains neutral, although I know she can't help but be charmed by him too.

His face is flush with worry, but he manages to hide it. "You wouldn't want to do that, Mrs. D. Then there would be nothing to hold up this handsome face."

Just as he is about to step inside, Aunt Vi allows the screen door to swing shut right in his face. As she turns to walk away, I see a grin creep across her lips and she says, "Careful, wouldn't want to mess up that handsome face."

I can't help myself—a loud guffaw escapes as Drake rubs his nose, opening the door again. "You're a cruel woman…a cruel, cruel woman," he says as if he is truly offended, but I can hear the adoration in his voice. He quickly grabs me around the waist when he's close enough. "And you—you're in big trouble!"

A fire ignites as it does every time he touches me, all thoughts of sadness gone—all thoughts of any kind gone. "We were supposed to study for our finals at my house hours ago."

Drake tries to place a stern look on his face until he notices mine. *Dammit.* The ugly, crying eyes curse! Now his face only shows concern. "Selene? Did something happen?" he asks as he glances over at Aunt Vi. She gives him a nod and turns to leave us alone.

When he looks back at me, I shrug. "It's nothing, I just got a letter..." He starts to say something, but I put my hand up to stop him. "From my dad, and before you say anything, just know I'm fine. I cried, I slept, and now I want to forget about it for a while." His fingers tighten around my waist, and I feel the tension pulsing through his long, strong fingers. I reach a hand up and gently pull his face until our eyes meet. I need him to know I'm all right. "I'm fine, I promise."

Slowly, I rise up on my tiptoes and press my lips to his. His eyes close, and I feel him relax as he pulls me into him, deepening the kiss. Two of my favorite things about Drake are his ability to understand me and the amazing way he unknowingly reaffirms his love for me just when I need it most.

chapter 35

Drake

I stuff my face with fresh strawberry scones as Selene pours the lemonade Mrs. Durham made this morning. It's hard to believe I'm not fat from all the time I've been spending over here, eating all of Mrs. D's cooking. I often tease Selene that food is the only reason I spend so much time at her house, but we both know that isn't true.

As she sets the glass of lemonade down in front of me, Selene reaches over and brushes a crumb from my cheek. "Pig," she states matter-of-factly.

"You love it," I say, grabbing a hold of her hand as she makes her way past me to pour her own glass of lemonade. I brush a kiss on her knuckles. "Besides, you find it charming."

She laughs as I release her hand. "Well, pigs are cute." She is unable to hold back a smile as she says it.

I jump up from the stool, knocking it over. Just as I'm about to dart around the island, Mrs. D clears her throat behind me.

Glancing over my shoulder, I see the trademark Durham lifted eyebrow even Selene has inherited. I straighten up and quickly set the stool right.

"Drake, I need you to help me in the garage with some boxes." She walks past me toward the back door, pausing just as she reaches it, and looks back at us. I lean forward and lightly kiss Selene on the cheek, letting out a low oink as I pull away.

She laughs out loud, and the sounds make me feel lighter. I realize Mrs. D is still watching us, and she has a strange look on her face. I move past her, and just as I push the door open, Mrs. Durham says one last thing to Selene. "Oh, and Selene, dear...uh...your father is here to see you. He's waiting in the living room." I stop cold in my tracks. Selene sucks in a sharp breath, and just when I'm about to turn back, I feel a delicate but strong hand nudging me forward. "She'll be okay. She needs to do this."

It takes me a moment to move again, but I don't turn around entirely. I only glance back at Selene. Her eyes are wide with fear, but she nods, letting me know she'll be okay. It takes every bit of strength in me, but I follow Mrs. D, leaving Selene to face her biggest fear.

Selene

I take a few deep breaths, trying to calm my nerves. I haven't seen my father for nearly a year, and our only communication was the handwritten letter I received a week ago, the letter he wrote asking for my forgiveness. I think about my decision every day and have still been unable to come to terms with whether or not I can give him what he is asking for. He is here now, though, leaving me little choice but to speak to him.

Walking down the hall, I stop just outside the living room. I grip the wall and peek around the corner, into the room. His back is to me, and he is looking at the pictures of me on the mantel of the fireplace. I watch as he moves to a photo of me and Mama from one of our many visits.

Finally, his eyes settle on one Aunt Vi recently framed. It's of Drake and me, and he's holding me from behind. I'm looking back up into his eyes while he looks forward, smiling into the camera. Aunt Vi said she couldn't help but love it because we both look so happy. I wonder what my dad sees when he looks at it.

I remain silent and continue watching, noticing his hand tighten a little. Drake looks so much like his father, and I like my mother; it has to be painful, and I'm sorry about that. I know what he said in his letter, the way he felt about my mother and Mr. Thomas's relationship, though he really doesn't deserve my sympathy. It isn't my fault.

Taking a deep breath, his grip visibly loosens. Placing the frame back on the mantel, he runs his hand through his hair. He does that when he is stressed, and I've seen him do it many times. Is he worried about what I might say? I'm not even sure what I will say.

Timidly, I take a quiet step forward. "Dad..." I say, pausing. He swings toward me and stares. "Hello," I continue. I can tell he's unsure of what to do, and I definitely don't know where to begin, so I wait.

It seems like an eternity passes before he says, "Hello, Selene. I...I'm sorry to just show up like this, but I was going crazy. I needed to see you." He takes a step forward, and my body tenses. He notices and stops, running a hand through his hair once more. "I shouldn't...have...come." The words seem to stick in his throat like they physically hurt him to get out.

Shaking my head, I step closer. "No, no, it's fine." I sit in an overstuffed chair close to the window. "I'm just not sure what the urgency is about. I didn't realize you needed a decision so quickly. You haven't seemed all that interested in me for nearly eighteen years, so I didn't think a couple more weeks would matter too much."

I slap my hand over my mouth, a little bit of regret prying its way into my heart. He looks shocked and a little heartbroken, and he flinched slightly at my words.

"Selene, please sit down. There are things that need to be said."

I quickly swallow the lump forming in my throat. I think maybe I should say sorry, but I don't. It's time to be honest and stand up for myself. "You told me all the things you have felt over the years. Now it's my turn." He stares at me for a moment, nods his head, and takes a seat on the sofa. I'm a little surprised he does so without a word. I look down at my hands and begin picking at my chipped nail polish. "I want you to know you hurt me. You hurt me with every missed I love you, goodnight kiss, and hug a father is supposed to give his daughter. I could see what I was to you—nothing." He starts to say something, but I raise my gaze to his and put my hand up to stop him. "I'm not finished."

His mouth closes, and his lips tighten into a resigned line. I can see it is hard for him to not defend himself, but it's my turn to speak.

"You're the reason I built walls and wouldn't let anyone in." I take another long breath before standing up and walking over to where he is. I sit next to him, and his eyes widen in surprise. I timidly place my hand over his where it rests on his knee, look up at him, and continue. "But someone broke down those walls. He showed me how to love and, most importantly, how to forgive. So…I'm going to try to forgive you…Dad."

A tear slides down his cheek, matching the ones that begin to fall down mine. He looks so scared. Slowly, he reaches over and pulls me into a tight embrace. We're both a little stiff; it's awkward and feels strange. I realize it will take time.

Pulling back, I want him to understand this doesn't mean everything is going to be easy between us. I'm working on forgiving him, but I never said I would just trust him.

"Dad, this is going to take time. I want to try. It's what Mama would want, and it's what I want." I take his hand and squeeze. A tiny smile spreads across my face at the knowledge that there are opportunities for second chances.

Drake

"**D**rake, get away from that window." Mrs. Durham's stern but gentle demand pulls my gaze away from the house where we left Selene with her father. I walk over to where she is digging through a box, looking for something she said she wanted to give to me. "Mike would never touch Selene in anger. He has finally woken up and seen what you and I have always seen in Selene." She pauses in her search and looks over at me. "Selene needs this too. She wants to forgive him. He was wrong and can never make up for all the years he neglected that girl, but he can work hard to love her in the future. You should know what it's like to forgive a father who let you down and did everything wrong when it came to you." She places her tender hand on my shoulder. Our eyes meet, and I see nothing but understanding.

I swallow the unease I feel for Selene. "Yeah," I say.

She quickly claps her hands together and turns back to the box she was searching earlier. "I know it has to be in here," she says as she rummages through the contents.

Suddenly, I'm overwhelmed by curiosity about what she is looking for, especially because she says it's for me. "I'll help you look if you tell me what you're looking for," I say as I reach for another box she had me pull down. Without glancing up, she states matter-of-factly, "A picture of Elizabeth and your father."

I swallow. "Elizabeth is Selene's mother…"

"Yes, Drake, now close your mouth. I'm well aware who Elizabeth is," Mrs. Durham says just as she lifts a photo from the box, grinning from ear to ear. "I knew it was in here," she says softly. I watch her face as she examines it, many emotions playing over it until she turns and holds the picture out to me. "Take it. I have one for Selene also."

I reluctantly take it from her, as if it might burn me. "You know, their missed chance is what I call a broken rule of fate." I look up at her, unsure of what she means. She can tell I'm not following her, so she continues. "I believe when destiny knows it's course, sometimes it can get ahead of itself. It feels the connection between two souls before they even come to be, and when the bond is so strong, it pulls everything and everyone that stands between them together." She sighs. "You and Selene are so connected, nothing can stop the fate of your hearts."

My heart beats rapidly at her words. I glance down at the photo in my hand and see two young teenagers. If I didn't know better, I'd think they were me and Selene. I can see the way they love one another by the look in the girl's eyes and in the way the boy is looking at her. In all my life, I've never seen my father look so happy. Looking up at Mrs. Durham, I nod my head. "Thank you."

chapter 36

Drake

T he picture shakes in his trembling hand. I didn't show
him to hurt him; letting him see the photo Mrs. Durham
gave me was my way of saying I understand, of saying I
can see what losing her did to him. I wanted him to know I understand losing her was like dying a slow, painful death—I know
because I had a taste of what life without Selene would be like
for me. The first thing I thought of when I looked at this picture
was that my dad loved Elizabeth Durham so fiercely. I never
thought a person could love another as much as I love Selene,
but my father did.

He hands the picture to me then turns, placing his hands on
the counter with his head down.

Stepping behind him, I place my hand on his shoulder, trying to comfort him. "Dad, I didn't mean to upset you."

Shaking his head, he murmurs, "You didn't. I just...it's just
seeing this picture makes me realize I was so lucky to have loved

her." Lifting his head, he turns and faces me. "I know you understand that feeling—I can see it in the way you look at Selene." He pauses as if contemplating something before speaking again. "They look so much alike, don't they?"

I watch his face as he talks to me. The common thread between us gets stronger as I listen to him while he looks down at the photo again. He's right—they do look nearly identical. The only thing missing from the face of the young girl in the picture is the tiny mole that rests just at the top of Selene's lip. I look back up at him, smiling. "Yeah...yeah, they do."

My dad smiles, too, and it feels so good to see it. I'm sure it's the first genuine emotion we've ever shared. "Tell me about her, Dad," I say, surprising him and even myself.

He nods then walks over to take a seat at the table. I follow him, sitting in the chair across from him.

Taking a deep breath, he begins fidgeting with the sleeve of his shirt. This conversation makes him appear vulnerable. "My God, Drake. Elizabeth was so good...so kind. She made me want to be better." My dad closes his eyes, and I know he has gone back in time. I watch him and wait. "Of course she was beautiful—you can see that for yourself—but she was more. She was funny, stubborn, and fiercely loyal. I was the luckiest guy because she loved me." Swallowing, I notice tears in his eyes. "She was mine for more than two years. I was going to marry her. We were going to be happy, and it's my fault none of those dreams came true."

Reaching across the table, I lay my hand over his. "Dad, I'm sorry, even knowing it would mean no me...no Selene." Dad looks up and begins to say something, but I stop him. "Don't. I know that's not what you're saying or even what you wish. I just get it, and I'm sorry for that alone."

Standing up, he comes around the table and kneels down, pulling me into his strong embrace. I settle into it, feeling his love for me. Pushing me back, he forces me to look directly into his eyes. "Drake, I love you. I'm more thankful for you and your sister than I ever showed you. If I can give you one piece of advice..." He blinks away the tears. "You love that girl—never give up on her. If she is what you want, then hold on tight so you'll never have regrets."

I give him one quick nod and we hug again. This moment is one I will play over in my mind for a very long time. It's the moment I completely forgive my father.

Selene

Crossing my legs and leaning up against the tall cypress, I take a long deep breath. "So, I asked myself why I felt the need to come here today, especially after the day I had." I'm feeling content. "I barely knew you, yet I feel drawn to this place." Swallowing, I add, "Maybe, it's our childhood friendship, maybe it's Drake, but honestly, I think it's your connection to Mama."

The breeze blows through my hair, as if trying to comfort me. "I can't even remember if I've said this or not, but I don't blame you. I realize Mama never would have, so really, why should I? Not to mention, you're a part of Drake, and I love him. I love him beyond reason."

I tilt my head up and close my eyes, breathing in and out slowly. When my father left, I went to search for Drake and Aunt Vi. When I walked into the garage, Aunt Vi was sitting alone, sifting through pictures. Without looking up, she told me Drake had gone home and told her he would be back later. Then whispered, "Good for you, Selene. You did the right thing." My heart seemed to slow, and an unexpected peace came over me. I left her sitting there, not even sure where I was going until I arrived here.

Suddenly, I'm aware of the body heat next to me as a hand lifts mine and laces our fingers. My eyes remain closed. "I'm going to give him a chance. I know it's probably crazy to do, but I couldn't help it. Even if his reasons were selfish, I want to love him now." Warm lips press against my cheek, and a deep sigh escapes my lips.

"I understand. I finally let things go and forgave my father tonight too. We needed to forgive if we want to be happy." He pauses, and his thumb caresses my hand. "They were wrong, Selene, but forgiving them was right. Their reasons were not malicious…just selfish. I can understand that. I just don't want to see you hurt."

Opening my eyes, I looked up at him, and I'm struck by this beautiful boy who is mine. He is more than I ever could have hoped for, and the bond I feel between us is everything I ever wanted with a person. "Drake, I don't want to see you hurt either. I'll never purposely hurt you again. If I have you, I'll get through anything." I lean my head on his shoulder. "Do you think this feeling between us will last? I need it to last."

I can feel him shake with laughter, but I'm not offended. "Selene, yes, I think this will last. It won't be easy, but that's because nothing that's worth it is ever easy. I don't believe we have a choice. Our paths were chosen for us long before we ever met." He kisses me on top of my head. "I need it to last, too."

I'm not sure how long we sit there in silence, just me, Drake, and the ghost of the girl who brought us together.

chapter 37

Drake

After eighteen years, I'm pretty sure my life is normal for the first time. Normal is a relative term, especially since everything leading up to my life today was a Lifetime movie on crack. Now, it is one day at a time. The best part is Selene and I are both finally breathing easier. It feels good knowing I have gone through the worst life can offer and made it. I can look forward and know that while things are always a gamble, I can hope.

There will always be a chance my mom will try to make trouble for me, but I don't fear the possibility. My dad told me I don't have anything to worry about anymore. He said she has started the life she always wanted. It doesn't hurt me that she never wanted me—I have plenty of people who do.

Graduation is in just a few days and will be the beginning of something new. Selene and I are headed to Austin in just a couple of months, and even with the unknowns, I feel confident all will be right.

Looking up, I watch Selene and Emme walk into class. Tommy follows close behind, rolling his eyes at their girlish banter. I can't help the smile that tugs at my lips as I watch them. All three are oblivious to the fact that without each of them, my life wouldn't mean quite as much. When they reach me, Selene leans over and kisses me. "Hey there." I breathe the words against her mouth.

It hits me that right now is that kind of moment—you know, the moment when the love that has been coursing through you finally reaches the center of your heart and takes deep root. It becomes the only source of energy that keeps your heart beating.

She looks down into my eyes, and I know she feels it too.

Selene

D rake follows me up to my room with a few boxes for packing. We'll be leaving for school soon, so I wanted to get a bit of a head start. He puts the boxes down and turns to me.

I smile as I press my lips to his, and I look into those deep greens eyes. It's the same look I noticed in class earlier—a promise. The best part is it's the first promise I haven't been afraid to believe.

"You sure seem to enjoy kissing me," Drake says as his lip curls up in one corner.

Generally, I would try to knock him down a few pegs for his arrogant comment, but not this time. "I do. I thoroughly en-joy kissing you," I say playfully as I wrap my arms around his neck.

"Don't you like kissing me?" I lift one eyebrow, waiting for his response.

I squeal as he pinches my backside and claims another kiss. We laugh with our lips pressed together and I jump up, encircling my legs around his waist. The movement is so abrupt we fall back on my bed. At first we are playful, and then our eyes meet. Suddenly, something in the air between us changes. All at once, my body is burning for him and his touch. Soon we are both moving, almost desperately, as our mouths collide. I can feel him on every part of me. It feels like so much and not enough all at once. I want to be closer to him but feel as if I could never be close enough. Before I realize what I'm doing, my hands are moving at the edge of his shirt, trying to pull it up over his head. He lets me. I look down at him lying beneath me, his eyes darkened with desire. I lift my own shirt over my head, tossing it somewhere behind me.

Pulling my lip between my teeth, my eyes roam over Drake's chest, up to his face. I slowly move my hands along his sides. I feel him squirm a little, and my lips tip at the corners. It feels good.

He puts his hands on my wrist and stops me from sliding them farther down. "Selene...maybe we should stop." He swallows as if those words were like fire scorching his throat.

I shake my head. "No, I don't want to stop, and Aunt Vi won't be home for hours. She's playing canasta with her ladies' group." I sigh when I see doubt in his eyes. "Do you really want to stop? Because, like I said, I don't." I've never been surer in my life.

Before I know what's happening, Drake is flipping me over and pinning me beneath him. I quickly recover, and my hands immediately move to the button of his jeans. Once again, my touch is frenzied as if my life depends on this moment. Drake's lips are making their way down my throat in slow caresses. "Let's go slow," he says on an exhale against my skin. As if on command, my hands still and then begin making more controlled motions. I slowly begin unbuttoning his jeans, and he does the same to me. He calmly and deliberately starts pulling my shorts down my legs and then stands, taking his own jeans off.

I lie on the bed, more vulnerable than I have ever allowed myself to be, yet feeling safer. I feel his eyes rake across my body just as mine roam over his solid form standing before me. He is mine, and I can see in his eyes that I'm his.

Slowly, he moves and covers my body with his until we're eye to eye, our mouths mere inches apart. "I love you," he whispers just as we connect. Then, he shows me just how much.

Drake

Selene is cradled in my lap as I rock us in a wooden chair, looking out over the back yard. My hand subconsciously strokes her thigh.

"This is nice," she declares then releases a low sigh.

The happiness I feel reaches my eyes. Selene is right—this does feel nice. "It's probably the best I've felt in my entire life," I confess. Saying that doesn't make me feel any sadness, only happiness. I actually feel content and happy, something I never thought would happen.

"Me too." She sighs. I squeeze her a little tighter against me, and she relaxes into my embrace.

I'm not sure how long we sit together in silence, looking out into the night before she asks, "Are you nervous about tomorrow?"

Shaking my head, there is no hesitation when I say, "Nope." I kiss the top of her head before I continue. "How can I be when it's one more step into our future together?" Selene looks back at me over her shoulder, tears glistening in her eyes, and just watches me. "Don't you see it, too? Don't you feel it?" I ask her, already seeing the answer in her eyes. She nods, turning and leaning back into me.

I hold her. Everything I went through up until this point doesn't matter. It's over. With Selene, I will finally know and give the kind of love that is unconditional.

Selene

Mr. Gibbons places the diploma in one hand and shakes the other as we turn and face the camera for our photo op. Although it feels good to know my life is moving forward and happiness is possible again, this moment is bittersweet. I can feel the tears threatening to fall until I look out and lock my eyes upon his gaze. He gives me that nearly unbearable heart-stopping smile, and I can't help but reciprocate.

Then my eyes drift out to the crowd just beyond my other classmates. Aunt Vi is standing, funneling her hands around her mouth and yelling my name. Next to her, my father is clapping wildly, wiping his eyes in between. It's weird seeing him out there, cheering me on. While it wasn't easy for me to agree to it, I'm glad Aunt Vi talked me into sending him an invitation. My heart feels so full of possibilities. My cheeks redden as I make my way back to my seat and notice Emme laughing as Drake punches Tommy in the arm. I'm confused until I see the sign Tommy is holding out of Drake's reach that reads, *Selene, forget Drake and marry me!* I roll my eyes, unable to stop myself from enjoying the moment.

The remainder of the day is a blur of hugs, smiles, and laughter. Drake and I never had a chance—it was always going to be this way in the end, just like one of Lacey's romance novels, me, Drake, and our happily ever after.

epilogue

Selene

I imagined this day completely different. I thought Mama would be here, but instead, Aunt Vi is by my side. Everything is different. In fact, I never could have predicted standing here with boxes and a suitcase full of my belongings at my feet in front of a co-ed dormitory—a dorm my boyfriend would be living in too.

Aunt Vi isn't exactly thrilled with the idea, but I convinced her I'd be safer with Drake close. She joked that she was more worried about Drake than anyone else. I laughed, but she didn't. Maybe she wasn't completely joking. Either way, she conceded to the idea.

My heart warms as she places check marks next to the items she wrote out on a list of things I would need. I'm so thankful she's here. My nerves are in overdrive as I watch the other students and their parents shuffling around me, excitement in their voices at the prospect of the anticipated freedom that comes along with moving away from home. Some parents are quietly patting their children goodbye on the shoulder while others are pulling their sons and daughters against them, saying tearful goodbyes and giving orders of daily phone calls. The chaos around me cannot take my mind off the one thing I'm waiting for.

My eyes search the crowd until finally my gaze falls upon the one person I can't make it through this day without: Drake. He doesn't see me. His eyes roam over the crowded campus until his dad walks up to stand next to him, saying something that draws Drake's attention to him. It still surprises me when I see them side by side. Their features are so strikingly similar, I can't help but imagine Drake at his father's age. I'm struck once again, as I have been often over the last several months, by the thought that my mama was in love with this man.

If they had made different decisions, Drake would not be Drake, and I would not be me. We would not have one another. Everything would be different. As often as I have wished for things to be as they once were, I know, especially now, I would never survive life without Drake, even if I'd never met him. Life is funny that way. I was once the girl so afraid to give my love, to take love, and to trust. I've changed, at least when it comes to Drake.

Continuing to watch them, I think about how much has changed. I watch as Mr. Thomas says one last thing to Drake before he draws him into an embrace. To a stranger's eye, it would appear to be a regular, father-son college farewell, but I know the history. I recognize the slightly awkward movements. I see the effort it still takes for each of them to show the other affection or trust in the other. It gives me hope.

As they pull apart, Drake turns, and our eyes finally meet. He lifts his hand in a wave before picking up his bags, saying a last goodbye to his dad over his shoulder then heading in my direction. I feel happier than I could have imagined. This feels so right. We're moving forward, and while we have more growing up to do, we have both already come a long way. I know what is in front of me, what I want, and what it will take for me to get there.

Looking up from Drake's stare, my eyes connect with a similar one. I grin when Mr. Thomas gives me a nod and returns my expression. Raising his hand, he gives me a sign of peace, and my heart swells with familiar warmth and love. I can't believe it, but he gave me the one thing I was missing from this day: a part of Mama. She never left me without flashing me the peace sign. A lonely, happy tear falls down my cheek as I lift my hand to return his gesture. With a tender look on his face, he slowly turns, gets in the car, and drives away.

Drake finally is standing before me, dropping his bags and pulling me against him. I hold him tight, feeling his breath against my ear as he whispers, "Are you okay? How do you feel?"

Pulling back, I look up into his worried eyes and say, "Peace. I feel at peace." Then I lift up on my tiptoes and place my lips softly against his, not caring who's around.

If someone had asked me a year ago if I thought I would ever be happy again, my answer would have been no. Truthfully, I've never been this happy, and even though Mama is gone, I can admit it without guilt. I'm not sure why my life and Drake's were meant to be one, but they are. I guess there isn't anything we can do to avoid fate, especially when our destinies collide.

Giving Thanks...

When Selene and Drake's story began taking shape in my mind, I never imagined I would one day be on the journey I'm on now. It began as a fun little way to entertain my friends. I would write a chapter and send it to them to read, and then as the story began to unfold, my reason for writing Selene and Drake's story changed.

About eight months after I began WDC, two of my very best friends and I discovered Colleen Hoover. After falling in love with her books and then with her journey into life as an author, I found inspiration. My friends encouraged me to finish my book and publish it. I've said this before, but Colleen was the water to the seed of my dream, but she wasn't the only one. It took many people to get me to where I am today. They each came into my dream journey at just the moment I needed them, each one helping me in different ways. They were all perfectly on cue when I needed them to be, and I am forever grateful to each of them.

First, I have to say thank you to my two biggest supporters and cheerleaders through this journey, **Trish Lyle** and **Kristen Teshoney**. Thank you both for sending me hundreds of threatening text messages about your need for me to get off my lazy bleep bleep and write you some bleeping chapters. So sweet. Ha.

Trish...this isn't the first time I 've wondered what I could have done in my life to deserve a friend like you. There are no words to describe what you mean to me or what your support has been to me. You're always there sharing and caring and being the truest friend I could ever hope for in my life. You have the biggest heart of anyone I know. I love you.

Kristen...your laugh is infectious and your optimism is contagious. I'll never be able to repay the love and support you have shown me. Your friendship is one that would be impossible to live without. I may get lost on my way to the post office with important packages, but I will always pull through for you in the end. Thank you for Facebook trolling on Super Bowl Sunday. Ha! You got my back, I got yours.

Murphy Rae...from the very first email we ever exchanged, I knew we were going to become friends. You are genuine and one of a kind. Thank you for taking me under your wing and wanting to help me. You have introduced me to a whole new world and a whole new book family. I will never be able to thank you enough.

Kristin Delcambre and **Chelle Northcutt**...how can I ever thank you both for your complete honesty and care with Selene and Drake? It was the hardest thing I've ever done when I attached my manuscript to an email and hit send to two complete strangers. Thank you for helping me see the humor in writing an imperfect book, and also for helping me see there is always room for improvement. Most of all, thank you for our newfound friendship.

Sara Ney and **Christine Kuttnauer**...holy poop on a stick! You two round out my lucky streak! Thank you for coming in at the end and helping me finalize all my loose ends. You both gave me the little extra courage and support I needed to make this happen. Sara, you're hands down the queen of blurbs, and possibly other things too inappropriate to discuss here. We'll save that for another book. Christine, your attention to the small stuff kept me in line. Your love for Drake makes me so happy.

Finally, to my family who allowed me to spend hours and hours alone with my computer. You're everything to me.

S hirl Rickman is a writer, a dreamer, and an optimist. A small-town Texas girl currently residing in the San Francisco Bay Area, Shirl adores her husband, daughter, and two crazy dogs. When she's not dreaming up new love stories, Shirl can be found reading, drinking her favorite coffee, Kona Blend with coconut milk. She loves kindness, laughing and meeting her readers.

Website link:
https://shirlrickman.wordpress.com/

Facebook:
https://www.facebook.com/shirlrickmanauthor/?pnref=story

Shirl's Girls & Cody Facebook Group
https://www.facebook.com/groups/1010382209000750/

Twitter:
https://twitter.com/shirl_rickman

Instagram:
https://www.instagram.com/shirlrickmanauthor/